NO BAD DAYS

by
J. STERLING

ISBN-10: 1-945042-06-0
ISBN-13: 978-1-945042-06-5

Please visit the author's website
www.j-sterling.com
to find out where additional versions may be purchased.

DEDICATION

This story is for all of us who have lived through broken hearts, broken promises, and broken dreams, as well as for the ones who fight to put us back together. Sometimes the ones who break us are the same ones who help us heal.

WELCOME TO MY LIFE

Nick

I WAS SITTING in the living room of my fraternity house, drinking an ice-cold beer with my brothers, when a quick knock on the door was followed by the knob turning. No one waited to be let into our house; it was always open. A girl with a pair of tanned legs stepped inside, and I had to stop myself from rolling my eyes.

Sheila.

She made a beeline in my direction, her expression serious as she stopped in front of me. "Nick, can I talk to you?"

I wanted to say no. Hell, I even fought the words from coming out of my mouth.

"Nick?" She cocked her hip and stared down at me.

I groaned. "What?"

"I asked if we could talk," she said, her tone whiny. And I hated whiny girls.

I took another swig of my beer. "So, talk."

She looked around, clearly taking stock of the ten or so guys all watching us with rapt attention. "Not here. I meant in private."

Glancing around at my fraternity brothers, I shrugged. "I'm going to tell them everything we talk about anyway.

Might as well just talk here."

She shifted on her feet, clearly uncomfortable.

I was being a complete dick and I knew it, but I hated it when a girl couldn't take a hint. I'd taken Sheila out three times before realizing she was just like all the rest, and I stopped calling her.

Ladies, when a guy stops calling, stops responding to your texts and avoids you, he's no longer interested. Do us both a favor and disappear quietly. Creating a scene just makes everyone uncomfortable.

"You don't have to be such a jerk," she said with a huff, then spun around and stomped back out the front door.

Colby, one of our newer fraternity brothers, glanced my way. "You aren't going to chase after her?"

I rolled my eyes. "It's always the same. 'Why haven't you called me? I thought we were having fun. Does this mean you're done with me? I thought we had something special,'" I said, mimicking a female voice, and my brothers all burst out into laughter.

Yeah, I was being an absolute asshole, in case there was any lingering doubt. I'd learned that for the *clingers*—the girls who wouldn't take a fucking hint—being a jerk was the only way to deal with them. If I gave them even the tiniest bit of attention, or faked even a tad of compassion, their grip on me retightened and we were back to square one.

Sheila needed to go away, and I was doing my damnedest to shake her off once I realized there was nothing behind her hot body and model-worthy face. She had over a hundred thousand followers on one of the social media sites, which was partially what drew me to her in the first place. I wanted to know exactly how she'd built her following. It didn't take me long to realize she'd racked up the likes by posting makeup tutorials and half-naked photos of herself.

"It's not like there isn't a line of girls willing to replace her anyway, brother." Darryl put his knuckles in the air from the other side of the room, and I air-knuckled him back.

I sensed pretty easily when a girl was looking for a replacement daddy, and tended to tap out as quickly as I'd entered the ring. And Sheila was one hundred percent looking for someone to take care of her. Yes, she had all those followers on that one site, but she did nothing with them except brag to anyone who'd listen. The idea of being someone's sugar daddy, filling whatever void they might have, didn't interest me. I had to admit that having some hot eye candy on my arm was nice for a week or two, but eventually even that got old when it was all there was. I actually liked it when a girl had ambition and goals.

Surprised I'm more than just a pretty face? Yeah, sometimes I am too.

I never shared those thoughts with my fraternity brothers, though. They assumed my policy was *fuck 'em and dump 'em*, and to be honest, I never cared enough to set them straight. I had to admit, I sort of enjoyed having that reputation on campus.

Only my closest friends knew the truth—that I stopped seeing girls the moment I realized there was absolutely nothing between us and never could be. It wasn't like I was completely heartless; it only seemed that way from the outside if you didn't really know me. And most didn't.

My own father would have a heart attack if he knew I felt

this way. He'd always taught me that a girl with ambition was the enemy of a successful man. But if that were true, why couldn't I see it that way? Why did the idea of a woman who had no drive repulse me? I chalked it up to the fact that I couldn't comprehend someone actually having no goals.

How could you want nothing for yourself in life?

Shaking my head as if to rid myself of the funk I was slipping into, I slapped the side of the couch before standing up. "All right, I need to shower before the party. DJ should be here in an hour," I said, nodding as I looked around the room. "Everything else looks great."

*

NINETY MINUTES LATER, I emerged from my room, all cleaned up and looking hot as shit, if I did say so myself. It wasn't that it took me that long to get ready. I wasn't a chick but I did like to make an entrance, so that meant I always joined the party once it had already officially begun.

The bass from the DJ's sound system thumped with each step I took down the hall. It was still early, but people were already gathered inside. I could hear girls laughing and guys yelling at someone to *chug*.

The living room had been transformed into what looked like a nightclub. Lights flashed against the walls, and an area was cleared off to provide a dance floor. The couches had been pulled against the walls, and couples were already making out on them. I swear, sometimes all it took was a darkened room for people to lose their inhibitions.

"Hey, Nick." A sorority girl named Brenda sidled up next

to me and reached for my arm. "Heard you were single again. Wanna change that?"

Brenda used to date Thomas, so I bowed out respectfully. "You know my rules, Bren. Can't," I said before walking away from her with my hands up.

I didn't date my fraternity brothers' exes, a personal rule of mine that I tried to live by. It was hard sometimes, considering how many guys were in the frat, but I seemed to manage.

"I hate your stupid rule."

When Brenda stuck out her bottom lip in a sexy pout, I couldn't get away quick enough. She was stupid hot, and a guy only had so much strength to resist. Removing myself from the situation—and her—was my safest option.

When I reached the kitchen, I noted the bar setup and the brothers assigned to man it. Everything looked great. We had a wide range of hard alcohol, mixers, and an ice-cold keg, thanks to my brothers. It took everything in me not to slip behind the bar with them, wanting nothing more than to play bartender like in that old Tom Cruise movie from the eighties.

Someone handed me a red cup filled with beer, and I nodded before turning around and smacking right into another hot little number named Monika, with a *k*. Who the hell spelled their name like that?

"Hey, Nick, I was looking for you," she said, practically purring as she grinned up at me.

I slid my arm around her waist. "Oh yeah? What for?"

"I wanted to give you something." She pressed her scantily clad body against mine, making me wonder exactly what I was going to get.

"What is it?"

"Me."

Monika smiled before standing on tiptoe to throw her arms around my neck. She pulled my head down and kissed me, her tongue pushing its way into my mouth a little too aggressively, but I decided not to give a shit as I kissed her back.

Pulling away a moment later, I forced a smile before downing my beer and tapping the empty cup on the counter, signaling for a refill. When it returned, I gulped down half before feeling up to kissing serpent-tongue again.

Apparently, I must not have hated kissing her that much, because I spent the rest of the night doing it.

CONFIDENT AND HOT

Jess

WALKING ACROSS THE sunlit college campus, I smiled to myself when I noticed Nick Fisher and his entourage heading in my direction. Never alone, he was flanked by at least a couple of other guys at all times.

Running my fingers through my shoulder-length blond hair, I made sure it was smooth, wanting to look good for him whether he noticed or not.

Even the blinding sun was no match for Nick's charms. Nick outshone her on every level, and I glanced up toward the gleaming fireball and realized that she knew it too. I didn't blame her for hiding behind that cloud as he passed beneath her. If there were clouds that I could hide behind, I might have done the same. But then I wouldn't get the chance to ogle his delicious body and possibly be noticed by him.

Nick Fisher was a senior at State, the president of his fraternity chapter, and had played on the football team until he quit last year. He'd claimed he had no intention of going pro, and didn't want to take someone's spot who did.

His frat was known to throw the best parties on campus, and that was solely due to his talents. If there was something Nick wanted to accomplish, he did, and you felt lucky when you got to be a part of the process. He was a marketing major, ridiculously skilled in all things social media, and seemed to know everyone in the entire freaking world.

Plus, the rumor was that his real brothers owned three of the hottest bars in Hollywood, so the drinks at his parties were always off the charts. I had no idea if that was true or not. There was a blurry line between fact and fiction when it came to all things Nick Fisher.

Staring down at my pink toenails revealed by my strappy sandals as I stepped across the concrete, I allowed my gaze to lift in his direction as he neared, his dark hair cut short and tucked under a backward baseball hat. With a quick glance at the other two guys, I realized that they were Nick's fraternity brothers, who I recognized from the party at their house last Friday night. Both of them were taller than Nick, who stood about six feet tall, but neither was built better.

Don't get me wrong, Nick didn't look like a total musclebound meathead. I couldn't stand guys who were nothing but hard muscle upon even harder muscle; I could never understand why anyone would think that was attractive. Who wanted to lean against something that felt like concrete? Not me.

Nick was built like an athlete—firm, defined, and blissfully chiseled without overdoing it. He looked good. And he knew it. His self-confidence was part of what made him so irresistible. When a guy could pull off being that self-aware of his effect on others—without coming off as a self-absorbed jerk—there was nothing hotter, in my opinion. And I wasn't the only girl who agreed with that assessment. Nick Fisher was wanted by at least half the females who went to State, or at least it seemed that way.

No, it was definitely that way.

Common sense warned me that I shouldn't want a guy like Nick the way every other girl did, but the rest of me refused to agree. I shouldn't like him, but I did. I shouldn't be interested in him at all, but I was. I was a fool for his charms, and I didn't even care. That was the thing about Nick . . . you knew you should stay away from him, but you didn't want to. If he wanted to give me his attention, I'd gladly accept it.

Not that he'd ever said more than two words to me before, but I'd seen him plenty of times since I started going to school here. Nick was bigger than life, magnetic in every single thing he did. Even something as simple as walking.

By the time his group was about ten feet away from me, all their eyes were locked onto some part of my body or face. His two buddies checked out my boobs and the sliver of my stomach exposed by my crop top, but not Nick. His blue eyes stayed firmly focused on mine. He shot a lopsided grin at me as we passed each other, and I hoped to God I smiled back. I could barely feel my own feet at that point, let alone my mouth.

I wanted to turn my head and enjoy the view as he walked away, but I forced myself to continue looking straight ahead. I might have been part of the Nick Fisher fan club, but that didn't mean I had to embarrass myself because of it.

Hurrying toward the white building in the distance, I refocused my attention on getting to the right classroom. The first day of the spring semester meant that I had left extra early this morning to avoid the potential awkwardness of walking in late. Truth be told, I was notoriously great at getting lost. I was directionally challenged, to say the least.

Scanning my schedule one last time, I matched the number for where my Speech Communications class was being held with the tall three-story building in front of me. I breathed out a sigh of relief before glancing at my cell phone, and realized that I was twenty minutes early. Shrugging to myself, I located the correct door and walked into the empty classroom, then chose a seat in the last row.

I had this thing about sitting in the last row in large rooms. It was completely stupid, but I hated the idea of people staring at the back of my head, even when I knew they weren't. The simple thought of them being behind me, looking at me, watching me, or seeing me when I couldn't see them, it all sort of freaked me out. It made no sense, and I wasn't sure where the illogical fear stemmed from, but I'd been this way for as long as I could remember. Just thinking about someone sitting directly behind me almost made me break out into a sweat.

Slowly, the classroom started to fill up with other students. I recognized a couple of girls from my classes last semester, but didn't know them by name.

The door eventually flew open with a crash, and the sound of male laughter met my ears. I turned my head in time to see Nick and his two friends from earlier walk in. His head swiveled to the left and back to the right, taking stock of the classroom before his gaze locked onto mine.

"Hey, Nick! Sit over here," a girl all but cooed at him from somewhere near the front.

"Hey, Stacy. I think I'm gonna sit in back." He nodded toward her as he passed and then settled into the desk right next to mine. His friends plopped down in the row directly in front of us.

Of all the empty seats to choose from, he had to pick the one next to mine?

"Is anyone sitting here?" he asked, his voice so low and sultry that I had to cross my legs to stop the want from settling between them. The last thing I needed was to daydream all through class about the things I'd let Nick Fisher do to me.

I swallowed. "Apparently you are."

He laughed and extended his arm. "I'm Nick."

I stared at his offered hand for a moment before reaching out and placing my hand in his. His fingers wrapped around mine easily, his grip firm, yet gentle.

"Do you honestly think I don't know who you are?" I smiled as I tried to pull my hand from his, but he only tightened his grip on me.

"It would be rude of me to assume. And how else would I get to know your name?"

Smooth.

"I'm Jess Michaelson."

"Yes, you are," he said, his voice low. He brought my hand to his lips and planted a kiss on top of my knuckles.

I pulled my hand away and couldn't help but scowl. "Are you for real?"

Who kisses someone's hand? I can't believe I thought he was charming two seconds ago.

"Do I look imaginary? Wait, don't answer that," he said with a grin, holding a hand in the air to stop me.

"You do seem like sort of a nightmare, now that I think about it. Those come from your imagination, right?" I pointed at my head, my tone playful, even if my words seemed otherwise.

He leaned back into his seat and grinned. "I like you, Jess."

I wanted to play hard to get, but I couldn't find the strength. I shouldn't have been so willing to feed Nick's ego, but I couldn't stop myself from doing it. The guy was hot, I was attracted to him, and I clearly didn't care if he knew it.

"The feeling's mutual, Nick," I said, falling into his eyes. They were so blue, they looked almost black in the lighting of our classroom, but I knew the truth—they were dark blue with a ring of lighter blue in them.

He smirked, and my cheeks warmed as I looked away.

Here's what I knew about Nick Fisher. He was a serial dater, the type of guy who always had someone vying for his attention. He wasn't the typical type of player who only screwed a girl once and then never spoke to her again. No, Nick actually dated girls. The "relationship," if you could call it that, never lasted longer than a month, but still, you had to at least give the guy props for trying.

Props for trying? What the hell was I thinking? This guy turned me into a complete traitor to my gender in two seconds flat.

Nick was currently in a "single" phase, but according to my roommate, those never lasted very long. Rachel had made it her mission to know everything about the guys worth knowing on campus. She called them GIMS, which stood for *Guys I Might Stalk*. She had a file on her computer with detailed notes and everything.

Poor Rachel, the girl would never have a chance with Nick. Apparently he lived by a set of rules, and one of them was that he never messed around with a girl who used to date one of his fraternity brothers. Rachel had dated Trevor for six months last year, and since he was in the same frat as Nick, she was now off-limits.

Much to her displeasure.

One night when she was drunk, Rachel told me that if she had known about Nick's stupid rule, she never would have dated Trevor in the first place. Then she asked me how any girl in her right mind would willingly pull themselves out of Nick's dating pool, muttered something I couldn't understand in Spanish, and then puked into the sink.

My roommate was all class, but at least she was honest. And I loved her for it.

SHE WANTS ME

Nick

J ESS MICHAELSON WAS hot as hell. How I'd never noticed
her before was beyond me.

She sure seemed to know me, which wasn't unusual, but
the fact that I didn't know her . . . well, that was. I prided
myself on knowing as many people as I could on campus. It
was part of what I deemed my *job* to get to know my fellow
students and make them feel like they mattered to me, that I
cared. It was part of what made me so good at what I did, and
how I earned the reputation of being the go-to guy on campus
for all things.

I was a marketer by nature, bred into the business by my
old man. I could sell anything to anyone. Literally.

Anything. To anyone.

Selling shit seemed to come naturally to me, so it only
made sense that I would major in it at State. My old man was a
marketing genius too, but he was old school and refused to
adapt to this century. He hired people to handle certain aspects
of the business instead of learning it himself and saving a
bundle. Where he failed, I excelled.

From an early age, I watched the way my dad would
charm people, making eye contact, always shaking hands,

giving people pats on the back when he passed by them. Small gestures like that made people feel he was invested in them. It was amazing what a little contact could do, and how people responded to it. If you gave them your attention and remembered small details they mentioned, people associated that with trust. And once you earned their trust, you held all the cards.

Taking his strengths and combining them with my own made me feel like a million bucks. I knew I was good. Hell, if being here at State had taught me anything, it was that I was even better than I'd thought. Even the professors came to me when they wanted to promote a new business venture or idea, needed help learning the newest social-media app, or wanted help thinking *outside the box*, as they liked to call it. Last semester, I gave a group of professors a crash course in all things Snapchat. It was slightly disturbing, to say the least, but they were grateful for my expertise. Each of them recommended me to everyone they knew who could use my help.

But back to Jess, the hot little number sitting next to me. I wanted to find out more about her, so I bumped my knee against hers. Damn, her skin was soft.

She glanced at me, her eyes narrowed slightly as her lips pulled into a straight line.

Tempted to reach out and pull her face toward mine, I leaned in slightly and whispered, "Have you ever been to any of my parties?"

She looked toward the professor before meeting my eyes again, and nodded.

I swallowed, racking my brain for any images of her. After coming up blank, I whispered, "When?"

She shook her head slightly. "Last Friday, stupid."

"Stupid?" I fought back the urge to laugh out loud. She was a mouthy little thing.

"I'm not surprised you didn't see me. You had your tongue down some girl's throat the whole night."

This time I did laugh. Out fucking loud.

The professor looked up from his textbook, adjusting the glasses on his nose as he scanned the room for the offenders before he continued, his tone broadcasting his annoyance at my disruption.

Half-tempted to pull out a piece of paper and start writing her notes to her like a fifth grader, I decided I'd have to talk to Jess later when I wouldn't get us both into trouble. The last thing I needed was to get screwed in this class and not have enough credits to graduate.

But even with the lingering threat, I still couldn't keep my mouth shut.

"Maybe next time that will be you," I said, hoping to win her over a little.

"I'm already seeing someone. Sorry," she said, her flat tone signaling the end of the conversation.

But it wasn't.

Not at all.

INTRIGUED

Jess

WHEN THE PROFESSOR slammed his book shut in a display of authority before dismissing the class, I fumbled with my notebook as I tried to stuff it into my bag.

Nick had distracted me, and after his questions, he spent the rest of class either staring at me with a shit-eating grin on his face, or touching my leg with his. I don't think I took a single note after that. Anytime his skin pressed against mine, I wanted to hop into his lap, tell him I surrender, and let him have his way with me.

Pushing up from my chair, I started for the classroom door and away from Nick when he shouted my name. I stopped and turned to find him and his two friends heading toward me in a rush.

"You always travel in packs?" I asked, lifting my chin at his frat brothers.

He turned to them. "I'll catch up with you guys in a bit."

"Are you sure?" one of them said. "We're supposed to meet Marcus at Bites."

"I'll meet you there," he said curtly with a nod. The guys walked away slowly and left Nick and me standing at the front of the classroom with the rest of the class hurrying out around us.

"They seem lost without you," I said with a smirk.

"It does seem that way, doesn't it?" He reached for my elbow and pulled me toward the glass doors. "Let's walk and talk."

Without responding, I started moving along with him, my body language telling him everything my mouth wasn't. He held the door open for me and I walked through, thankful that the sun was hidden behind tree branches. I didn't want to put my sunglasses on when Nick wasn't wearing any. Call it another quirk of mine, but I always considered it rude to wear sunglasses during a conversation if the other person wasn't. There was something intimate about eye contact.

"So you were at the party last Friday. And I was too busy making out with Monika to notice."

"Oh, so you do remember her name," I teased, and he stopped walking to laugh a little, which caused me to stop as well. Whatever his body did, mine seemed to mimic.

He leaned in close, his mouth mere inches from mine. "I'm not a total scumbag, Jess. I do remember the names of the girls I kiss."

"How nice for them," I said with a little more snark than I'd intended, feeling absolutely bipolar with my emotions. One second I was wanting to throw myself at this guy, and the next I was a snide brat basically calling him a pig.

Pick a side. I mentally chastised myself, wondering if I even could. Nick seemed to bring out warring emotions in me, even if the side that wanted to jump into his lap was definitely favored.

"So mouthy," he said, staring at my lips.

Pretending not to notice the chills his attention sent through my body, I blurted, "Sorry. I don't know what's wrong with me."

Wait . . . why the hell was I apologizing?

"Don't apologize. I like it." He started moving, and again, my body automatically followed. "So, Jess, tell me about yourself."

I swallowed hard and hoped he didn't notice. How on earth was I supposed to even answer that question?

"What do you want to know?" I cast a glance in his direction, taking in the way he moved with an air of confidence most guys only pretended to have.

A few choruses of *Hi, Nick* broke through our otherwise private conversation. He cast smiles at the girls and bumped knuckles with a few guys, but never stopped walking or focusing his attention on me.

"What year are you," he asked, "and why have I never seen you before?"

"I'm a sophomore, and I don't know."

"Did you live in the dorms as a freshman?"

"Yeah."

"Well, there's one reason. I don't hang out at the dorms. Did you go to any of my parties last year?"

"No."

"Why not?"

I considered telling him a lie to sound cool, but opted for the truth instead. "I was so terrified that I was going to fail out of school, that I didn't really have any fun at all last year."

"I find that hard to believe."

"Which part?"

"All of it. You don't strike me as the type of person to fail or not have any fun."

His gaze raked the length of my body, making me feel very underdressed in my crop top and shorts. It was the first time since we started talking or flirting or whatever it was we were doing that he made me feel like a potential notch in his bedpost with just a glance.

"You don't even know anything about me," I shot back, my defenses coming up.

"That's all going to change, Jess Michaelson. I'm going to get to know you. Very well."

"I told you I'm seeing someone," I reminded him.

"For now," he said, his confidence oozing out of him as easily as breathing. "I've gotta go. See you in class." With those words ringing in my head, he took off toward the small group of guys clustered in front of the student store.

That was hands down the single most confusing, exciting, and weird conversation I'd ever had. And I loved almost everything about it.

*

"RACHEL, ARE YOU home?" I shouted as I walked through our apartment door, hoping to hear her Latina accent fill my ears. Silence greeted me instead and I groaned, dying to share today's happenings with her.

I had ninety minutes between classes and instead of hanging around school, I decided to come home, grab something quick to eat, and hopefully talk my roommate's ear off. I was too excited to stay on campus with no one to talk to.

Scanning the fridge for something to eat, I fired off a text to Rachel, asking when she'd be home. She responded immediately that she was on her way.

I made a grilled-cheese sandwich for each of us while I waited. Right as I stuffed a gooey cheese-filled bite into my mouth, she burst through the door, a smile on her pretty face as her long dark ponytail swung back and forth.

Rachel was a little thing, only five foot two, but filled with more piss and vinegar than should legally be allowed to fit into one person's body. She always claimed it was her mother who made her so feisty, so she couldn't be held responsible. All I knew was that I loved her for whatever it was that made her a force to be reckoned with.

"What's up? Get lost yet?" she asked before tossing her bag onto the couch.

"No, smartass, but you'll never guess who was in my first class."

She pursed her lips, glancing up toward the ceiling as she pretended to think. "Hmm, Julio Cavanaugh? Jacob Styler? David Wescott?"

"No, no, and no," I said before taking another bite of my sandwich. I pushed the other sandwich across the counter toward her as she made her way into the kitchen.

"*Ay, dios mio!*" She groaned, already sounding exasperated with me. "I could go down the entire list of GIMS by class, but it will save time if you just tell me. Thanks for the sandwich, by the way," she said as she refilled her water bottle, then took a big swig.

"Nick Fisher," I said, trying not to smile.

She choked and spit the remaining water into the sink.

"But he's a senior. Shit, Jess, tell me you sat in full view of that body all class. And next time, take some pictures so I can get through mine."

Laughing, I shook my head at her craziness. "He sat next to me. There were a ton of empty seats, but he plopped his happy ass right next to mine."

Rachel grabbed me by both arms and turned me to face her, her expression shocked and serious. "Shut the hell up. Are you lying to me?"

"Why would I lie to you?"

"He sat next to you? Did he talk to you? Tell me everything right now."

This was exactly why I couldn't wait to tell Rachel about my encounter. I knew she'd be more excited than I was. I filled her in on our little whatever it was, all the while waiting for the redness in her cheeks to fade.

"Are you holding your breath?"

"I can't help it. You're blowing my mind right now." She shook her head quickly before exhaling.

"What do you think it means? You're the stalker, so you tell me. What does he want with me?"

"Want with you? Duh, Jess. You're obviously going to be the next girl he dates. I thought that much was obvious." She reached for my hands and clasped them in hers, releasing a high-pitched squeal that only dolphins should be able to hear.

"I told him I was seeing someone," I blurted.

"You what? Why would you tell him that?" She dropped my hands and eyeballed me like I was insane.

Hell, maybe I was.

"I don't know, it just came out," I said about the lie I'd

told. "He said something about kissing me at one of his parties, and he was so cocky about it that I just—" I blew out an irritated breath. "I told him I was taken. It seemed like the right thing to do at the time."

"So now he thinks you're dating someone. Might not be a bad thing." She tapped a finger against her lips as fear filled me from the inside out.

Did I want to date Nick Fisher? Hell yes, of course I did. At least, I think I did.

But did I want to completely wreck myself and my heart in the process? Absolutely not.

I was conflicted, torn between wanting to be chosen by him, but not wanting to be tossed away like all the others. The tossed-away part was probably the real reason why I told him I was dating someone. My subconscious was clearly all about my sense of self-preservation, even if the rest of me wasn't.

"I don't know if I can do it," I said in a low voice, filled with self-doubt.

"What don't you know if you can do? Go out with Nick Fisher?" Rachel frowned, clucking her tongue at me. "Are you dead? No, you're not. So of course you can." She pinned me with her brown eyes, seeing right through me.

"I'm already stupidly crushing on him, no thanks to you. But if I go out with him, he's going to break me. I'm sensitive, Rach. I want the guy I go out with to actually like me back."

"Who says he doesn't?"

"He doesn't even know me."

She rolled her eyes and took another sip of water before groaning. "That's the whole point, *gringa*. How else will he get to know you if he doesn't take you out? Stop reading into this and just have some fun. We're in college; it's not like we're looking to get married."

"Definitely not looking to get married," I repeated. "So I'd date Nick for fun?"

"Yes, for fun. Don't go into it with any expectations. You know his reputation. He doesn't tend to date anyone for very long, but nobody knows why. And when Nick does ask you out—and trust me, he will—say yes and then we'll work on convincing you that it's no big deal. That you're just going out as friends and nothing more."

I nodded along with her crazy train of thought, my brain doing its damnedest to agree with her. "I like it. Just friends. I can do that."

"Of course you can," she said, obviously more sure of me than I was.

"Yeah. Friends don't break friends' hearts because you're just a friend, and it's just friendly feelings there," I said, trying to convince myself.

"Exactly," she said with a dismissive wave of her hand. "Friends. Because a heart has no place in dates with Nick Fisher."

My heart pounded inside my chest.

Shit. I was doomed before we even began.

FLIRTING MASTER

Nick

L UCKY FOR ME, the class I shared with Jess met three times a week. Unfortunately, today wasn't one of those days.

I found myself scanning the campus while I walked through it, hoping to catch a glimpse of her. I realized that I left her sort of abruptly yesterday, but I really did have to go, and leaving people wanting more was always a good game to play.

Hearing her say she was dating someone annoyed the crap out of me. Not that I couldn't handle a little healthy competition, but I definitely wasn't used to it. So I wasn't ashamed that I cyberstalked the hell out of Jess once I got home, but batted zero because she had all her social media accounts set to private.

Smart girl.

I then made it a point to ask a few of my fraternity brothers about her, trying not to arouse too much suspicion. But when they were a little too intrigued for my liking, I backed off and pretended I only needed to find her to ask a question about class.

Who knew what those knuckleheads would do if they thought I was into her. One of them would probably try to get to her before I could, just to say they did. And then I wouldn't be able to date her at all, and the thought of that pissed me off.

You see, I might have certain rules when it came to my personal life, but that didn't mean that the rest of the guys in my fraternity followed suit. In my opinion, being a jerk to girls sometimes was one thing, but being a dick to my brothers was another thing entirely. I didn't want to be someone the other guys didn't trust or couldn't put their faith in.

All through the day, I looked around for Jess. Admittedly, I might have stayed on campus a little longer than necessary in the hope of running into her, yet I never did. But not seeing her gave me more time to come up with a game plan for the next day in class.

A plan that flew right out the window the second I saw her.

Jess sat down first and I moved to sit next to her again, knowing she'd be surprised. I watched as she flinched slightly, no doubt assuming that the last time had been nothing more than a fluke.

"You again," she said, trying not to smile.

"It wasn't so bad last time, was it?"

"Depends on your definition of bad."

"I think you secretly like when I sit near you, Jess Michaelson," I said, saying her full name so I could watch a blush spread over her cheeks.

One shoulder lifted in a small shrug. "I might like it a little."

I leaned close, my lips almost grazing her ear as I whispered, "Go to lunch with me today."

She jerked away and turned to face me. "I can't."

I knew she was lying. What I didn't know was why. "Why not?"

"I have plans," she said, then turned away as if she was in control of the conversation.

She wasn't.

"What kind of plans?"

Her lips flattened as her gaze met mine. "Plans that are none of your business. I can't go to lunch with you. I'm sure you'll survive."

Releasing a long breath, I slumped back into my chair. "I'm not."

She smiled, shaking her head and focusing her attention on our professor.

Inside, I reeled with questions. Why she was trying to stay away from me? I knew when girls were interested in me, and Jess Michaelson was definitely interested. I remembered her mentioning that she was seeing someone, and wondered what the lucky bastard was like and if I knew him.

"Is this because of your boyfriend?"

She leaned closer to whisper without turning to look at me. "No, why? Can't fathom a girl actually not being interested in you?"

I held back a laugh. "No, I can fathom that," I said, mimicking her word choice. "But you are interested. So what I *can't* fathom is why you're pretending like you're not."

"Anyone ever told you that you're arrogant?"

"You say that like it's a bad thing." I raised my eyebrows at her, trying my best to flirt as the professor cleared his throat and glared at us.

Shit. This girl was going to get me in all kinds of trouble. I shut my mouth and decided I'd leave her alone.

For now.

*

THE NEXT TIME Jess walked into class, she was wearing a sweet little blue dress, and I had to tamp down the hormones that raged at the sight of her. If I didn't know any better, I would almost think she was dressing this tempting on purpose just to wind me up.

Fingering the poker chip in my pocket, I watched her from our regular seats, which I'd commandeered in the hope that she'd willingly come and sit next to me. She glanced around the room before drawing in a long breath that made her chest rise. Rolling her eyes at me, she headed my way. When she sat down, I resisted the urge to rest my hand on her exposed thigh, as if she were my girl and I had every right.

Staring at the dusting of freckles across her nose, I thought how they only added to her attractiveness, and again, I had to stop one of my body parts from brushing against one of hers. I wanted to touch her, longed to know what her skin felt like under my fingertips.

But when class ended, she practically sprinted out of her seat. No doubt trying to get away from me, but I was quicker than her escape plan.

"Jess, wait up." When she slowed her pace but didn't stop, I hurried to catch up. "Where you headed?"

"The student union."

"Me too. Maybe we could go together?"

Jess stopped walking altogether and turned to face me,

forcing the other students to dodge and weave around us as they poured out of the classroom.

"What do you want, Nick? With me, I mean? Why this sudden interest?"

Shit, she was direct.

And then I knew why she'd tried so hard to stay away from me—she'd heard about my reputation and didn't trust me.

"Hell, I don't know, Jess. I just wanted to get to know you better," I said, not used to being put on the spot in that way.

Her eyes, so blue in the sunlight, locked on mine in challenge. "Know me *better*? You don't know me at all."

"Why do you keep stopping me then?"

"Because."

"Because of your *boyfriend*?" I spat out the word as if it tasted bitter on my tongue.

"He's not my boyfriend."

When she stared down at her feet, I knew she was keeping something from me.

"Did you guys break up?"

"Something like that." She brushed her hand over her dress, not meeting my eyes.

Despite the fact that her tone was still off, I wanted to break out into a little dance like an idiot. This was my *in*, my chance. I couldn't let her walk away so easily this time.

"When's your next class?" Hopefully, she had a break long enough for me to take her to lunch.

"Not for ninety minutes."

She finally lifted her gaze, focusing on something behind my shoulder. I half wondered what the hell was so interesting beyond me, but I stopped myself from turning around to look.

"So you have time then."

Her head cocked slightly as her eyes finally met mine and stayed there. "Time for what?"

"Time for us," I said, and watched with amusement as her smile faltered for a second before returning. "Come on, spend the next ninety minutes with me."

I was nothing if not persistent. Jess had become a bit of a challenge, and I owed it to myself to see if that's all she was, or if there was something more there.

She studied me. "I'm afraid if I tell you no, you'll just ask again."

"I will."

Her lips twitched. "Then how can I refuse?"

"You can't. Let's go; we're wasting precious minutes here."

As she gave me a big smile, I had to fight to hold in my own so I didn't look like too big of a wimp. The two of us walked through the student union, each eyeing the various fast-food concessions before agreeing on the campus's only fresh deli.

After waving my hand, I followed behind her toward the short line. I moved to grab a tray for her, but she reached for it at the same time and our hands brushed before she pulled away. It was a small thing, our fingers touching, but it sent shots of *what could be* and *what if* throughout my already tense body.

I handed her a tray before grabbing one for myself and sliding it across the metal countertop close to hers. A second later, I changed my mind and returned my tray to the stack.

"We'll just put it all on one tray, okay?" I asked Jess, who was now staring at me with a confused expression.

Her cheeks turned pink as she looked away. "Okay."

The guy working the counter was short and had his longish blond hair pulled up on his head in some sort of cross between a ponytail and a bun. He brightened at Jess with a smile that seemed a little more than just normal politeness as he asked, "What can I get started for you?"

When he leaned toward the glass that separated them, his smile not dimming in the slightest, I wanted to pick him up by the shirt collar and toss him across the room, just for the way he was looking at her.

"I like your man bun," Jess said with a polite smile of her own.

Man bun? There was an actual fucking term for this dude's hair? Seriously? What kind of douche wears his hair in a *man bun*?

"Thanks. I like your dress." The dude winked before scanning the length of Jess's blue sundress, noting the way it clung to the curves of her breasts and her hips.

Furious, I cleared my throat, wanting to remind him that not only was I in the room, but I was standing right fucking next to the girl he was flirting with.

Man Bun shot me a murderous glare. "Be with you in a minute, bro."

"That's not why I was clearing my throat, and I'm not your bro," I shot back, annoyed at his disrespectful behavior and a little confused by my violent reaction to it.

Jess looked at me with a crooked smile and nudged my shoulder with hers before she turned back to the man-bunned douchebag. "I'll just take a turkey Swiss on sourdough with lettuce, pickles, and mustard."

He made her sandwich slowly, methodically, as if he was making love to the damn thing, then had the nerve to throw in a bag of chips *on the house*. Man Bun was asking for a beat-down.

Jess took her wrapped sandwich and bag of chips and set them on our shared tray.

Man Bun made my sandwich with the hands of a man going to war, slamming the bread down hard enough to leave finger dents in it before stacking the ingredients haphazardly. I eyed him the entire time to make sure he didn't include a side of spit. Lucky for him, he didn't. And he didn't toss in any free chips with my order either.

I reached for Jess's bare shoulder as she stood next to me, wanting to show the douchebun that I was allowed to touch her and he wasn't. Bread Boy needed to know who was in charge.

"Can you grab us a couple of drinks, Jess? I got this." I reached for my wallet before she had a chance to protest.

"It's okay. I can pay for mine," she insisted.

She was adorable. I wanted to kiss her square on the lips for being so fucking cute.

"I got this," I repeated as she tilted her head at me, obviously weighing her options. "I want to." I pitched my voice at its most sincere, doing my best to calm whatever storm was currently raging behind her blue eyes. "Just grab me a Pepsi, please. And whatever you want."

"You're sure?" she asked one last time.

"I'm sure."

She walked to the glass-front fridge as I attempted to pay for our stuff. I say attempted because I got distracted by the sight of Jess's sundress rising up her thighs as she bent over to grab a drink from one of the lower shelves.

"It's ten eighty-three, please."

The cashier's voice pulled my attention away from the gorgeous pair of legs for only a moment. But it was a moment too long because when I glanced back, Jess was already heading my way, two drinks in hand and a smile on her face.

"Hey, Nick, come here."

A girl I'd dated briefly last year called to me as we crossed the crowded student union and I stopped, fully aware that my presence here would attract too much attention, too many questions, too many *other* people. It was how it had always been with me. I had information and knowledge that people wanted, so when they ran into me, they all wanted to pump me for it.

A game of questions was sure to follow. It's what always happened.

What was going on this weekend? Did I had an *in* to the newest nightclub? Did I know the bouncer at that club in Hollywood? Were we throwing a party that weekend? It could be any number of things.

On any other day I wouldn't have minded nearly as much, but not today. Today I wanted to get to know Jess, to see if we had anything in common.

My reputation preceded me, but I actually did have standards. My dating a lot of girls simply boiled down to not having found one good enough to stick around for. It wasn't my fault. It was hard to find a decent match when you were in college and girls were looking for all the wrong things—a guy with money or a nice car, someone who had famous parents or something you could offer them. Yeah, it's true, guys wanted all the wrong things too, like an easy lay or a pretty face. But I honestly tried to be better than that.

"Jess, we aren't going to get any privacy in here. Will you go somewhere else with me?" I narrowed my eyes, willing her to say yes.

"Of course," she responded easily.

I nodded toward the exit and headed in that direction as she followed a step behind. Once we were through the double glass doors, I set our tray on top of a trash can and grabbed our food.

"Come on." I motioned, holding both of our sandwiches as she carried our drinks.

"Where are we going?" She squinted before juggling the drinks so she could lower her sunglasses over her eyes.

"That's a surprise, but it's not far."

Eh, it was a little far but it would be worth it, and I had a suspicion that Jess wouldn't mind the walk. I glanced at her shoes, noting the sandals on her feet.

"I might have lied," I said.

Her smile dropped. "About what exactly?"

"The distance. It's on the other side of campus."

"Where exactly are you taking me, Mr. Fisher?"

Jess snagged her bottom lip between her teeth as she waited for my response. She might have been waiting a minute, ten minutes, or a year, I couldn't be sure. I was so focused on that lip.

Shaking my head slightly to regain my focus, I said, "The field."

"The football field?" she asked, clearly confused.

"Yeah."

"Weird, but whatever." She shrugged one shoulder and picked up her pace.

I knew no one would be there, and even though I wasn't on the team anymore, the field was still sort of a sanctuary for me. It was the one place I could hide out when I didn't want to be found, which wasn't very often, but still, everyone needed a safe place. The football stadium at State was mine.

We slipped through an opening in the gates, then climbed all the way up to the last row and sat in seats beneath the press box. It was the only area in the whole place that had any sort of shade.

Jess settled in the seat next to me, and I kicked my feet up on the chair in front of mine and scooted lower into my seat. She handed me my Pepsi and I handed her her sandwich, and her stupid chips.

"Why the football field?" She glanced at me as she pushed her sunglasses on top of her head, trapping strands of her blond hair behind her ears.

"It's the one place on campus where no one bothers me," I admitted, far too quickly and easily to someone I barely knew. "If we'd stayed in the student union, we'd never be able to have a real conversation."

"You used to play, right?"

I nodded, taking a bite of my mangled sandwich. "Up until last season."

"Yeah, I heard something about that. You don't want to play anymore?"

She lifted her mile-high sandwich to her lips, making me wonder how on earth she was going to take a bite without spilling the contents down her dress. That mystery was solved when she pressed it between her fingers, making it as compact as possible before moving it to her mouth and taking the smallest bite I'd ever seen. I would have bet money she only got lettuce in that bite.

"I'll look away and you can just shove it in there," I teased, not purposely avoiding her question.

"Excuse me?" she mumbled, still chewing.

"Asshole Man Bun made your sandwich too big. I'll look away so you can get a good bite in."

She started laughing, or maybe she was choking; I couldn't be a hundred percent sure. She reached for her water and took a swig.

Once she had herself under control, she said, "Asshole Man Bun?"

"Yeah, didn't you read his name tag? That's what it said." I gave her a sly smile.

"Must have missed it. Okay, so . . . seriously, turn away so I can get down and dirty with this sandwich without you watching."

I turned away from her and stared at the seats in the stadium, remembering how they used to fill up when I played. Nothing compared to a Friday night under the lights, but that time in my life felt like eons ago instead of only last year.

"You can look back now."

I turned back and grinned at the spot of mustard that rested on the tip of her nose. Leaning closer, I reached out to wipe away the offending condiment, letting my fingers brush her cheek as I did.

"You had a little mustard there."

She swallowed hard. "Oh. Thanks. So much for not embarrassing myself. Quick, do something distracting so we can pretend this never happened."

"It was just a little mustard, Jess. I think we'll be okay."

I tossed my arm around her shoulders and tugged her toward me. Being with her was easy, not tense and awkward. I wasn't used to things with a girl being so easy, so carefree. There was always a hidden agenda, but Jess didn't seem to have one.

"Are you going to tell me why you stopped playing football?" she asked again.

"What'd you hear?"

She sighed. "Do you always answer questions with questions? Why are you so evasive on this topic?"

I spit out a laugh before removing my arm and reaching for my drink. "I'm not. Sorry, it's just that I thought everyone knew the answer to that one already."

Her gaze softened. "I did hear something, but I'd rather hear it from you."

"I didn't want to go pro," I said as my chest tightened. "Honestly, I don't even know if I was good enough, but plenty of guys on the team were, and that was their dream. I couldn't, in good conscience, continue playing every Friday night over someone else who wanted it more than I did, who wanted their future to include football when I didn't."

Jess nodded, her hand suddenly resting on my thigh as she gave it a light squeeze before taking it away.

Immediately, my mind screamed, *Put it back.*

"That's very . . . I want to say *noble* of you, but who calls people noble these days? But that's sort of what you are in that situation. I don't know if many guys would do what you did."

I drew in a slow breath. Jess made me proud about my decision, yet my old man had practically disowned me for it. Which made absolutely no sense whatsoever, because he had always complained about how much of my life football consumed, insisting it was a waste of time.

He even threatened once to stop paying for school completely if I didn't, so I did. I quit. And I thought he'd be happy but he still seemed disappointed, as if I'd let him down in some way. I couldn't win with him.

That theme seemed to be the story of my life. *How to Disappoint Your Father*, starring Nick Fisher. Yes, I had the leading role.

I gulped down the rest of my drink before angling my body toward Jess. "Ready for twenty questions?"

She popped the last of her sandwich in her mouth and chewed slowly before saying, "Um, I guess."

HOLY HOTNESS

Jess

*W*HOSE LIFE IS THIS?

How was I sitting in the stands of the football stadium with Nick freaking Fisher right now, playing a game of Twenty Questions that he'd initiated? And why with me, of all people?

One minute we were in class, and the next time I blinked, Nick had bought my lunch, gotten a little jealous of the deli-counter guy, and claimed he wanted to get to know me better. Instead of psychoanalyzing everything, I went along with it.

Because I wanted to.

Because if Nick freaking Fisher wanted to get to know me better, then I was going to help him do it. The overanalyzing could wait until later with Rachel.

Nick grabbed his baseball hat and flipped it around so it was facing the right direction. The move shaded his eyes, and I mourned the loss of being able to see them clearly.

"Where did you grow up?" he asked.

Easy enough. "The Valley. You?"

"Orange County."

I nodded, but then wanted more specifics. "Where in Orange County?"

"Laguna Beach. Where in the Valley?"

"Studio City. The nice part."

He smiled. "Parents still married?"

"Yep. Yours?" I had no idea why, but I figured Nick would say his were divorced.

"Yep."

"I think we're like a rare breed or something," I said, keeping my tone light. Very few people I knew had parents who were still together.

"Tell me about it. But their relationship is so fucked. I almost wish they'd split up."

"Really?" I thought about asking more, telling him to give me reasons and examples, but it seemed too personal a topic to press, so I added a little bit about my own. "Not mine. They're ridiculously in love, and it's gross. And sweet. But mostly gross."

"Siblings?"

"Nope, you?"

"Two brothers. Older," he explained before I could ask.

"How much older?" I cocked my head to the side as he grinned.

"Ryan and Frank are eight and ten years older than I am, so I don't see them as much as I'd like. I was definitely an accident." Nick snagged one of my chips and tossed it into his mouth, chewing while I processed his words.

"I always wanted an older brother," I confessed, feeling silly.

He swallowed, his Adam's apple bobbing. "Not a sister?"

I shook my head sharply. "No. I wanted to *be* the younger sister. It always seemed cool to have an older brother watching out for you. You know, beating up the guys who tried to date you, and stuff like that."

"You want someone to beat me up?"

Nick's mock hurt made the already gooey parts of me melt even further.

I laughed. "I just want him to give you a hard time."

"Cruel. Any pets?"

"One dog and three fish," I said with a big smile. I loved those stupid fish.

"Fish? Really?"

I punched his shoulder. "Hey, I won them at the carnival and they're still alive. That was six years ago, and that's a major accomplishment."

He wiped the back of his hand across his mouth. "That is a major accomplishment. I think those things are meant to die the second you bring them home."

"Well, Ron, Snape, and Harry are never dying," I said over his laughter as he repeated the names of my goldfish. "Shut up, Nick. Stop laughing at me."

"Harry, Ron, and Snape? Seriously?"

"I was going through a phase."

"Please tell me your dog isn't named Dumbledore?" he all but snorted, and I glared at him.

"My dog's a girl. Her name is Bettina. What about you? Do you have any pets that I can make fun of?"

Nick stopped laughing and shook his head. "No. Sorry. My dad claims to be allergic to dogs, but I think he's full of shit. No pets for me, not even as a kid. Not even a stupid fish."

I couldn't help it, but in that moment I actually felt sorry for him, and said so. He shrugged but didn't say anything.

After an awkward pause, he asked, "What are you majoring in?"

"Film production," I replied, trying to stop myself from smiling at him like an idiot, but failing.

He let out a little groan. "Ah, that must suck."

Confused, I squinted at him. Did he think my choice of major was lame? "Why does it suck?"

"Because I thought they were dropping it after this semester."

I sat up straight in the hard stadium chair as my body instantly stiffened. "What are you talking about? Why would they drop it?"

He brushed his thighs, sending crumbs from his long-gone sandwich to the ground at his feet. "Shit, I could be totally wrong. It's not my major, so . . ."

"But they have all the equipment, and three separate studios. It doesn't make sense," I said slowly, not wanting to believe that State would actually cancel the program.

"Jess?"

Nick's voice was clear, but my thoughts felt muddled.

"Jess, look at me."

When I looked up, his deep blue eyes made my heart lurch like they always seemed to do.

"I'm sure I heard wrong. Check with your counselor, but don't take my word for it, okay?" When I didn't respond, he grasped my hands, giving them a quick squeeze. "Jess."

"Sorry, I'm just silently freaking out here."

"Don't. I'm sure it's nothing." He waved a hand as if dismissing the entire idea. "So, tell me what you want to do in film production."

My smile slowly returned. "I'm not a hundred percent sure yet since I haven't ever done any of it. I was thinking I might want to direct or produce, but there are so many other things that go into making a film, who knows which direction I'll choose." The possibilities seemed endless, and that filled me with hope. Hope that I'd follow my dreams and have a career I loved.

"What about you?" I asked.

"I'm a marketing major. My dad owns one of the top marketing firms in three states, so I'll go to work for him as soon as I graduate." His words seemed forced, not filled with the kind of excitement one would expect.

"You don't want to work for your father?"

Nick's brows pulled together briefly before relaxing, as if he wondered how I'd picked up on such a subtle detail. "No, I do. It's just . . ."

When he didn't continue, I asked, "What? It's just what?"

"It's just that there's a part of me that really wants to work with my brothers. Working with my dad would be great, but . . ."

He stopped talking again, and I urged him on.

"Your brothers don't work for your dad, right? They own a bunch of bars or something?" I'd heard they did, but since the information was secondhand, I wasn't sure.

His face lit up. "They own one bar in Santa Monica. It's called Sam's."

"So you said that working with your dad would be great, but . . . but what?"

"It's just that if I could do anything, I'd work with Frank and Ryan, buy into the bar with them. I love being there. And

I'm good at it." His gaze finally raised and connected with mine. "I helped them create and design their new drink menu, and I've handled all their marketing to date." A cocky grin emerged. "And I'm pretty good with people, in case you didn't know."

I laughed. "I'm well aware."

Nick looked so happy talking about the bar, it made me wonder how he could just walk away from it. He didn't seem to be the type of person who wouldn't fight for the things he wanted, but then again, I didn't really know him.

"Why don't you work for them instead?"

At my question, his entire expression darkened. He blew out a breath that was long and painfully slow as I waited for him to say something, anything. This was the kind of good stuff in a conversation that really let you peek inside the character of a person. And it was rare that a topic like this came up between two people so quickly.

"That was never in the plan, Jess. It's been set in stone for as long as I can remember that I would work for my dad and run the company one day. I wasn't really raised to question that, you know?"

"Not really. My parents are super encouraging, and they're excited that I'm following my dreams."

My parents were middle-class working people who raised me to hope and dream for whatever it was that I wanted. When I expressed an interest in film production a couple years ago, their attitude was *Well, someone has to produce films, so why not our daughter?* I used to believe that everyone's parents were this way, but sitting here with Nick now, I realized just how naive my assumption had always been.

"Mine raised me to believe that his dreams *were* my dreams," he said with a solemn expression that placed a tiny crack inside my heart.

"So, do it anyway," I insisted as if that was an option.

"Do what exactly?" Nick looked at me, his eyes shadowed by the bill of his hat.

"Work with your brothers."

He shook his head. "I can't. At least, it feels like I can't. Maybe at some point later on, but not right now. Maybe not ever. Hell, I don't know."

"Why not? I don't mean to pry, but won't your brothers stick up for you? What do they think about this? They didn't have to work for your dad, so why do you?" I wanted to hear his answer, longed for it, held my breath waiting for it.

"My brothers never had to deal with any of this stuff. My dad's company didn't hit it big until about ten years ago. Both of them were out of the house already, doing their own thing. I never stood a chance with them gone."

"So they get to own the bar and your dad doesn't care? He doesn't pressure them to quit and work for him?" None of this seemed fair to me as an outsider looking in.

"No. He'd never try to tell them that."

"Why not?"

He smiled. "Because neither one of them would take it. They'd tell my dad to fuck off. Which is something I couldn't do if you paid me." When I grimaced, he added, "Don't get me wrong, I want to tell him to *fuck off* all the time." He shrugged. "I just can't."

It wasn't something I could relate to, but I'd never been in the kind of situation he was in. It felt awful for me to disappoint my parents, so I could only imagine the kind of pressure Nick felt.

"You need your brothers," I said and he nodded. "To help you stand up for yourself." I hoped I wasn't crossing a line.

When he agreed, saying, "I hate that you're right," I wanted to take him into my arms and hug him.

"Tell me about them. Your brothers," I asked, not wanting our conversation to end. Ever.

Nick's face lit up again, and I wanted him to see himself the way that I did. How just the mention of his brothers or their bar made his face come alive in a way nothing else had.

"Frank is the oldest," he said with a smile. "He's definitely the quietest of us three. He's an observer, you know what I mean? He got a scholarship to Arizona to play baseball right out of high school. He played until he got hurt. I always thought he'd move back home after that, but he ended up staying there. Thank God Ryan wanted to buy that bar, because otherwise I think Frank would still be there."

I smiled too. I couldn't help it. "That's awesome. I bet you're glad to have him back. So they both own the bar? Just them?"

"Yeah. When Frank got hurt, he changed his major to business management and finance. He keeps the books for the business. He's really smart."

"And you do all the marketing. What does Ryan do?"

A throaty laugh escaped as Nick shook his head. "Ryan, shit, where do I start? Ryan's the biggest flirt I've ever met in my life. You think I'm good with girls? Ryan's a god."

"I can't even imagine that." I smiled as I tried to picture an even more charming guy than Nick.

"It's true. The ladies can't get enough of him. Anyway, he's twenty-nine. He went to school down in San Diego and fell into bartending one night, filling in as a favor for a friend. He loved it so much, he never stopped. He told me once that he made more money in tips that night than he'd made in a month at his regular job."

"No way," I said, my tone incredulous.

"Honest. But that's not why he does it. He truly loves it. He makes the most incredible drinks you've ever tasted. They're a fucking art form. Ryan's more of a mixologist, you know? I've never seen anything like it before in my life. The time it takes to make a drink, the way he uses herbs and citrus to assault your senses before the alcohol ever hits your tongue. Wait until you try one, Jess. It'll change your life."

Wait, what?

I tried not to choke on my excitement, but failed. Words escaped me as I pictured hanging out with Nick and his brothers.

"Are either of them married?" It was a fair question, I thought, but Nick just shook his head with a slight grin.

"Frank has a girlfriend who moved out here from Arizona with him, but none of us think he's really happy. It sucks. And Ryan couldn't keep a girl if he tried. He's constantly dating, and constantly single."

"Sounds like someone else I know," I said, nudging Nick's shoulder with mine.

"Hey, it's not my fault that I can't meet the right girl."

I stopped myself from rolling my eyes. "That's what you're looking for? The right girl?"

He let out a quick laugh. "I'm just tired of dating all the wrong ones."

I wasn't sure what he meant, and to stop myself from reading into it, I turned the subject back to Nick's career. "I don't mean to keep going back to this, but they both got to choose their career, but yours got chosen for you? It doesn't seem fair." I didn't mean to continue poking at it, hitting a nerve, but I couldn't seem to stop.

"Frank and Ryan weren't raised the way I was. The childhood they talk about isn't something I can even relate to. It's so different from mine. The dad they talk about doesn't seem anything like the dad I grew up with. It's almost like they're two completely different people."

"Who got the better version?" My question came out without a second thought.

"I don't know, to be honest. All I do know is that if there's one person on Earth that I don't go up against or say no to, it's my old man. I don't like to disappoint him, but I feel like it's all I ever do." He finished off his can of soda as I filed away that bit of information somewhere between my heart and my head.

"I'm sure that's not true. How could he be disappointed in you?"

Nick shrugged but didn't respond, and I stifled my own disappointment that he didn't feel comfortable sharing it with me.

"Maybe you'll learn more from working with him. Maybe he can teach you everything you need to know, and it will make you better when you do go to the bar." I chewed on my bottom lip, hoping Nick wouldn't think my positive spin was stupid.

His head jerked up and a smirk appeared. "I like the way you see things," he said as he pulled something out of his pocket, rubbing his thumb across it before he tucked it away again.

"What was that?" I asked.

He looked at me like I was half crazy. "What?"

"What's in your pocket?"

"Oh." He reached in, pulled it out, and placed it in my hand—an old five-dollar poker chip from a Vegas hotel that didn't exist anymore. "It's sort of my lucky charm. My grandfather gave it to me before he passed away. Told me he used to always carry it with him, and I just started doing the same thing."

"That's sweet," I said, loving the sentimental side of Nick.

"My grandpa met my grandma in Vegas, at a poker table at this hotel. That's why he saved this chip. Said it brought him the best luck he could have ever hoped for."

"Your grandma?" The sweet story warmed my heart and made me smile.

"Exactly."

"So now you carry it?"

"I always thought it was cool."

"It is cool," I said, handing him back the chip before reaching for my cell phone.

"I always thought I could make it into a necklace or something, but that's probably a dumb idea."

I shrugged, trying to imagine Nick wearing a necklace with a giant poker chip on it, and laughed.

"To be honest, I can't really picture it, but I get what you're saying." Glancing at my phone, I noted the time and remembered how far away from my classrooms we were. "Shoot. I have to go or I'm gonna be late."

Nick stood up and extended his hand to me. I took it,

allowing him to pull me up as I tugged at the bottom of my shorts.

"I'll walk you," he said.

"You don't have to." I tried to resist, but secretly hoped he still would.

"I know I don't have to, Jess. I want to."

Best. Answer. Ever.

When we finally arrived at my building, ten minutes before class started, I was thankful that Nick had walked with me. I would never have found it on my own on time.

"Thanks for lunch." I clutched my bag against my side, not knowing what to do with my hands.

Nick leaned in to hug me and kissed my cheek. "It was my pleasure. Really." He gave my arm a little squeeze, then said, "We're having a small party at the house tomorrow. Come. And bring Rachel."

"Rachel?" I said with surprise. "Like my roommate, Rachel?"

He laughed. "Yeah, like your roommate, Rachel. I think Trevor misses her."

As Nick walked away, I stood there with my mouth hanging open, wondering just how much research he had done on me. He not only knew that I lived with Rachel, but he knew she was Trevor's ex-girlfriend.

He turned around to face me as he turned his cap backward. "Say you'll come, Jess, or I'll just harass the living shit out of you until you do."

Now I was the one laughing. "I don't doubt that. I'll be there."

With bells on, Nick Fisher.

With. Bells. On.

FRAT-BOY SCENE

Jess

AFTER CLASS, I walked back to my apartment and tried to focus on my homework, but Nick's face kept popping up in my head instead. He had completely taken me by surprise today, and our conversation kept playing in a loop in my mind.

The door was locked, so I fished out my key before unlocking it and stepping inside. I decided that it was good that Rachel wasn't home yet, so I'd have a chance to get started on my homework before she talked my ear off about today's Nick-tivities.

I grabbed a cold soda from the fridge and headed into my bedroom. After piling all the pillows against the wall, I leaned into them. Reaching for my laptop, I fired it up and began searching for information on my assignment.

The front door slammed far sooner than I had expected. I hadn't even read a single article yet.

"Jess?" she shouted into our apartment.

"In my room," I shouted back.

Rachel's curvy frame appeared in my doorway before she hopped onto my bed, making my laptop bounce up and down on my legs. "What's up?"

"Just working on this assignment for Psych."

"Ugh, core curriculars suck," she said, referring to the classes I had to take to fulfill my general-education credits. She pushed back off from my bed and walked out of my room without warning. "I need a drink. And I'm starving. Come out here with me and I'll make you food."

I couldn't resist her offer, so I bookmarked the site, closed my laptop, and grabbed my soda before heading toward the other room. "The class is actually really interesting, but it's also really hard."

"That's why I took Sociology instead of Psych."

"Well, maybe if you'd taken Psych, you could analyze the day I had today," I said with a slight huff.

"Why? What happened? Are you okay?" Her eyebrows drew together with concern, which surprised me. I hadn't expected my comment to worry her.

"It's nothing bad. Sorry. I just spent the entire break between my classes with Nick today," I said in a rush. I popped open the can, taking a sip to silence my babbling.

Rachel choked on her words. "You what?"

I grinned, my smile feeling like it took up my entire face. "You heard me."

She grabbed my hand and pulled me toward our couch in the living room. Forcing me to sit down next to her, she released my hand before angling her body toward mine. "Tell me everything immediately. And don't leave anything out."

"He wanted to hang out with me after class, so I told him I had ninety minutes."

"Wait." She held up her hand. "What about your fake boyfriend?"

"I told him we broke up," I said with a laugh, and she laughed with me.

"Okay, go on."

"He bought me lunch, and then we went to the football stadium and talked."

"Talked?" She cocked an eyebrow as if she didn't believe me.

"Yeah. *Talked.* He's . . ." I paused, searching for the right word, and Rachel jumped in.

"He's what, hot? Horny? Great in bed? He's what, Jess?"

Shrugging, I said, "He's really cool."

Really cool? That's the word I use to describe him? #Fail, Jess.

"Cool?" Her lips curled up with distaste.

"I don't know. He was nice. Super nice. And normal. I don't know what I thought he'd be like, but this wasn't it."

"What did you guys talk about?"

I didn't want to tell Rachel about Nick's family life or his dad's business, so I decided to keep those things to myself. Even though I didn't know him all that well, some things shouldn't be shared without permission.

"I don't know, everything. We talked about where we grew up, our families, our majors, what we want to be when we're real grownups."

Rachel swept her dark wavy hair off her shoulder with a flick of her wrist before leaning back against the cushions. "Did he ask you out?"

I sucked in a quick breath as I remembered. "He invited us to a party tomorrow. Both of us. He said it was small, and he specifically mentioned you and said that Trevor misses you."

"He what?" she shouted as she leaned in close. "How would he even know that?"

"They're fraternity brothers. I'm sure they talk. Although I have no idea how he knew you were my roommate."

"I guess." She tapped her bottom lip with her finger. "This is all very interesting."

"Why'd you guys break up, anyway? You never did give me a straight answer about it."

I thought back to last year when Rachel and Trevor had dated. I liked Trevor the few times I'd met and hung out with him. Rachel and I had both lived in the same dorm building as freshmen, but we weren't suitemates, so I didn't get to see her every day until we moved in together this year.

Trevor had always seemed like he was really into Rachel whenever I saw them together, and when they stopped dating, I never knew why. That was the thing about Rachel, she tended to keep certain details about her life private. When she wanted to share, she shared—overshared really—but when she didn't want to, no amount of prying could get the information out of her.

"It doesn't matter," she said, looking past me and out the sliding glass doors.

"Will you come to the party, though?" If she said no, I wouldn't go either. There was no way in hell I'd go to a frat party alone.

Her gaze darted back to mine. "Are you kidding? And miss the chance to watch Nick Fisher flirt shamelessly with my roommate? Of course I'll go." She stuck her tongue out before pushing off the couch. "It's going to be epic."

I blew out an exaggerated breath. "We'll see."

"I hope your fake boyfriend doesn't show. I heard he's the jealous type."

"Shut up," I said, swatting her shoulder. "But you're right. He's super possessive. That's why I had to end things."

*

SINCE NICK HADN'T asked me for my phone number, that meant I didn't have his either. It also meant I had no way of texting him to ask what time the party started, or tell him we were on our way over, which we were. I prayed that arriving close to eleven would be a safe enough bet, and that the gathering would be in full swing by then. It was a little late, but I had to focus on some homework first.

I sat in the passenger seat of Rachel's old Civic, my knees bouncing up and down.

Rachel shot me a glare. "Stop shaking your knees like that."

"I'm nervous," I bit out.

"You should be."

I snapped my head around to look at her, but she burst out laughing before I could speak. "I hate you."

"You don't. Don't be nervous. It's just a party and he's just a guy," she said, obviously trying to downplay the entire situation as she made a right turn. The frat house was down the block, but I could already see people gathered on the front lawn.

I chortled out a laugh. "Just a boy? You're one to talk. You've been building him up since we got to school here last year. It's like you think he's part god or something."

"You never know. All those mythology stories have to come from somewhere."

"Yeah, good writers' imaginations." I huffed, absolutely refusing to believe that Nick was anything other than human, no matter how hot and charming he was.

Rachel pulled the car to the curb, and I smiled at the four guys playing beer pong out front as I got out of the car.

"Nick! Your girl's here," one of them yelled.

My cheeks burst into flames. How the hell did they know who I was, and that I was here for Nick?

"Did you hear that?" Rachel whispered as she locked arms with me.

We walked inside where the lights were dimmed, the music blared, and more than a few people had gathered in the house. A lot of people.

This wasn't what I considered a small party. This was a *party*.

I scanned the crowd of bodies swaying to the music in the living area, and then checked out the group of guys hanging out in the kitchen, but didn't spot Nick.

Trevor suddenly appeared at Rachel's side, focusing on her as he said, "You came."

"Nick said you wanted me to," she said, her tone down-right bitchy.

"Can we talk?" He motioned over his shoulder, and she looked at me.

"Will you be okay if I leave you alone?" She raised her eyebrows in that way that meant she wanted me to say yes.

I scanned the room again before waving them off. "I'll be fine. You two go."

She gave me a quick best-friend squeeze before following Trevor into the crowd and disappearing from view.

I navigated my way around the sweaty dancing bodies and headed toward the kitchen, where I figured I'd grab a drink and ask if anyone had seen Nick. As I moved through the group of dancers, a guy grabbed me by the waist and spun me around.

"Hey."

"Hi," I said awkwardly, not recognizing him, but definitely realizing that he'd had way too much to drink.

"You're really pretty," he slurred, pushing his face too close to mine.

"Thanks." I gave him a tight smile as I pulled out of his grip. It took a little wriggling, but I finally broke free and bolted away from him in search of the one guy I came here to see.

Marching up to the group of guys in the kitchen, I noticed six of them circled around a keg. They were trying to convince one of their brothers to do a keg stand, and before they talked him into it, I interrupted.

"Do you guys know where Nick is?"

They all turned to stare at me, and I recognized two of the guys from the class I shared with Nick.

"Hey, you're Jess, right? I'm Todd." He extended his hand to me over the counter that separated us and gave it a firm shake. "Everyone, this is Jess."

My cheeks immediately heated again with the ridiculous shouting that followed. Drunk guys were the weirdest. Once the cheering died down and I found my voice again, I repeated my question.

"Do you know where Nick is?"

"I think he's in his room. Down the left hallway, last door

at the very end," Todd said, pointing me in the right direction.

Suddenly realizing that Nick might not be there alone, I asked, "Uh, do I want to go in there?"

"He was alone when I saw him," Todd said, and I turned just as they lifted the other guy by his legs and held him upside down, chanting his name.

Shaking my head, I took a left at the dark hallway and noticed several couplings happening against the walls. I watched my feet, navigating my steps carefully, not wanting to step on anyone's feet or discarded clothing if I could help it. The hall was ridiculously long.

"I remember you."

I looked up to find the guy from the dance floor in front of me, blocking my way. I had no idea where he came from; it was like he appeared from thin air.

"Uh, okay." I moved to slip past him, but he reached out to stop me. When I tried to sidestep him, he moved in front of me again.

"Where are you going?"

"I'm just going to get Nick," I said, hoping that the mention of his name would deter the guy.

It didn't.

"Nick's busy," he bit out with a slur.

My stomach tightened into a painful knot. Maybe Todd was wrong, and Nick was in his room with some other girl. Why would he invite me here if he was only going to hook up with someone else?

"But I'm not. I'm not . . . not even busy."

The drunk guy shoved me against the wall and extended his arms on either side of me, trapping me as he propped himself up with his palms. His words were mangled as he continued speaking to me.

He was drunk. *Really drunk.*

And he was strong. *Too strong.*

No matter how I twisted or ducked, I couldn't find a way out of the human cage his arms formed around me.

His voice was drowned out by the sound of my heart frantically pounding in my ears. Not that his words were truly threatening; they were mostly filled with stupid things that drunk guys said when they didn't want you giving your attention to someone else. It was his body language that caused my current heart palpitations.

It was as if he wasn't quite aware of his own strength as he refused to let me get away from him. The more I struggled, the tighter his hold on me became. That's what scared me more than whatever words were currently spewing from his mouth. His words couldn't hurt me, but his hands could. And they were.

"Please stop," I pleaded, my voice shaking. "You're hurting me."

"Hurting you. How's I hurting you?"

His words were nonsensical as he moved his face dangerously close to mine. Then he licked his lips before diving straight at my mouth.

I turned my head quickly, cringing with disgust as my cheek was kissed and licked. *Gross.* I tried to push him away, but I wasn't strong enough.

"Get off," I said, my voice soft. Too soft.

"Stop pushing at me."

He breathed drunkenly into my face, using his body to

press me even harder against the wall. I was half surprised it didn't swallow me with the force. When his hand moved down the length of my body, I stifled a cry as his fingers grazed my breast. Suddenly feeling ill, I froze as panic coursed through me.

A handful of people were nearby, close enough to help me, but I couldn't find my voice. I'd been told what to do in situations like this, but my body refused to do it. I simply went numb. Too intimidated to move, too panicked to scream, too shocked to do anything but stand there, pressed against a wall in the dark with tears filling my eyes as some drunk guy tried to grope me.

"What the fuck?" I heard before feeling the release of pressure.

All at once, I was free. I slid to the floor, struggling to right myself, my knees weak with relief and my legs shaking.

A loud thump drew my gaze as I saw Nick pinning the drunk guy against the other wall, his muscular forearm pressed against the guy's neck. The drunk struggled, probably the same way I had, but this time Nick was the one who was stronger.

"You like cornering women? Make you feel like a tough guy to know that you're stronger than a girl? How about now? Not feeling so tough now, are you?" Nick spat out, and I noticed the guy's cheeks turning an unnatural shade of reddish purple.

"Nick!" I pounded on his back. "Nick, let him go. He can't breathe. He's just drunk. Nick!"

I shouted and pulled at his flexing shoulder, his muscles taut and hard. He glanced at me, and when our eyes met, he dropped the guy like he'd never existed in the first place.

"Jess, are you okay?"

Nick's strong arms that only moments ago were being used to inflict pain now wrapped around me, and his hands gentle as he comforted me, touching me with care.

I started to cry; I couldn't help it. The emotions over what had just happened overwhelmed me. It was everything—the drunk guy's actions, my fear, my shame over my inability to help myself, and Nick's reaction to it.

"Nick," I whispered, but the word barely came out.

"Come on. I got you."

He lifted me into his arms, cradling my body as he walked me down the rest of the long hallway toward what I assumed was his room.

FALLING OR SOMETHING LIKE IT

Nick

WHEN I SAW my frat brother David pressed against Jess in the hallway, I almost lost my fucking mind. And it wasn't only because I didn't like seeing her in the arms of someone else.

No, it was the way she struggled against him that really set me off. She tried to move, to get away from him, but she wasn't strong enough. And he refused to let her go, his face and body inching closer with every second that no one stopped him.

I saw red, blood fucking red, and it took Jess yelling in my ear to get me to calm down. I wasn't sure what would have happened if she hadn't gotten me to stop, but I had an idea.

I'd never been so out of control before. Usually I was too preoccupied sticking my tongue down someone's throat, as Jess would say, to pay attention to what was really going on at my parties. The thought made me wonder if this type of thing had ever happened before, but either way, I sure as shit was going to make sure it never happened again. I had no tolerance for that kind of behavior toward girls. It did everyone in our gender a disservice.

Shaking my head to rid myself of those dark thoughts, I

turned and focused my attention on Jess, who was now sitting on top of my king-sized bed, staring down at her hands.

"Are you okay?"

"I think I'd like to go home," she all but whispered.

She looked up at me, her blue eyes brighter now they were swimming in tears. When a few slipped free and started to spill down her face, I sat next to her and rubbed my thumb along her jawline before pulling her close and giving her a tight hug. She gulped in her breaths and trembled a little in my arms. Watching her wade through her emotions and not be able to help was one of the worst things I'd ever experienced.

As president of the fraternity, I was always expected to attend our parties and act as host. So when the party was in full force earlier, I knew I should have been out there socializing, but I'd started feeling sorry for myself when I realized Jess wasn't coming. Or at least, when I thought she wasn't.

Assuming she had blown me off, I'd moved my pity party to my bedroom and stayed out of sight, not wanting to see everyone else having a good time when I wasn't. Alone in my room, I was idle but my mind was busy, coming up with scenarios of her and her stupid ex-boyfriend getting back together, or thinking that maybe she hadn't enjoyed the time we spent together the day before.

It all came back to Jess not caring enough to show up at the party tonight, and I couldn't fucking handle it. And because of that, because of my stupid fucking ego, I wasn't there to protect her when she needed me.

"I'm so sorry I wasn't there," I said. Reluctantly, I released her, but ran my palm over her back, up and down and back again, keeping my movements slow and easy. "I'd been out there waiting for you all night. I actually thought you weren't going to come, so I was sitting in my room. Sulking, to be honest. I'm so sorry, Jess."

And I was. I felt responsible in some way. Even though I knew logically that it wasn't my fault, my mind refused to give me a reprieve. Certain things were my responsibility, and this felt like one of them.

"It wasn't your fault," she said softly.

When her eyes moved to meet mine, I knew in that moment that I'd do whatever I could to keep this girl safe. She was vulnerable, yet strong, but I'd be damned if anyone would ever hurt her on my watch again.

"I should have been there."

"I wanted to tell you that I was on my way, but I didn't have your number." She tried to smile, but it slipped away.

"Where's your cell?"

I held out a hand and waited as she pulled her phone from her back pocket and handed it to me. After typing my name and phone number into her contacts, I sent myself a text from her phone so that I'd have her number as well. My phone pinged in response, and I returned her phone.

"That's taken care of. I have your number, and now you have mine."

"Was that a pity handout?" she said with a sniff, and I smiled.

"No. I meant to ask you for it when we had lunch yesterday, but I forgot." I reached for her free hand and gave it a squeeze, but didn't release it. "Do you want me to take you home?"

One slim shoulder lifted in a shrug. "I came here with Rachel."

"Any idea where she is now?" I asked, but there was no way Jess could know. She couldn't possibly know anything after what she just went through.

"She went off with Trevor when we first got here."

"Can you call her? Or send her a text?" I suggested, looking at the phone still in her other hand.

"Duh. Yeah, I'm an idiot. Sorry." She shook her head, frowning at her herself, and pecked out a quick text to Rachel.

My heart beating fast, I shifted a little closer next to her on the bed, half afraid that my closeness would alarm her. When she leaned against me, I relaxed a little.

"You're not an idiot. You're shaken up. Anyone in your position would be."

The cell phone vibrated in her hand, and she jumped as if it had scared her half to death. It killed me to watch her react that way to something as simple as a text message notification.

"Is it her?"

Jess looked down, pressed a couple of buttons, and looked back at me. "She said I can go with you. She'll see me later."

My pulse finally started to settle into a normal rhythm. "So I can take you home now?"

"On one condition."

At this point, she could ask for anything and I'd give it to her. I'd do anything Jess asked me to.

"What's that?"

"Will you stay there with me for a little while? Please." Her brows pinched together as I tilted her face up with my fingertips. "Don't just drop me off and leave. I don't want to be alone; I just don't want to be here."

"Of course. I'll stay however long you want me to."

Staying with Jess was an easy thing to agree to. I was only a man, after all, but the need to protect her, to make her feel safe, far outweighed anything else at this point. I wasn't sure why it was suddenly so important that this girl knew that she could feel secure with me, but it was. I felt like it was my mission to make sure she knew I wasn't some douchebag who would hurt her.

"Thank you," she said, looking tired as I pulled her up from my bed.

"Come on. I got you." I wrapped an arm around her and tucked her in close to me.

Ignoring the shouts of my drunken frat brothers calling my name, I navigated us away from the party. Her body tensed in my hold with the shouts. She was uncomfortable, and I hated the way it made me feel. I was the one who had invited her here; I had put her in this position. I furiously scanned the room like a crazed lunatic, looking for David, and when I didn't see him anywhere, I tried to calm my breathing.

We left the house and crossed the poor excuse for a lawn. When we neared my truck, I pulled my remote from my pocket and clicked the unlock button. Jess seemed to relax a little as the lights clicked on.

"Jesus. This is your car?" she asked as I opened the passenger door for her.

"My dad bought it for me," I explained, tamping down my discomfort as I helped her up into the seat.

It wasn't that I didn't love my truck; I did. But I'd wanted something a little less flashy for my eighteenth birthday, half expecting a car with a little more age and dust, but my dad showed up with this one—a brand-new, fully loaded, customized model that cost more than most new BMWs, and was just about as luxurious and comfortable as one.

When I hopped into the driver's seat, Jess added, "It's really nice. I've never seen a truck so nice on the inside before."

I nodded, wanting to disagree with her, but couldn't. It was nice as hell, and I knew it.

"Thanks. I try to take good care of it," I said, thinking of all the times I'd detailed the interior myself, as if I had something to prove to everyone. Or maybe I was just trying to feel like I deserved the damn thing.

"Well, you do. It looks brand new."

CONNECTED

Jess

W E PULLED INTO the parking lot of my apartment complex, and I directed Nick into a visitor's spot. He held my hand the entire drive, and even though it didn't take us long to get to my place, the gesture was comforting. I appreciated it more than I could tell him.

What had happened at the party was mostly uncomfortable and jarring. I wasn't entirely sure how far things would have gone if Nick hadn't shown up to stop the guy, but the fact that I completely froze in the midst of the incident wasn't lost on me.

Honestly, that was what stuck with me the most. I had always assumed if something like that ever happened to me, I'd fight back, or at the very least yell for help. It had never once occurred to me that I might be the type of person who was too shocked to react rationally, or to even react at all. I was mad at myself, embarrassed even. Or maybe it was mostly disappointment that I felt.

I unlocked the front door and stepped inside, flipping the light switch to illuminate the entrance and kitchen area. The tension I felt eased at the relief of being home.

"Cute place," Nick said as he looked around at our beachy

decor.

"Thanks. Rachel found it for us last summer."

"It's really nice. Two bedrooms?" he asked, peeking his head into the first room that came into view, which was Rachel's.

"Yep."

"And two bathrooms?"

"Uh-huh. Two master suites. Makes things so much easier."

It was nice not having to share a bathroom like I did in the dorms last year. Even though Rachel and I ended up in the same one whenever we got ready, it was nice having our own private space where we could be as messy as we wanted without pissing off someone else.

"Your room?" he asked, still looking into the darkened space.

"Rachel's." I tilted my head in the opposite direction, where my door was.

Nick entered my bedroom, flipped on the light switch, and plopped right down on my bed as I headed to get us some water.

"Comfortable?" I shouted from the kitchen.

"It'll do," he shouted back.

I smiled to myself before walking in, trying to calm the nerves that had started to break through all of my other warring emotions. As I handed him a glass, our fingers touched.

"It'll do for what, exactly?" I cocked an eyebrow, teasing.

He sat up straighter and lifted his free hand in the air in surrender. "Nothing, nothing. I was just kidding."

"Me too. I'm okay, Nick. I'm not going to break."

"Are you sure?" He frowned. "How can you be okay? Hell, I'm not okay."

My heart melted a little with his admission.

"It was just a drunk guy. Yeah, he was strong and a little scary, but nothing *really* happened."

Nick scowled at me. "He tried to kiss you. He pushed himself on you and wouldn't let you move. That's not nothing, Jess," he insisted, his voice rising with each word.

I shifted my weight from foot to foot as what he said sank in.

"I don't know what you want me to say. I don't mean that it's *nothing* nothing, but it's not like he—" I stopped, not wanting to say those words out loud. The thought of what could have happened, hell, what *did* happen all the time to other people, was too horrible to consider.

"Don't diminish this, okay? I realize that it could have been worse, but it was bad enough. What he did wasn't okay."

"I know that." Averting my eyes, I took a sip of my water.

"I'm sorry, Jess." He leaned back into the stack of pillows as he relaxed. "I'm just a little worked up."

"I understand. And thank you." I sat on the bed next to him and placed my glass on the bedside table. "For everything tonight. I don't know what I would have done without you."

Nick's tight-lipped smile faded as he gritted his teeth, making the muscles in his jaw jump. "I can't even think about it."

Wanting more from him, I asked, "What do you mean?"

"I can't think about what would have happened if I wasn't there, Jess, if I didn't come out of my room at that moment.

You don't understand what it was like to see you like that. Pinned against the wall, frantic, trying to move but not being able to." He tossed his baseball cap on the bed and raked his fingers through his hair. "God, seeing how David was controlling your body and the way he was touching you . . ." He winced, squeezing his eyes shut for a second before staring at me. "I wanted to really fucking hurt him."

My breath hitched in my throat as my heart stuttered. "I'm glad you were there, but I'm even gladder that you didn't kill him."

Nick's eyes met mine, something unrecognizable in them. "Only because you stopped me."

"Wouldn't want you going to jail." Forcing a grin, I added, "You're too pretty," trying to lighten the conversation.

He rubbed a hand along his scruff-lined jaw. "You're right," he said and huffed out a laugh.

I didn't know what else to do, so I laughed along with him, praying it would release some of the tension. All the emotions, the drama, it was exhausting.

"Should we play more Twenty Questions?"

I shook my head. "Not tonight."

My response surprised even myself, but I was too tired for games, even if they would help me get to know Nick better. His reaction to my situation tonight had told me plenty. Plus, with the adrenaline starting to wear off, I felt like I was crashing. Hard.

"Do you want me to take off?" he asked, his tone hesitant.

"No," I said quickly, not wanting him to go any more than he seemed to want to. "Maybe we can just watch TV?"

"Netflix and chill?" he said with a smirk.

The implied suggestion that we have sex was ridiculous, which was exactly why he said it. Obviously, Nick was trying to lighten the mood too.

I swatted his shoulder. "You wish, Fisher."

He cocked an eyebrow. "I might, but not tonight. Why don't you go do whatever it is that girls do when they get ready for bed, and I'll find us something to watch while we don't *chill*."

"Smartass."

I pushed off the bed and headed for my bathroom, a little uncertain what to do. Part of me was dying to wash off all my makeup and be clean after feeling so dirty, but the rest of me wanted to leave it all on so that Nick thought I looked this put together all the time.

It became a moot point when I saw my tear-streaked face in the bathroom mirror. The notion of me looking put together at this point was a total joke. I couldn't stay like this, not with my foundation streaky and my mascara runny.

After scrubbing my face clean, I shrugged at my reflection before giving myself a little pep talk. If Nick Fisher didn't find me attractive without makeup, then he could fuck off, right? I tried to make myself believe it was that simple.

After brushing my teeth, I changed into a pair of boy shorts and a tank top. Nick was stretched out on my bed when I came back, one arm slung behind his head as he watched the flat-screen television on top of my dresser.

"All done?" He rolled over to his side to look at me, his gaze roving from my bare legs to my chest and back again.

"Yep."

I crawled onto the bed and reached for a blanket, pulling it over me as I tried to get into a comfortable position that didn't seem awkward. Nick was practically lying down, his head propped up by a bunch of pillows, so I did the same.

Glancing at my face, he said, "I like your no-makeup look."

Then he looked me in the eye before dropping a sweet kiss on top of my head. A part of me might have melted a little in that moment, but I couldn't say for sure.

"Come here." Nick wrapped an arm around my waist and pulled me gently toward him. His body heat hit me like an oven.

I propped myself up with my own set of pillows and pretended to be interested in the TV, but all I could think about was Nick lying next to me, his fingers moving lazily across my waist.

"This is nice," I admitted, and his hand moved from my waist to my hair.

As we watched TV, he ran his fingers through it, over and over again without saying a word until my eyes got heavy. I wasn't sure how long it took me to actually fall asleep, but I woke to the blare of an infomercial so loud, I practically jumped out of the bed. I glanced at the clock to find it was 2:34 a.m., and clicked the remote to turn off the television, leaving the room in darkness.

"Jess?"

Nick's voice startled me as I turned my head to face him. I'd completely forgotten that he was here.

"Shit," he said. "I fell asleep. I'm sorry."

"It's okay. I did too," I said with a sleepy smile.

"I should go."

When he shifted to get out of bed, my insides ached.

"You don't have to. I mean, you can stay if you want," I said, hoping he would.

"Are you sure?"

"I'm sure."

"Okay. I need to pee, though," he admitted.

Relieved, I released a quick breath. "You know where the bathroom is. And I think I have an extra toothbrush in the drawer, if you need one."

"You have extra toothbrushes?" The bed dipped as he rolled out of it.

I glanced up at his muscular frame silhouetted in the dark. "They're for me, but I'm willing to share with my knight in shining armor."

He huffed out a laugh as he walked away. "I could live with that title."

"Figures," I teased as he flipped on the light.

Nick walked out of the bathroom a few minutes later looking ridiculously hot. He had run water through his hair, leaving it standing in messy spikes. I'd rarely seen him without his baseball hat on, so the wet spikes were utterly adorable.

"Can I take my shirt off, or will that make you uncomfortable?" he asked before flipping off the bathroom light.

Is he serious? "Nothing about you makes me uncomfortable, Nick. You can take it off."

Without another word, he peeled off his shirt and tossed it on the floor before crawling over me to get on his side. Once he was under the covers, chills raced through me, even though his body heat warmed every inch of my exposed skin.

"Jess." From behind me, he breathed my name against my

neck, his lips near my shoulder.

I realized that if I turned to face him, we'd be practically mouth to mouth, but the way he said my name sounded so earnest, so sincere, I couldn't resist. When I rolled over to face him, we were so close we shared the same air, and I tried to steady my racing heart. Even in the dark, I could see where he focused his gaze.

"I like you," he said, his gaze drinking in my lips.

"I like you too."

That little affirmation was all Nick needed, and he reached for my hip at the same time his mouth brushed against mine.

"Is this okay?" he whispered against my lips.

When I nodded, trying not to tremble, his fingers deepened their grip on my hip as I moaned against him. His body was like fire, it was so hot, and hard in places I never realized that bodies could be hard before. Nick had muscles everywhere, and I liked the way they molded against all the softer parts of me.

I wrapped my hands around his neck, pulling at his hair and deepening our kiss. It was emotional, filled with desire, want, and need. But I wasn't ready for anything more than kissing, and I knew instinctively that Nick wouldn't push it.

In that moment, I realized that I trusted him. After everything that had happened tonight, Nick had earned my trust faster and more completely than anyone ever had before.

We held hands as we kissed, linking our fingers as we held on to each other as if we were afraid to let go. When we finally did break apart, I blinked hard, trying to steady my heart. There were no words for kisses like those; they were intimate, conveying a depth of emotion that forged bonds between us.

I was afraid to say anything, not wanting to break the spell, hoping that if anyone broke the silence, it would be Nick. His breathing echoed my own, rapid and shallow.

"Jess?" He said my name softly, giving it an unspoken question that floated between us in the darkness.

"Yeah?" I inhaled deeply, trying to slow the breaths that still came out in quick bursts.

"That was really nice."

I smiled, so glad he couldn't see the blush I knew was creeping into my cheeks. "It was something, all right, but I'm not sure I'd call it nice."

Nick laughed and leaned forward to press his lips against my forehead. "I don't know what else to call it without ruining the moment."

He was probably right. Calling it *hot* wouldn't have fit, nor would anything else I could think of. Nice would have to do.

"Good night, Jess."

"Good night, Nick."

He sighed as he wrapped his arms around me, and I closed my eyes and dreamed of him.

*

I WOKE UP the next morning emotionally spent, yet also refreshed. It was a contradictory feeling that I didn't understand at first until memories of every moment from last night hit me at once.

How would I ever be the same after everything that had happened? Not only because of the altercation at the party, but because of how Nick handled it, how he handled me. I'd never been in that kind of situation before—thank God—so I wasn't sure what other guys normally did. But I was pretty certain that almost strangling someone with your bare hands probably wasn't the most normal reaction. Then again, what did I know about guys and their tempers?

I felt connected to Nick now. He'd comforted me, taken care of me, fought for me. He made me feel safe, and I never knew before last night that a guy could make you feel like that. Honestly, I never knew before last night that I *wanted* to feel that way.

Focusing my sleepy eyes on my bedroom wall, I'd almost forgotten that I'd asked Nick to stay with me until I rolled over and practically crashed into his hard stomach. His arm moved around me and he pulled my body against his. I was certain he was still asleep until his lips curled into a devilish smile.

I swatted at his chest. "Nick, are you awake?"

"If I say no, will you stay like this?" he asked, knowing damn well what was currently pressing against my thigh.

Smiling, I tried to pull away from him, but he held me in place. "Nick," I said with a groan.

"Jess." He groaned back, mimicking me.

When his eyes opened and he stared at me, drinking me in, I wasn't sure how I stopped myself from quivering, because that look sent a fire through every part of me.

"I'm going to kiss you now."

It wasn't a request, yet it wasn't a demand either. Nick's words were simple, direct, and non-negotiable.

My eyes closed instinctively as I parted my lips and waited for him. The bed moved under me as Nick got closer. His thumb stroked the length of my cheek before brushing across my lips.

"Do you know how beautiful you are?"

I dipped my head but said nothing, squeezing my eyes shut a little tighter. I wasn't great at accepting compliments, and this was no exception. His breath was closing in, I could feel his exhale around me, and yet I still waited for the feel of his lips. When his hands moved away from my face, his mouth was suddenly there, meeting mine.

God, his lips were soft. So soft.

We kissed until we found our rhythm and fell into it, our bodies coming together, touching and stroking as we explored each other, everything working in unison as if we were made for each other. Kissing Nick was like eating your favorite ice cream on a hot summer day—taste-bud overload and way too good to stop.

His hands threaded through my hair as my fingers found themselves firmly embedded in his shoulder blades. Our movements were sensual, slow, and passionate, both of us taking our time to explore the kiss, the curve of each other's back, the hardness of muscle. I squeaked when he accidentally bit my bottom lip, and he pulled away, a smirk on his face.

"Sorry."

"It's okay," I said, practically out of breath. "But we should probably get ready for class."

His grin stayed put as he glanced between us, his gaze roaming the parts of me that weren't covered by my sleep attire. "Mind if I shower?"

I caught my bottom lip between my teeth and bit down. "Go ahead. There's an extra towel under the sink."

"Extra toothbrushes, extra towels . . . I almost think you've done this before," he said playfully as he headed for the bathroom, and I blushed at the thought that he might actually believe that.

"I'm kidding," he said.

When he closed the door behind him and turned on the shower, I reached for my pillow and squealed into it, trying to hide the stupid excitement I felt at Nick Fisher being naked in my shower.

A light knock on my door startled me. *Rachel must be home.*

"Come in," I said softly, not wanting Nick to hear.

Rachel poked her head around the door, her eyes wide as she scanned the room. "Is that Nick in the shower? I saw his truck outside."

I smiled. "He stayed the night."

"I can tell that, dummy. Oh my gosh, he loves you, doesn't he?"

"Shut up. He took me home after something happened at the party." I swallowed, realizing that my best friend didn't know yet.

She sat down and stole a quick glance at the bathroom door, which was still closed. "I knew he took you home, but what do you mean, something happened? What happened?"

"This guy attacked me at the party. I mean, he didn't really *attack* me, but he sort of did. I don't know." I shook my head. "He wouldn't let me go, and he tried to kiss me. It sounds so stupid when I say it out loud."

Rachel gave me a concerned look. "It does not sound stupid. Are you okay?"

I nodded. "Nick stopped him."

"Really?"

"I thought he was going to kill him."

Her lips curled into a snarl. "Should have let him."

"I'm serious." I swatted her shoulder.

"So am I."

The shower turned off and Rachel hopped off the bed. "I'll go. I'll talk to you later. You're sure you're okay?"

"I think so," I said right as the door opened and Nick stepped out, drying his hair.

GOSSIP AND GIRLS

Jess

NICK HELD MY hand as we walked from my dorm toward the tall white buildings in the distance. When I shivered in the cool morning air, Nick pulled me against him, our bodies fitting side by side as if they were made for each other.

Once the campus sidewalks were more crowded, he held on even tighter. I wasn't sure what I expected, but it wasn't that. I sort of figured that once other people came into view, he'd let go of my hand. But I was wrong. And if I thought that last night was a one-time thing or a fluke, he was proving otherwise with every step we took.

"You okay?" he asked.

I nodded, a small smile playing on my lips.

I was more than okay. What had happened at the party had rattled me, but it could have been so much worse. And it had been for other girls; I knew that for a fact. But right now, being with Nick like this made everything better.

Two guys that Nick apparently knew fell into step beside us and said hi to me before asking Nick what happened to him last night.

He shrugged. "I took Jess home and stayed with her."

They whooped and hollered before offering him high-fives. He shrugged at me before giving in to them with a shit-eating grin on his face.

"Um, hello! I'm standing right here." I pretended to pout, so the guys turned to me and offered me high-fives as well. I laughed as I slapped their hands in quick succession.

"Idiots," Nick said as they walked away in the other direction.

"But they're your idiots." I leaned into him.

"So are you," he said, and I smacked his shoulder.

"I'm not an idiot," I said through my laughter. "Well, I am holding your hand right now, sooo . . ."

"So that makes you the smartest girl on campus. Obviously." He pulled my hand toward his mouth and planted a quick kiss on the back of it.

Whispers swirled around us as we walked, and I couldn't help but notice the looks we were getting. People seemed to be noting our locked hands, not that this was unusual for Nick, but it still tended to attract unwanted attention. I tried to pretend that no one else was around, but it was hard to ignore the death stares.

"You sure you're okay?" Nick asked as my body tensed.

"It's just the girls. They're all staring."

"Let 'em stare." He stopped walking and pulled me against him. "Or we can really give them something to stare at."

"Stop," I said, unable to stop smiling.

"I think you're embarrassed to be seen with me, Jess Michaelson."

"Well, you are wildly unattractive."

He choked on his laughter as he dropped my hand, and I almost started running away from him, but quickly realized that he'd only chase me if I did that. Running from Nick wouldn't be a good attention-avoiding tactic.

Nick stood in place and pressed a hand to his heart as I started walking again toward our class. "You wound me, Jess."

"I'm pretty sure you'll recover," I shouted back at him, and he jogged to catch up. "See? All better."

His smile seemed to grow even wider as he raced ahead to reach the building's door before I did. He pulled it open and waved me inside.

"Such a gentleman."

He cleared his throat. "It's *knight in shining armor*, thank you very much."

I huffed out a quick laugh. "My bad. I forgot."

We took our regular seats as Professor Manal started his lecture, his fingers weaving through his long dark beard while he talked. Nick rested his hand on top of my knee.

How was I supposed to concentrate on anything with him touching me like that? I turned my head to glance at him, but he was staring at me.

"What?" I whispered, feeling the heat rise into my face.

"Nothing," he whispered back. "You're fun."

The professor cleared his throat, and I glanced up to find him glaring at us . . . again.

Crap.

Nick squeezed my knee, his lips pressed together as he tried not to laugh. I was too scared to do anything, but he leaned toward me. "You heard me, right?"

"I heard you. You're fun too," I whispered back.

Professor Manal hopped down from the small stage he lectured on and immediately headed our way.

"Ten." Frowning, he stalked toward the last row where

Nick and I sat. "Nine. Eight. Seven." He pointed at the two of us and then at the door, all while continuing the countdown.

Confused, I turned toward Nick, mortification flooding through me.

The professor rapped his knuckles on my desk and pointed at the door once more. "Five. Four. Three."

After grabbing my bag, I rushed toward the door and left the classroom just as Professor Manal called out, "One!"

Nick burst through the door right behind me, and I exhaled a relieved breath. We waited for Professor Manal to come out of the classroom and give us a lecture, or yell at us, but he never did. We stood in the hallway outside the classroom and waited a few seconds more.

"Did we just get kicked out of class?" Nick asked.

"I think so. Who gets kicked out of a college class? I didn't even think that could happen." I started pacing back and forth, trying not to freak out.

"Well, shit. Breakfast?" he asked before tossing an arm around my shoulders.

"I guess so." I didn't really think I could eat, but what else was I going to do?

We walked like that toward the student union, his arm draped across me, until Nick burst out laughing. I stopped walking to just smile at him, unable to help myself.

"I can't believe that just happened," he choked out, still laughing. "I know everyone in that fucking class. I'm going to get so much shit later."

Frowning, I folded my arms over my chest. "Well, maybe you should learn how to behave."

"I think it's your fault we got kicked out. I've never been

kicked out of a class before, and I've been here two years longer than you. So by deduction, this is all your fault," he said, pretending to be serious.

I rolled my eyes. "Fine. I'll take the blame. I can handle it, since you obviously can't."

"You're so mean to me." He jutted out his bottom lip, and I fought the urge to attack it with my mouth in public.

"You like it," I teased, and forced myself to look away from his mouth.

"I might." He dropped his arm from my shoulder and reached for my hand, pulling me into the student union.

Sitting across from Nick a few minutes later, I watched as he inhaled a plate filled with eggs, bacon, and hash browns.

"Sure you're not hungry?" he asked as he swallowed.

"I'm sure," I said, eyeing the separate plate of toast he hadn't touched yet.

After taking another bite, he shifted in his seat and looked at me. "What?"

"Just wondering where it all goes," I said without thinking.

He winked. "I'll show you sometime."

"Gross."

"Kidding."

I pushed out of my seat and stood. "I actually should go to the library. I need to research a paper I'm working on, and you're distracting."

"Really? I haven't even tried to distract you yet." He gave me a cocky smirk as he took a bite of his toast.

I waved my hand toward him. "Your whole being is distracting."

"My whole being?" He laughed. "So is yours. Come on,

I'll walk you."

He stood up and took his leftovers to the trash, dumping them in the appropriate receptacles. The library was right next door to the student union, so it seemed like we arrived there in two seconds.

We stopped at the entrance, and Nick seemed different. Something odd suddenly filled the space between us, and I couldn't quite put my finger on it.

"Is everything okay?" I asked, wondering what had just happened.

He shifted his weight. "Yeah. No, it's nothing. I'll see you later, okay?" He leaned over and planted a quick kiss on my lips.

"Are you sure?" I felt uneasy, like there was something he wasn't telling me, but I had no clue what.

Flashing his trademark smile, he said, "Sorry, I just remembered something I had to do. It's no big deal."

Confused, I murmured, "Okay."

"I'll talk to you later," he said as he walked away.

I watched him go before I turned and walked through the library doors.

*

I STAYED AT the library until my next class, and once that ended, I headed back to the library. My professor had insisted that we use actual books for reference on this paper, not just the Internet. Admittedly, I sort of loved that we had to do that. I couldn't remember the last time I'd gone into the library to do actual research. It was pretty cool.

By the time I got home, it was dark. Rachel was already in the shower, prepping for Friday night.

Rubbing my eyes, I pulled a premade salad out of the fridge and headed for the couch, where I plopped down.

"Jess?" Rachel shouted my name from her bedroom. It almost sounded like a question, as if she wasn't sure if I was home.

"I'm here," I said, not wanting to move from my comfortable spot in the living room.

She came out of her bedroom, holding her cell phone, and stopped just outside her door. "So," she said, then hesitated.

What the hell was wrong with her?

"So . . . what?" Taking another bite of my salad, I chewed as I gave her the side eye. She was acting weird.

"Do you know where Nick is?" she asked, her tone cautious.

"I have no idea. Why?" I shifted, her wariness making me uneasy as I placed my salad on top of the coffee table.

"Because—"

When she stopped and took a deep breath, I cocked my head to the side as I waited for her to continue, but she didn't.

"Oh my gosh," I yelled. "Just spit it out, Rachel."

"He's out with Carla Crawford," she spat out in a rush. She came toward me slowly, taking small steps, as if I might jump out of my seat and attack her if she approached too quickly. "He's out with her right now. My phone won't stop blowing up."

I shrugged, trying to play it off like it was no big deal, but the burn of humiliation mixed with shame swirled inside me, a nauseating combination.

Nick wasn't my boyfriend, so technically he could date whoever he wanted, but for some reason I had stupidly assumed that he wasn't. Or that he wouldn't, especially not after what happened between us last night and this morning.

Jesus, was it just this morning that we'd walked to school hand in hand? Now it felt like forever ago.

"Jess, did you hear me?" Rachel's voice broke through my inner turmoil, her eyes reflecting her concern.

"I heard you," I all but whispered, training my eyes on a stained spot on the carpet.

"Are you okay?"

I swallowed, surprised that it was difficult, as if my throat was closing up.

"I don't know. I guess I should have known better, right? You probably think I'm pretty stupid," I said, projecting my own feelings onto her. I was the one who felt stupid. Idiotic, actually.

Rachel sat down next to me. "I don't think you're stupid. He's an asshole."

I sucked in a quick breath. "That's the thing, Rach. He hasn't been like that to me. He's been anything but."

She reached for my knee and gave it a light squeeze. "He's good at this kind of thing. Nick could sell ice to an ice farmer, and we both know it."

"An ice farmer?" I tried not to smile at her odd choice of words, but then they sank in and began rattling around in my brain. "Wait—you think that I was just some kind of game? Like he didn't mean anything he said to me?"

"No, no, no," she said quickly before throwing up her hands. "I just meant that Nick knows what he's doing. He's a great salesman. And if he didn't want you to think he was an asshole, then you wouldn't think it. Shit, does that make sense?" she mumbled under her breath as her phone beeped.

"Let me see it."

I took the phone from her and opened up the newest text message. A picture appeared that showed Nick and Carla facing each other in a restaurant booth, his arm draped lazily around her shoulders. The slight smile that played on Nick's lips made my stomach roll.

They looked comfortable together. Carla's long dark hair accented her naturally bronzed skin. She was exotic and breathtaking to look at. I could never compete with a girl who looked like a Hawaiian Tropic model.

I handed the phone back to Rachel. "She's really pretty."

"Who cares how pretty she is? She's a *puta*," my roommate spat back.

Calling someone a bitch was satisfying, but it sounded even better calling them one in Spanish.

"You know her?"

Rachel propped her feet on the coffee table, narrowly missing my salad as she crossed her ankles. "I had a couple of classes with her last year. She walks around like she's some sort of princess because her dad's loaded and owns all those TV channels. I remember she was late to this one class almost every day. The professor stopped mid-lecture once to tell her that it was in poor taste to be habitually tardy, and that she should consider being more considerate to her classmates. That girl freaking said that she and her classmates paid his salary by attending school here, so she would arrive and leave whenever she saw fit. And then she stood up and walked out."

My jaw hung open as I formulated a response that contained actual words instead of amazed grunt-like sounds. "Wow," was all I seemed to muster.

"Right? And even if what she said was true in any way, which I don't think it is, it was the way she said it. Her tone of voice." Rachel crinkled her nose in disgust as she relived the memory. "Like Professor Santero was completely beneath her, and she was appalled he would even think to address her at all."

And this was the type of person Nick liked? "I can't believe Nick is out with someone with that."

"Nick's dated all kinds of girls, Jess. And they're not always nice."

"I know that," I lied. Actually, I didn't know that. "I guess I just thought he was different. He seemed different with me."

"I'm sorry. In all honesty, I thought he was different with you too. I mean, he spent the night here last night, and you guys held hands today at school."

My head snapped around in her direction. "How do you even know about the hand-holding thing?"

"Duh. I hear everything, Jess. You know this. And not that him holding hands is odd, but I just thought it meant you guys were dating now and not dating other people."

I groaned. "I thought that too, that we were starting something, and now we're over before we even really began."

Her phone beeped again, and she glared at it. "Enough people, jeez! I already know." She turned to me. "You'd think I ran an online gossip site or something."

"Maybe you should. Just don't start with this story. Please."

A sharp knock at the door pulled us from our conversation.

"You expecting anyone?" Rachel asked.

As she moved to get up, I stopped her. "No. You?"

"No."

"I got it."

When I opened the door, Nick took a step toward me before I could even react. Without a word, he cupped the back of my head with his hand as he planted a kiss on my lips like he owned them . . . like they belonged to him.

Quickly, I pulled away, wiping my lips with the back of my hand. "Don't touch me!" I said, wondering how he was here when I could have sworn he was just at a restaurant.

Nick's brow furrowed. "Jess? What's wrong?"

The clueless act only pissed me off more. Clearly, he assumed I had no idea where he'd just been and with whom.

"What are you doing here?" I demanded.

"What do you mean? I wanted to see you." He took a step toward me, and I pulled back. "Jess?"

"Get out of here, asshole," Rachel called out from the living room. "I swear to God, I'll put a curse on you, Nick Fisher."

Nick jerked his head toward her. "Asshole? What did I do?" His gaze pinged between us, his expression all innocence when everyone knew he was guilty.

I crossed my arms over my chest. "I thought you were on a date with Carla Crawford?"

He blanched, his body language immediately changing. "How'd you even know about that?"

When he didn't deny it, my heart sank. Not that he could

deny it, anyway—I'd seen the pictures—but part of me hoped . . . Hell, I didn't know what I had hoped.

"I was informed," I said, not wanting to rat out my roommate.

"I told her," Rachel said before pushing off the couch and heading into the kitchen. "My phone's been blowing up all night with stupid pictures of the two of you at Shakes."

He shook his head as he tried to process the information. "Your phone? Why? Why is my having dinner with Carla so text-worthy?"

Rachel groaned before rolling her eyes dramatically. "Jesus, Nick. You can't walk around campus holding hands with Jess, and then go to dinner that same night with a girl who isn't her, and think that people aren't going to talk about it."

"Shit." He pulled out a chair at the kitchen table and sat down, dropping his head into his hands.

"I don't think you're welcome to stay," Rachel said before I could.

And she was right. Nick had admitted he'd just been on a date with another girl, and he thought he could still hang out with me like nothing was wrong with that? *Everything* was wrong with that.

"Why is everything always so complicated?" he muttered as he gripped his head between his hands.

"Because girls are gossipy. And nosy. And more than that, they're competitive," Rachel told him.

Nick lifted his head, his eyes pleading with me. "I did take her out, but it's not what you think, Jess. I promise."

My heart sped up as his gaze met mine, but I refused to give in or believe him so easily.

"Hell, I didn't even take off my hat." He pointed at the baseball cap he always wore, still firmly on his head, as if that meant something.

"So? Then what was it, exactly?" I asked.

I walked into the kitchen where Rachel stood, needing her support. Plus, the more space between Nick and me, the better. I didn't trust myself with him; my desire to believe him was too strong.

"We already had that date set up before you and I were—" He stopped before pushing away from the table and moving toward the countertop that separated us. "Well, whatever we are. I couldn't just cancel on her. Our dads set us up. But I did tell her that I was seeing someone, and that this would be our first and last date." He reached for my hand, and this time I didn't pull away when his fingertips touched mine. "Actually, I told her it wasn't a date at all. But I still paid for dinner, so maybe she thinks it was."

I stopped myself from smiling before glancing at Rachel. She smiled too, reassuring me that I wasn't being stupid or naive for believing him.

"Does she hate you now?" If he had done that to me, I'd probably hate him.

"I don't really care," he said, his eyes holding mine as his thumb rubbed small circles on the top of my hand.

I didn't care either.

"Excuse us for two seconds."

Rachel shattered the moment as she grabbed me by the hand and yanked me into my bedroom, closing the door behind us.

"What are you doing?" I asked her, feeling frantic.

"Do you believe him?" she whispered.

I nodded. I did believe him. The moment he mentioned his dad, I believed him.

"I do too. I've heard about Nick's dad setting him up on dates before, so I don't think he's lying."

"Then why are we in here whispering when we should be out there?" I whispered back.

"I just wanted to make sure we were on the same page."

"Are we both dating Nick now?" I said with a laugh before we left my bedroom.

Wait, am I dating Nick?

Nick hadn't moved an inch. His eyes tracked me as I returned to my spot in the kitchen, keeping the counter between us.

"Why did your dads set you up?" I asked, wanting to hear his reasoning.

"My dad sometimes tries to set me up with the daughters of his business associates. He's been doing it since high school."

"Seriously?" I couldn't even wrap my head around that kind of weird archaic thinking. "So he thinks it's good if you date someone whose family could help his business?"

"Honestly, I don't even know his real reasoning," he said, exhaling a long breath. "He tells me to take someone out, and I do it. It's not like he really gives me a choice."

"Sounds like a bad movie plot," I added, remembering what Nick had told me in the bleachers about not being able to tell his dad no. I hadn't seen it in action before, but now I understood a little better. Nick wasn't exaggerating when he said he couldn't do it.

"Welcome to my life."

"Is he stuck in the forties or something?" Rachel asked, her gaze swinging between us. "Seriously?"

Nick shook his head. "I think it's just another way for him to control me. He has plans for me, the company, and my life. He doesn't give me a say, and I don't always know what to do to make him happy."

He stopped abruptly, but I didn't push him. I knew talking about this made him uncomfortable, and was surprised that he'd shared that much in front of Rachel.

"Jess, tell me you forgive me."

"I forgive you."

"Can we go talk in your room now?" he asked, then glanced at my roommate. "No offense, Rachel."

"None taken." She waved her hand at us. "Go away."

So we did.

WE'RE DOING THIS

Nick

I HEADED TOWARD Jess's bed and sat down the way I had last night.

Shit, had it just been last night? It felt like days ago instead of only hours.

Jess stepped toward me, stopping once she positioned herself between my legs. I wrapped my arms around her and pressed my face against her stomach. She tugged off my hat before raking her fingers through my short hair. That simple gesture felt so damn good, I think I moaned out loud.

"I don't understand this thing with your dad," she said, her tone hesitant.

"What do you want to know?"

I realized in that moment that I trusted Jess enough already to confide in her. Hell, I'd already told her that afternoon in the bleachers more than I told most people. Something about her comforted me. Her presence was steadying, and I was drawn to it.

"Do you guys have a bad relationship? I can't quite figure it out. It seems like you idolize him one minute and then hate him the next," she said, and her words struck a chord with me.

"That's how I feel half the time. I love him because he's

my dad; he's extremely smart and successful, and I know he wants the best for me. But I hate him because he's controlling, and I don't feel like I get a say in my own life sometimes. I never know what to do to make him happy. Whatever I do, it's never enough. When I played football, he's pissed that I'm playing. So I quit, and then he's pissed that I quit. I join the same fraternity he was in when he was in college, but I had to be the president. Because just being in the same fraternity as him wasn't good enough, I had to run the damn thing."

Sighing, he added, "I date girls, but they're always the wrong girls. That's why I stopped bringing anyone home to meet him. He's nice to everyone's face, but then behind closed doors he rails the living shit out of me." I dropped my head in my hands before continuing. "If the girl doesn't come from money, he tells me I'm being stupid. That love has no place in business, and to get my head on straight."

"I don't know what to say. Obviously, I think that's all insane. Him, not you."

Time to change the subject. Take it away from my fucked-up father and back to us. "Jess, are you sure we're okay? I'm really sorry. I should have told you about the date."

I really was sorry that I hadn't mentioned it to her, but the truth was that I was terrified she wouldn't listen to reason. Most of the girls I'd dated in the past had run on emotion instead of logic, and instead of hearing me out, they'd just scream and yell. It was exhausting.

"Why didn't you?" she asked. "About the date, I mean."

"I wanted to. I almost did when I walked you to the library this morning, but . . ." I paused, thinking of exactly how to word it. "I thought you'd be pissed. Or wouldn't understand,

and I wasn't allowed to cancel on her. I didn't want you to be mad at me." That was some more truth right there. The last thing I wanted was to piss Jess off. I liked her too much already.

She tugged at my hair until I looked up at her. "You can't lie to me, Nick. Or keep things from me. Otherwise, this doesn't work." She winced, clearly more than a little uncomfortable.

"You're right. You're absolutely right." I looked her in the eyes, noting how the blue of them seemed to cast a spell on me I refused to fight.

She leaned down, trying to plant a quick kiss on my lips, but I pulled her on top of me, deepening the kiss. I refused to let her get away that easily. I gripped the back of her neck, spreading my fingers through her blond hair as my mouth tasted her, loving every second of it and never wanting it to end.

"Nick," she said softly, her breath feathering my lips, and I reluctantly stopped kissing her.

"Yes?"

"What are we doing?" She tilted her head as she stared at me.

"I thought we were kissing," I said with a smile, and she scrunched her nose.

"You know what I mean. Don't you?"

"You mean about us. What are *we* doing, right?"

She caught her bottom lip between her teeth, something I'd noticed she did when she was uncomfortable. "Yeah."

Shit. She was nervous.

"Well . . ." I moved her body off of my lap so I could

think straight. No guy in his right mind could think at all with a hot girl sitting on his junk. "I like you. A lot. And at this point, I have no desire to see anyone else."

"At this point?" She swallowed before scooting away from me.

Damn. That didn't come out right.

"That's not what I meant. I want to be with you, Jess. I want to date you. Only you. I can't stop thinking about you, okay?"

"So we're dating then. And we're not dating other people?"

"Right. I mean, if that's what you want." *Please say that's what you want.*

"Is that what you want?" she asked, her expression so unsure that it almost hurt to look at.

I laughed. "Yes, Jess. That's what I want. I thought I said that already."

"I know, it's just . . . you have a reputation, and I like you a lot. Probably more than I should."

I reached for her hand and pulled her closer. "I like you more than I should too."

"You do?"

I tugged on her arm, wanting her even closer. When she did as I'd hoped, I pressed a kiss against her cheek.

"Yes." I kissed her forehead. "You're fun and you make me laugh." I kissed the tip of her nose. "And your motivation is sexy as hell. Most girls just want their MRS degree, but not you."

She pulled away from my lips. "Their what? What the heck is an MRS degree?"

"Spell it out. Say it." I raised my eyebrows, holding back my laughter as I waited for her to catch the joke.

"M . . . R . . . S . . . Mrs." She tapped her finger against her lip. "Oh my God, like they're married? What the hell are you talking about?"

"You've never heard that before, seriously?" I ran my thumb down her cheek, and her eyes closed in response to my touch. She was so pretty, and I didn't think she realized at all how pretty she was.

"Huh-uh. Is that a real thing?" she asked, her eyes still closed.

I leaned forward and kissed her lips because I couldn't resist them anymore. "It's a very real thing. Some girls only go to school to find a husband."

"That's the stupidest thing I've ever heard," she said with a grimace, and I kissed her lips again. "What a waste of money."

"Some people have more money than they know what to do with," I said with a sigh.

"Like your dad."

I swallowed hard. "Yeah. Like my dad."

"I hate that he sets you up with girls. It sucks and it's weird." Her bottom lip jutted out in a fake pout, and I resisted the urge to run my tongue across it.

"At least it doesn't happen very often, but I agree with you."

"What happens if he tries to set you up now? Will you tell him no?" She leaned against my shoulder, and I wrapped my arm around her lower waist.

"I don't know, Jess," I answered honestly.

My relationship with my father was beyond comprehension at times. I felt like I was living in a shadow I could never escape or outgrow. No matter what I did, I was always in the shade of his presence.

Jess moved slightly, angling herself more toward me. "Really? You don't know?"

"First of all, he doesn't do it that often. And second, I've never been dating anyone seriously when he's asked me before. So I've never had any conflict or reason to say no."

"Until tonight," she deadpanned.

"Until tonight."

"Will you get into trouble for walking out on Carla?"

"I took her out. I did what he asked, but I don't know. What's he going to do? Force me to date her?"

Honestly, I had no idea what my father would do, but I prayed he'd let this one slide. I would never date a girl like Carla otherwise. She was a grade-A pain in the ass, a total snob, and I hated even being seen with her tonight. But her dad owned a bunch of television stations, and my dad wanted that account more than he wanted anything else.

"Only if you let him," Jess said matter-of-factly.

The truth of her words hit me in the gut like a sucker punch.

I knew I'd perpetuated the fucked-up situation between myself and my dad by not standing up to him. It had always been easier to give in, to cave to the old man's requests. It was easier not to start an argument, not to make my mother upset, not to be blamed for everything that went wrong in the damn house all the time.

It was times like these when I really wished my brothers still lived at home so I had more of a support system. Or that my mom would help me out for once, but that would never happen. She hated rocking the boat as much as I did.

"You know, Nick—" Jess paused as if she was gathering her thoughts. "All the things he's asked of you so far are little things. Insignificant, really, I'm assuming. But I can only imagine that one day it won't be so insignificant, because it won't be what you want. At all. I think there's going to come a time, like a defining moment, when you know that if you agree to what he's asking you to do, it will change everything. And it will be the moment there's no coming back from. You know what I mean?"

Sledgehammer, meet chest.

Breath, meet your exit.

Heart, meet your doom.

I soaked in her words, allowing the cold, hard truth of them to enter my mind and swim around in there before drowning.

This was too much. Too much truth for one evening, too much feeling. Too much everything. I was desperate for a subject change, feeling oddly uncomfortable in my own skin.

"You're right. But let's talk about something else, girl-friend."

"If you want, boyfriend." She smiled slightly as she said it, but to me, it was enough to light up the whole room.

"I want. And I need to ask you something. But you have to say yes."

She laughed. "That doesn't seem fair."

"Maybe I don't play fair."

Her face scrunched up as she crossed her arms. "Well, are you gonna ask or what?"

"We have formal coming up in a few weeks, and I refuse to go unless you come with me."

I smirked, hoping she'd be unable to refuse. The truth was that I had to attend because it was a frat event and I was the president, but I'd hate being there if Jess wasn't. I wanted her by my side.

"What's formal? Like a prom?" She gave me a perplexed look.

"Basically a formal dance and dinner. We bring dates. It's a lot of fun. We'll have a good time; I can promise you that."

"And we get dressed up? You'll be in a tux?"

"A suit. But a really hot suit."

"How could I pass up seeing you in a really hot suit? I'm there." She smiled, and I loved knowing I put that smile there.

"Yeah?"

"Yes."

Jess leaped into my arms and moved to straddle me again. All thoughts slipped away as her lips met mine, sending my blood flow straight to my groin. When her tongue met mine, I instantly hardened and gripped her ass, and her hips moved slightly, grinding into me.

"Wait!" she exclaimed and hopped off of me as quickly as she'd gotten on.

"What?" I groaned, half wanting to die.

"Will David be there?"

David, the fucker who put his hands on my girl? "No."

"No?"

"He was suspended from the fraternity today."

"For how long?"

"I'm not sure yet. But I'm thinking permanent removal."

"Really? When did this happen?" She crossed her legs and sat on the floor.

I moved from the bed and sat directly across from her. "This afternoon. I met with David and told him to get out before meeting with the rest of my fraternity brothers. I'm supposed to take a vote, but I overruled it."

"What do you mean?"

"When something happens, we're supposed to vote on the punishment. But I didn't take a vote. I just told him to leave."

I could have issued David a warning and allowed him to stay in the fraternity, but I knew I'd never be able to look at him without wanting to pummel him. And he needed to learn that his behavior wasn't okay. I realized he was drunk out of his mind at the time, and he apologized profusely when he saw me later, but he needed to learn how to hold his liquor. Yeah, this was college and we all made mistakes, but that was one mistake I refused to condone.

My decision didn't earn me any friends. The guys in the house were pissed at me over it. We were supposed to be a democracy and take a vote on whether he should be kicked out. When I removed him without the vote, they said I was making an example out of David because it was Jess he did it to. They claimed that if it had been some other girl, any other girl, I would have been more lenient, more willing to listen to reason.

I didn't want to think about just how right they might have been. I wanted to believe that no matter who it had happened to, my reaction would have been the same, but the truth was that I didn't honestly know. And I didn't like the way that made me feel about who I was as a person.

There had been so much about my character that I'd struggled with lately that this only added to it. One more thing

I needed to do some soul searching about, but I pushed it deep down inside instead. It was easier avoiding the hard truths than meeting them head-on.

EPIC EMBARRASSMENT

Jess

NICK AND I had been officially dating for a couple of weeks now, and the death stares from other girls had pretty much stopped.

I knew the routine. They were probably biding their time until our relationship ended, which was what usually happened when it came to Nick and the girls he dated.

That fear stayed firmly rooted in the back of my mind at all times, that we had an expiration date. I wanted to think that this was different, that I was different, but what if that was how every girl felt when they were with him? I assumed they must have.

I tried to keep my feelings within reason when it came to him, but I struggled. Everything Nick did made me fall for him more. The confident, arrogant guy I'd seen from afar was still both of those things, but there were so many more layers underneath those two superficial ones. There was much more to Nick than I could have ever imagined, and I found it hard to believe that he had shared the things he had with me with all those other girls as well.

Rachel walked through the front door and slammed it behind her. "Please tell me that Nick asked you to formal," she shouted as she entered her bedroom.

I could have sworn I'd already told her that he had. I knew for a fact that I had told her; there's no way I would have kept that to myself.

"What's formal?" I shouted back to her, completely teasing.

"Shut up, dummy. I know Nick asked you. You told me already."

"Then why are you acting like you don't know?" I sat there confused as all hell.

"Because I'm going crazy right now." She wrung her hands as she entered the kitchen.

"Why?" I asked, still not having any idea what her deal was.

"Because Trevor asked me to go with him."

I squealed like an annoying girl. "Shut up! Wait a second, you and Trevor? Are you two back together? What happened with you guys last year, anyway?"

She smiled and squirmed a little. "I was an idiot. I broke up with him because I never thought he really liked me."

"Wait, what? Anyone with eyes could see how crazy he was about you."

"I always questioned everything. The parties, the other girls, the constant presence of the sorority girls. All of it. I felt like I was always competing for his attention, so I took myself out of the equation completely. It seemed easier that way, but it hurt a hell of a lot."

Her admission shocked me. Rachel wasn't the kind of girl who lacked confidence or seemed competitive like that—she was one of the fiercest girls I knew. I never realized that under her tough Latina exterior lay a girl with normal fears like the rest of us.

"I would have never guessed."

"What can I say? I was an immature, idiotic freshman. Also, first year is super overwhelming. I didn't handle anything that year very well."

"It was a huge adjustment."

I nodded, thinking back to how living on our own for the first time felt. To be honest, it was weird not having my mom around to wake me up for school, to ask me if my homework was done or if my grades were good enough. It was the first time I'd truly felt somewhat like an adult, minus paying bills and working full-time.

"Thankfully, he was willing to forgive me, and we're trying again."

"I always thought he was nice."

"He is."

When she gave me a dopey smile, I resisted the urge to tease her. Instead, I basked in the fact that she seemed happy.

"So, what's formal like?"

"Pretty much what you'd expect, but with lots of sorority girls. Which is annoying because when you're not one of them, you're fully aware that you aren't one of them."

"Are they mean?" I asked, suddenly wondering what I had gotten myself into.

"Not really. You're not in the Greek system, so they'll most likely ignore you."

"Okay then." I laughed uncomfortably. "I'm excited about it, anyway."

"You should be. You'll have the hottest date there." She

waggled her eyebrows. "And now we can go shopping for dresses together."

"Thank God. You know I can't be trusted to shop alone."

I was a terrible shopper. The second I walked through the mall doors, I wanted to turn around and go back home. While most girls seemed to live for all things fashion, I couldn't care less about any of it. My style was definitely more comfort over anything else.

Rachel grinned. "You are a bad shopper. But you have cute fashion sense, even if you don't realize it. You would have done all right for yourself."

I shook my head, smirking at her assessment.

"All right, gotta jet to class. See you later." She gave me a quick hug before running out the door.

*

LATER THAT EVENING, I had my books spread out across the kitchen table, my laptop open, and handwritten notes everywhere. My cell phone beeped a text notification while I was in the middle of writing, but I ignored it. After the fourth text in less than a minute, I finally tore myself away from my studies to read it.

Please tell me you're listening to KRAS right now.

I scrolled through the other texts to see they all basically said the same thing, demanding I turn on the radio. I jumped from my chair and hurried to the stereo in our living room to click the power button before turning the dial to the right station.

Nick's laughter filled the living room.

"So, tell us your question for Grand Master Paz, Nick," the DJ asked.

"All right." Nick cleared his throat. "I was calling because I wanted to get your advice on something about my girl."

His girl? Me? What on earth could he possibly want to know from a Compton rapper about me?

"Ask away, Nick. I'll see if I can help."

"Well, I was wondering if . . . How can I convince my girl to have a threesome with me? She isn't into it, but I'd like to change her mind."

My ears started to ring as his words reverberated through my head.

What the hell? A threesome? And he was asking this on the radio, where everyone in the general area could hear and was most likely listening?

I didn't wait for Dickmaster Dickface's response before I pressed the power button again, shutting it off, and started pacing back and forth.

My text messages blew up again.

Nice boyfriend.

Tell me you heard Nick on the radio.

Heat spread throughout my body as I fumed with my embarrassment. How was I supposed to study now with my idiot boyfriend's question replaying over and over again in my mind? The texts just kept coming, so I shut my phone down in order to save its life, since each new message tempted me to see how hard I could chuck it against the wall.

Rachel rushed through the front door minutes later, and

wrapped me in a hug before I could even say a word.

"I heard Nick on the radio when I was driving back from class." Frowning, she pulled back to study me. "I'd ask if you heard, but I can tell that you did."

"Hell yes, I heard. And I can't stop hearing about it." I pointed at my stupid cell phone.

"Has he ever talked to you about having a threesome before?" she asked softly, and I bristled.

"No! Never." I moved back to my seat at the table and sat down. "I can't believe he did that. I'm mortified."

"Mortified? I'm pissed. I really am going to curse that boy before the year is through," she threatened before breaking off into a Spanish-filled rant I didn't understand.

"I'm sure I'll be pissed in about an hour. Just give me time to get there."

Anger came a lot quicker than I had anticipated. It mixed with the other emotions rolling through me, and within a few seconds, I was so upset I couldn't even see straight. I felt so stupid.

"Are you okay?" Rachel asked as she sat down in the seat across from mine.

Shaking my head, I replied, "Not really."

"I'm sorry, Jess. This really sucks."

I sat there staring at my homework on the table. Finishing it now was out of the question.

Finally, I said, "I think I'm going to go to sleep. No sense staying up when I can't focus on anything other than his stupid voice asking that even stupider question."

Rachel got up and headed toward her room. "I understand. Good night."

"Night."

I hated Nick for embarrassing me and for being so disrespectful. I was half tempted to turn my phone back on and call him, but I was still too shocked to think clearly, and I had no idea what I'd say to him other than yell and swear like some psycho girlfriend. Not that he didn't deserve it, he absolutely did, but I wanted to maintain some semblance of self-control.

My emotions continued to swing between being pissed off and completely embarrassed, so I climbed into bed and closed my eyes, hoping for a sleep-filled reprieve.

*

I HAD TOSSED my cell into a drawer so I wouldn't be tempted to turn it on and use it. Now as I walked across campus toward my class, I realized that I had left it at home, still turned off.

Nick's easily recognizable frame was in the distance, and I watched as he altered his course to head in my direction.

Part of me wanted to turn around and run away from him, but I knew he'd only chase after me. And I couldn't avoid him forever. People had already started to slow down as they noticed us heading toward each other like two trains meeting head-on. No doubt they'd heard all about Nick's asshole request last night on the radio.

Once he was within a couple of feet, I raised my hand and smacked him across the cheek. Gasps filled the air around me but I tuned them out, my focus purely on the jerk-off in front of me. When a smirk spread across his face, I lifted my hand to slap him again, my anger only growing.

He grabbed my wrist and pinned it to my side. "Calm

down, Jess."

I squirmed, trying to pull my arm away. "Fuck you," I spat, still trying to pull my arm out of his grasp, but it was no use.

"Jess, listen to me." His voice was calm, almost soothing, and I wanted to hate him for his ability to be so in control while I clearly wasn't. "Listen to me," he repeated, demanding I do as he asked.

I glared at him, wishing my eyes had the power to shoot darts so I could pummel him with hundreds of them at once. "I hate you!" I yelled with as much venom as I could muster so he'd believe it, even if I didn't.

"I was just fucking around," he said.

I set my jaw and glared past him, refusing to meet his stupidly perfect blue eyes. One look in them and they'd soften me, and I refused to be anything but tough in this moment. His fingertips touched the bottom of my chin and tilted it up.

"Look at me, Jess," he begged until my eyes finally found his.

"What? I'm looking," I said, my tone bitchy and annoyed.

"I wasn't being serious. Grand Master Paz is one of my favorite rappers of all time, and I just wanted to talk to him. I'd called a minute before, and they asked me what I wanted to talk to him about. When I told them something stupid, they hung up on me. So I called back with something better. It's all I could think of that might work."

My heart rate slowed its frantic pace as his words sank in. I relaxed a little as my anger faded; I wanted so badly to believe him.

"Seriously?" I asked cautiously, not wanting to believe him

if it wasn't true.

"I swear. It was just so I could talk to him. I didn't mean it." He shifted his weight. "I mean, unless you wanted to," he suggested with a slight laugh, and I socked him in the shoulder as hard as I could. He threw his hands up in surrender. "Joking, Jess. Still joking. Stop hitting me."

A small smile took over my lips before I could stop it, and I felt myself leaning into him, the comfort of his body no longer something I wanted to resist. I believed him.

Nick's arms circled me as he pulled me against him and kissed the top of my head. "You would have known all of this already if you'd answered any of my calls last night. Or read my text messages."

"Yeah, well, I was too pissed."

"Because you're stubborn."

"Maybe a little." I had never wondered if I was stubborn or not, but in this moment I knew Nick was right. "But, come on. Put yourself in my shoes."

He gave me a big grin. "My girlfriend wants to have a threesome? I'm in."

"You're a pig," I blurted, pulling away from him.

"I'm a guy," he said with a shrug.

I glanced around at the students still gathered around us, watching us with intense stares.

Moving my mouth to his ear, I whispered, "All those people heard you last night. And if they didn't hear you themselves, they heard from their friends. They all know what you said. You made me look like an idiot, and right now they're all standing there judging me, thinking I'm stupid for forgiving you."

I focused on his mouth as I waited for a response, not wanting to see the glares being cast my way by all those who didn't understand what had happened in the last ninety seconds.

Nick looked around at the crowd before clearing his throat. "Morning, everyone. I'm sure by now you all heard me on the radio last night." He paused when a few guys started cheering and hollering, and held a hand in the air for them to stop. "I've pretty much worshipped GMP since I was a kid, and I just wanted to talk to him. I didn't mean what I said, so you can all stop judging Jess right now for still being with me. It was a fucking joke. This is the first and last time I'll ever address my relationship with any of you, but I wanted to clear the air." He looked down at me with a sincere smile. "For her sake. Now, leave us the fuck alone."

My insides were on fire at the combination of Nick's declaration and my embarrassment at being the center of attention.

"All better?" He gripped my waist and pulled me against him before lowering his lips to mine and kissing me in full view of anyone who was still around to watch.

I groaned against his mouth. "Thanks for that."

Nick smirked as he moved away slowly. "Anything for you. What time are you done with class?"

"Two hours."

"I'll pick you up after."

He branded me with his lips one more time before heading in the opposite direction. You'd think I'd be used to him doing things like that by now, but the guy constantly left me dumbfounded and struggling to breathe.

How could I go from such lows to such extreme highs so quickly? This relationship was exhausting at times, but so worth it.

HOPELESS

Nick

NEVER IN ALL of my twenty-one years had I created the kind of spectacle that I did this morning with Jess. At least, not to my knowledge. And I never would have given that sort of speech for any other girl besides her. My feelings for Jess grew every day. I was finding it harder and harder to keep them in check, but I needed to.

Falling for someone wasn't part of the plan. My father would probably go into cardiac arrest if he knew about her. His romantic plans for me had always included the daughter of a wealthy business partner.

Love didn't factor into the equation, as he'd told me on more than one occasion. *"Love doesn't pay the bills, son. And it fades. You need a nurturer, someone who wants to take care of you, focuses on you, and gives you everything you need to succeed in business. In the end, it's what you've built that matters, and if you happen to find some sort of love along the way, kudos to you."*

I was convinced the guy had no heart, that all he cared about was money, and whatever got him more of it was all that drove him. He didn't care who he hurt in the process, including me. When my father looked at me, all he saw was more ways to grow his empire. I'd never heard him give similar advice to Frank or Ryan when it came to their love lives, but apparently everything was different when it came to me.

I could tell that Mom hated the way Dad tried to control me, but she never once stood up for me. Instead, she allowed him to set rules, restrictions, and parameters for my life, always sitting on the sidelines with her glass full. No matter how much my mom might end up loving Jess, and I knew she would absolutely adore her, it wouldn't matter. Jess wasn't wealthy, didn't come from a prestigious enough background. She was "unsuitable."

No, my parents would both force me to end things. And it was the last thing I wanted to do.

But right now, while I still had time before I graduated and started working for my old man, I planned to enjoy every second with Jess. I knew she thought that I'd grow tired of her the way I did all the other girls, but she had no idea how different she was from them. She was so normal, so fun.

The girls I'd dated in the past reminded me too much of what my future was supposed to hold for me, all spoiled, entitled females who were used to being treated like princesses, or girls who never got enough attention from their daddy and were desperately aching to fill that void. It took me a few years to notice the pattern I had been setting for myself subconsciously, but once I realized what I was doing, I'd stopped.

Which was why I was single when I did meet Jess. And why she made me feel things I'd never felt in my life, never been allowed to feel. It was also why I'd do anything for the girl, including apologizing on her behalf to the whole damn student body if I needed to. I'd make a fool of myself if it meant she'd forgive me.

I started laughing when I thought about Jess slapping me. No girl had ever hit me before. I deserved it, for sure, but it had been worth it. Talking to Grand Master Paz was one of the greatest fucking moments in my life, and I'd do it all over again.

APOLOGY ACCEPTED

Jess

NICK WAS WAITING for me in the parking lot as I walked through it heading toward my apartment. I spotted him sitting in his black truck before he noticed me. When I knocked on the driver's side window, he startled before opening the door.

"Scared the shit out of me, Michaelson."

"Parking lots are super dangerous in the daytime," I teased.

He smacked my butt as I walked away. "I'm starving. Please tell me you're hungry."

I glanced back at him. "I could definitely eat."

After turning the handle and finding it locked, I fished my keys from the bottom of my bag. I unlocked the door and tossed my stuff on the counter as Rachel came out of her room.

"You're home?"

She looked around. "Obviously."

Laughing, I said, "The door was locked, so I just assumed you weren't here."

Rachel sat on the couch as I passed by her.

"I'll be right back," I said to both my roommate and my boyfriend before running into my room to change clothes.

"So, Nick," I heard Rachel say. "I heard all about your epic speech today. Addressing the crowd? Nice touch."

I tossed on a clean top and headed back out as Rachel gave me a wink followed by a pointed look that said she needed to hear all the details.

Nick wrapped an arm around my waist. "Yeah, well. Didn't want people thinking Jess was a—" He turned me around so that I faced him. "What'd you say, babe? An idiot?"

I laughed, nodding in agreement.

"Yeah. I didn't want anyone to think Jess was an *idiot* for staying with me. But she got a good hit in there first," he said, rubbing his cheek.

"I heard about that too. The slap heard around campus." Rachel covered her open mouth with a hand dramatically. "I'm shocked at your unladylike behavior, Jess."

I shrugged. "Hey, I never claimed to be a lady."

"I'll say," Nick said, still rubbing his cheek.

I shoved at him. "All right, we're going to get something to eat, and then I'll be back. I think." I glanced at Nick, not knowing what he had planned.

"She'll be back later. Much later." He smiled before moving to give Rachel a quick hug good-bye.

"Don't do anything I wouldn't do," she shouted as we neared the door.

"That's not very limiting, Rach," I shouted back as I stepped outside.

*

WHEN WE PULLED into the nearly full parking lot of a local

Italian restaurant known for having the best pizza and pasta in town, Nick glanced at me. "You like Italian, yeah?"

I smiled. "What if I said no?"

"I think part of me might die. Jess, this place is the best."

"I know it is. I love it here. The gnocchi." I moaned like I was in heaven before kissing my fingertips and lifting them toward the sky.

"Don't moan like that unless I'm underneath you. Or on top of you. Or kissing you. Or touching you," he said, his gaze lingering on my mouth.

"I can't help what good gnocchi does to me." I licked my lips.

"You're trying to kill me," he said before hopping out of his truck.

When I turned to get out, he said, "Stay put," so I stopped and waited as he opened my door and extended a hand to help me down.

Such a simple thing, but it meant a lot to me. Guys didn't do that kind of thing anymore. Those small gestures mattered; they truly did.

We held hands as we entered through the red-and-white-checkered door, and once we were seated in a booth, it was as if no one else existed but the two of us. Nick had a way of making you feel like you were the most important person in the room. When his attention was focused on you, you felt invincible, larger than life, and important.

"I'm really sorry again about last night," he said.

I cringed a little, wanting to forget the radio bit that I'd heard. "I know. God, I was so pissed."

"I know." He pointed at his cheek. "Aren't you going to

apologize for striking me?"

I laughed. "Striking you? No. You deserved it."

His jaw fell open. "Deserved it?" He started to say something else, but then stopped and shrugged one shoulder. "You're right."

"I'm sorry, what did you say?" I smiled and leaned toward him, cupping my ear. "Could you repeat that, please?"

"You heard me the first time, woman." He leaned away from me, his eyes narrowed playfully.

"No, I don't think I did."

"I said you were right," he mumbled, looking toward the floor as I laughed.

The waiter greeted us, took our drink orders, and informed us of the specials that evening. Every word he spoke made me want to drool, but somehow I refrained. I loved food, and Italian was my weakness.

After dinner, Nick reached across the table to cup my cheek. My eyes closed automatically at his touch. I tilted my face against his fingers, loving the strength and warmth they brought.

"Let's get out of here," he whispered.

My eyes flew open. "Your place or mine?"

"Mine."

His response was quick, too quick, which caused me to panic. Nick lived in a fraternity house, where anything any of them did quickly became public knowledge. I didn't want whatever was about to happen to be something that a bunch of guys I didn't know talked about behind my back.

"But you live at a frat house," I said, trying to backpedal. "With like a hundred guys."

He barked out a laugh. "And?"

"It's embarrassing," I admitted.

"What is?" He cocked his head to the side, his blue eyes boring into mine.

"There's not really any privacy."

"Jess, I have my own room. No one will be around. And I'll hurt anyone who makes you feel uncomfortable."

Nerves shot through me. I knew what this meant, going to his room, to his house. We hadn't gone that far yet, but after all the emotions and stupid things we'd been through already, I couldn't say that I wasn't amped up, or unwilling to solidify our connection.

Nick's room had a back entrance, so no one even saw us going in, aside from the two guys who were playing some sort of drinking game on the front lawn. I'd been in Nick's room before, but never with the silent anticipation of what was to come. We both knew it, but neither of us addressed it.

Then he shocked me by pulling out two candles from somewhere in his closet, and lighting them. I couldn't help but wonder how often he'd done that for a girl.

"Stop, Jess," he said, interrupting my thoughts.

"What?" I sat gingerly on the edge of his bed as he placed one candle on his dresser and the other on the nightstand near me.

"Stop thinking about who else has been in this room, or who else I've been with. Your emotions are written all over your face."

How the hell did he read me so well? Was I that transparent?

"It was just the candles. They're a nice touch," I admitted.

"I bought them the other day. For you. For us. I don't pull them out for every girl who comes along, okay?"

My breathing hitched. "Okay," was all I could find the strength to say in response.

"Do you believe me?"

"Yes," I answered without hesitation.

I wanted to rush, my need and want for him overtaking every single one of my senses. In all my fantasies, Nick and I had ripped each other's clothes off and scattered them on the floor in our haste to taste each other as quickly as possible. But the reality was so much better than anything my mind could cook up.

Where I was inexperienced, he was more skilled. He refused to let me do anything without his help. And he implored me to take my time, all the while constantly reminding me to slow down.

My clothes left my body a single item at a time, as did his. Neither of us removed anything without the other's help. And each time a piece of my clothing was dropped to the floor, his eyes lit up like he'd never seen anything like me before. He stared in awe and appreciation. I'd never felt that way naked with a guy before. It was empowering.

"You're beautiful, so fucking beautiful. Do you know that?"

As he kissed my exposed skin, I wondered how he'd gotten so good at this. Having sex was one thing, but being romantic about it was altogether different. The mere touch of his fingertips across my stomach sent flutters shooting through every nerve ending in my body. I'd had sex with other guys before, but they were nothing compared to this. They seemed so immature, such a waste of time. Because this, this was something I'd been missing out on.

Once we were both naked, Nick pulled me onto the bed and settled next to me. His fingers tangled in my hair as he kissed me slow and deep as if he didn't want to stop. Each time our tongues touched, both chills and heat raced down my body. It was a blissful contradiction, all the feelings crashing into one another. I never wanted it to end.

He positioned himself above me, our skin touching in all the places the clothes had just covered. When I felt the tip of him near my entrance, I stopped him, closing my mouth to end our kiss.

"I'm not on the pill."

"That's why I put this on," he said, motioning toward the condom covering him.

"When did you do that?" I asked, shocked that I had absolutely no idea when the hell he'd slipped that on.

"Two seconds ago." He smiled and leaned back down to kiss me. "Can I continue?"

Nervous, I smiled back. "Yes."

I braced for him, not knowing at all how he would feel inside me. But like with everything else this evening, he took his time, clearly savoring every moment between us. He pushed inside me with care, moving inch by inch before giving one last thrust.

I threw my head back, a moan escaping my lips at the feel of him. No longer concerned with how many guys were in the house or if they could hear me, my only thoughts were of Nick and this moment. The way he felt when he was inside me, I'd shout it from the rooftops when we finished.

His hips moved back and forth and I rocked against him, trying to find our rhythm. The way our bodies moved together was like a perfectly timed slow dance. In the past, sex had been awkward—I had been uncomfortable and self-conscious, worried that I wasn't good enough or pretty enough, but not with Nick. Nick made me feel sexy, made me feel wanted, and the way our bodies fit together felt right.

"You feel amazing. You're so perfect," he mumbled against my neck, pressing his lips to my skin after each declaration.

"You feel so good too. Don't stop." I moaned, my lips parting as his mouth neared. When his tongue entered my mouth, I squeezed my eyes shut at the touch, the taste, the sensation overload.

His hips moved faster, pushing and pulling in and out of me, and I sensed he was close. I lifted my hips and rubbed against him as he moved, each thrust hitting that perfect spot in me.

My own orgasm started to build, and I knew it wouldn't be much longer for me either. Two more pumps and I arched my back, pleasure ripping through every part of me until I trembled with the aftermath, and realized that Nick had almost slowed to a stop. I opened my eyes to find him watching me, his mouth open slightly.

"You're so fucking gorgeous, Jess. Everything about you."

Nick leaned down and claimed my mouth with his, nibbling on my bottom lip. He kissed me like he owned me as he began moving inside me once more. It all felt so good, like he was made just for me.

His body tensed and then quaked and jerked as he came inside me. Between my legs, I felt him pulse and throb as I continued to rock gently against him. He sucked in a breath and collapsed on top of me, the weight of his body almost too much, and I let out a quick *oomph*.

"You okay?"

"No," I huffed out. "I'm dead."

He pushed up onto his elbows and pressed his lips to mine. "That was amazing."

I nodded in complete agreement.

It was. It was so much more than amazing, but I couldn't find another word.

"I had planned on waiting until formal, but something about tonight just seemed right." His breathing still erratic, he moved off of me and lay on his back, peeling the condom off and then disposing of it in a trash can next to the bed.

"Tonight was perfect." I lay my head on his chest and listened to the sound of his heartbeat as he ran his fingers through my hair.

"You're not mad we didn't wait?" His body tensed as he pulled back to look at me.

I tilted my head. "Yes. I'm really upset that you just gave me the best sex of my life. Horribly upset."

"The best sex of your life?"

"I just want you to feel good about yourself," I said with a laugh as I came down from my post-sex high.

"I have you in my arms. I feel fucking great about me."

My heart grew two sizes bigger in that moment. Because . . . Nick Fisher. I knew that nothing would ever be the same again.

FORMAL

Jess

NICK AND I had definitely grown closer since having sex. As much as most people tried to claim that it didn't change anything, I knew with complete certainty now that they were full of shit.

Having sex changed *everything*.

It made my feelings for Nick grow tenfold. There was something vulnerable about being completely naked with another person and letting them inside you. We had connected in the most intimate of ways that you could never take back. It was as if we had a secret bond, an invisible string that tethered us to each other, and only grew stronger.

I knew I cared about Nick before having sex with him, but now it all felt like so much more. Sex with him made my emotions swell. And everyone seemed to know the minute it happened between us, like I'd sprouted a giant flashing neon sign on my forehead that read I GAVE IT UP TO NICK FISHER.

Maybe it was the way he held me now . . . *tighter*.

Or the way we stood when we were around each other . . . *closer*.

Everything between us was simply . . . *intensified*.

There was more affection, more touching, more intimacy

in every interaction. We gave our own selves away without even trying.

I was falling in love with him, even though I wasn't sure that I should. My mind cautioned me to slow down whenever Nick came near, but my heart sped up at the sight of him. My mind flashed warning signals with his touch, but my heart grew wings and flapped like a wild bird begging for more. My mind sounded alarms anytime it thought I might be falling too fast, but my heart tumbled over the edge without question.

That was the thing about falling in love—it couldn't really be helped or stopped. It wasn't like my mind could talk itself out of the things that my heart decided to beat for. And it had definitely started beating for Nick Fisher.

I liked the way it felt. If my heart wanted to fall in love with him, I was going to let it, my mind be damned.

*

THE ONLY FORMAL affair I'd ever attended was my senior prom, and even though Rachel had filled me in, I still had no idea what to expect when it came to a fraternity formal. Thank God she was going to be there with Trevor; at least I'd know someone other than Nick at this event.

Nick told me that most of the guys brought girls from sororities as their dates, so there wouldn't be a lot of non-Greeks there. Remembering what Rachel had said, I hoped that the night wouldn't be awkward or uncomfortable. It was hard enough being Nick's girlfriend sometimes; I didn't need the extra crap from girls I didn't know at my first formal event on Nick's arm.

First? Wishful thinking, Jess.

We arrived at the hotel and checked into our room. Nick had booked a suite for a group of us, so it was party central in our place. I didn't mind, but I had thought that we'd get some alone time together. Now I wasn't sure that was even a possibility with the current state of the place.

"This place is awesome!" Rachel shouted from the full-sized bar in the corner of the room as she poured some shots.

"So does everyone get ready in here?" I asked as I surveyed the number of people in our room.

Nick leaned toward me, his lips close to my ear. "Yes, Miss Michaelson, but we have our own bathroom. You won't have to share with anyone unless you want to."

I smiled at the way he seemed to think of the small details before I had even considered them. Nick's thoughtfulness was something that made me feel special.

"Except for me. You have to share with me." He winked before wrapping a strong arm around me. "And after we get changed, we'll take pictures and head out."

"Take pictures?" I asked, getting lost momentarily in the depths of his blue eyes.

"Hell yeah. If you think I'm not documenting this evening, you're crazy," he said before planting a kiss on my forehead. "Go get ready." He smacked my ass and sent me in the direction of our room.

"Rachel, come get ready with me," I yelled over the music that was now blaring from someone's travel speaker.

"Be there in a minute," she shouted back, then downed another shot.

Rachel and I took over the bedroom and hogged the bathroom, forcing Nick to change in another bedroom with

Trevor. Rachel helped curl my hair into beach-like waves that fell loose over my shoulders, but her normally wavy long dark hair had been straightened.

I had to smile at the sight of us in the bathroom mirror. Each of us had done the opposite of our normal styles. "Thanks so much for your help."

"Of course. Your hair looks pretty like this." She reached for a few strands and ran her fingers through them, making the waves even looser.

"My dress is in my room with Trevor. I'll just change in there," she said, and gave me a hug before walking away.

Outside my room, I heard her tell Nick that he couldn't go inside, that I wasn't done yet and would come out when I was ready. I laughed to myself as I put the finishing touches on my makeup.

The smoky eyeshadow made the blue in my eyes stand out even more, and the contouring I'd done on my face pronounced my usually undefined cheekbones. I finished the look with a practically nude lip and smiled at my reflection.

Reaching for my dress hanging in the small closet, I pulled it off the hanger and stepped into the black-and-white fabric. The top was fitted, hugging every one of my curves until it reached my hips and flared out slightly, stopping short well above my knees.

After one last spritz of hairspray, I headed toward the closed bedroom door and pulled it open. Nick happened to be standing right outside of it, and when he turned to face me, his jaw immediately fell open.

"Jess." He scanned me from head to toe. "You look beautiful."

My cheeks burned, and I gave him a once-over, approving of his black-and-gray suit. "Thank you. You look gorgeous." When my gaze settled on his dark hair, I said with a wink, "But I miss the hat."

"You do not. Do you really?"

"Kinda." I shrugged. Nick was hot as hell, but something about him in a baseball hat really worked on him.

"Can I wear it? My hat?" He sounded almost timid, like I might yell at him for even suggesting such a thing.

"I don't care. Why not?"

His face lit up like a little kid who'd just been told he could have a puppy.

It was just a fraternity formal in college; it wasn't like we were going to an event at the White House. Who cared if he wore a baseball hat or not? Certainly not me.

"You're the best damn girlfriend in the world," he said before kissing my cheek and disappearing into our room. He walked back out a second later, wearing his black baseball hat turned backward.

I smiled. "You look even hotter now." And he did.

"No other girl would ever let me wear a hat to formal. I fucking love you," he said, and we both froze as his words sank in. "Y-you know what I mean."

I averted my eyes, pretending my heart hadn't just soared out of my chest and was currently playing hopscotch in the clouds. "I know what you meant," I said, biting my lip to keep the dopey smile off my face as I tried to rein my heart back down from the sky.

Nick gathered our group and we headed downstairs. We took a ton of pictures in the courtyard of the hotel, surrounded by lush flowers and green shrubbery. I was secretly thrilled at the idea of having pictures like this with Nick. His arm was tight around my waist, pulling me close against him at all times.

"Let's eat," Trevor announced in a loud voice, then reached for Rachel and tugged her toward the double doors.

"Guess we're done taking pictures," Nick said with a laugh as he took my hand.

The ballroom where the event was being held was decorated like for prom, but with less fanfare. A DJ was set up in one corner, spinning tunes in the background that were pretty low-key. The round tables were covered with dark blue cloths, with centerpieces of multiple ivory candles in various heights. The decor was elegant in its simplicity.

Nick and I took our time wandering through. When we reached our table a few moments later, I was thankful to see Rachel and Trevor already seated, eating salads.

"Guess he really was hungry," I whispered to Nick, motioning toward Trevor.

"Never stand between a man and his stomach."

"Good tip."

Nick pulled out a chair for me next to Rachel, and I smoothed the back of my dress as I sat down. "Thank you."

He leaned down and placed a soft kiss on the side of my head before sitting to my left and placing his napkin in his lap.

Glancing around at the rest of our table, I might not have known anyone else by name, but I recognized the evil eye when I saw it. And boy, was I seeing it. The girl across the table kept staring at me through a narrowed gaze, her upper lip forming a snarl every so often. I would have bet money that I'd never seen her before now, but I'd be lying if I said it wasn't a little unsettling.

The last two empty seats at our table filled as my stomach instantly dropped. Carla Crawford, the girl Nick's dad had asked him to take out, took the empty chair on the other side of Nick. I tried to control the pangs of jealousy that worked their way through me, but she was so striking that I couldn't help but compare her long list of beautiful features to my much shorter one.

Her naturally tanned arms enveloped Nick's neck in a tight hug as her exotic almond-shaped eyes met mine over his shoulder. I tried to give her a small smile, but an evil grin appeared on her face before she touched the scruff on Nick's jaw and leaned in toward him. Nick pulled away, removed her hand from his face, and then turned his back on her and his attention toward me.

"I didn't know she would be here. Sorry about that," he said in a low voice.

I softened, my jealousy flitting away as he leaned in to kiss my lips. My eyes closed at his touch, and everyone else in the room disappeared.

"You okay?" Nick asked when he broke the kiss.

I nodded. "I just think I might hate her," I whispered, and he laughed.

"No need," he reassured me before forking a bite of Caesar salad and feeding it to me.

"You two are gross," Rachel said with a frown.

I gave her the evil eye. "You're gross," I shot back like a five-year-old with no other response.

She widened her eyes meaningfully and leaned toward me.

"I'm not the one sitting here being fed by my boyfriend while the rest of the girls at the table plot my murder."

I choked on the anchovy dressing, or maybe it was Rachel's words, but I reached for my water and gulped half of it down. "They are, right? It's not just my imagination?"

"Oh, they hate you. Since the moment you sat down," she said with a nod.

"Cool."

"I got your back." She grabbed a butter knife and mimicked stabbing someone with it.

I reached for the unsharpened knife and placed it on the table in front of her. "Let's just leave that here," I said as I patted the table.

"I'm just saying. Don't fuck with my girl is all." Then she launched into a tirade of rapid Spanish.

I assumed it was a tirade based on her tone of voice, but I had no idea what she was actually saying.

Right after I ate the last bite of my grilled chicken, Nick hopped out of his chair like something bit him. He grabbed my hand so hard that it shocked me.

"Dance with me," he said before yanking me out onto the otherwise empty dance space.

Whistles and hoots came from everyone before a few brave couples decided to join us, their bodies moving slowly with the music.

"Are you okay? What was that?"

"Carla grabbed my dick under the table," he said against my ear.

Enraged, I pulled back, my fists clenched. "She *what*?"

I looked back, but her seat was empty. Scanning the rest of

the space, I saw her at the opposite end of the ballroom and moved to head toward her, but Nick tugged at my hand, forcing me to a stop.

"Don't. She's not worth it. And she'll make your life hell. Trust me."

"That's rude and disrespectful. Who does that?" I all but shouted at him, not wanting to create a scene, even though I was seething.

"She's just jealous." Nick rolled his eyes and shrugged, downplaying it as if this sort of thing happened to him all the time.

"Jealous? Of me?" I scoffed. "Does she own a mirror?"

Nick's hand cupped my cheek. "You're a thousand times more beautiful than she is. In every way. Carla's not a nice person, Jess, and she doesn't like to lose. She's not used to it."

His tone was so soothing, so calming, that I almost forgot the whole thing had just happened. *Almost.*

"Don't let another girl touch you like that. I don't care who she is. Smack her hand. Do something."

"I did. I jumped up and reached for you," he said, as if that was enough.

Was it?

Why did girls have to behave like this around my boyfriend? Why did girls behave like this at all?

"This is so ridiculous," I said, unable to hide my annoyance.

He tilted my chin and leaned in, giving me a sweet, soft kiss. "Don't let it ruin our night."

I melted with his touch and looked into his blue eyes. "I want to punch her in her stupid face."

He laughed. "I know you do. And it's adorable."

"It's not adorable. It's tough. And gangster. I'll cut a bitch," I said, trying to channel Rachel, but I sounded silly instead.

Nick laughed again as he held me close, our bodies moving in perfect rhythm, not only to the music, but to each other. Even our breathing was perfectly timed. Nothing felt the same as it did when I was in Nick's embrace.

"I need a drink. You want something?" I asked, pulling out of his arms.

He placed his hands on my shoulders to steady me. "I'll get us drinks. You wait right here. What would you like?"

I briefly considered a vodka with Red Bull, but cast that aside when I remembered Rachel once saying that everyone who drank that concoction ended up smelling like cedar chips from mouse cages. The last thing I wanted was to smell like a mouse cage for the rest of the night, so I opted for the next best thing.

"I'll just take a beer." When Nick turned away, I called out, "A *light* beer!"

"Such a girl," he teased before walking away.

"You're just temporary, you know," a shrill voice said, tearing a hole straight through my happy bubble.

I turned to face Carla, who stood a few inches taller me and made sure I knew it by the way she looked *down* on me.

"As opposed to what?" I shot back.

She sneered. "As opposed to what I am."

I rolled my eyes, shifting my weight in an attempt to appear uninterested. "Which is?"

"His future. Do you think for one second that his dad would let him end up with someone like you? A girl whose parents own a *deli* in the *Valley?*"

She said the words *deli* and *valley* like they were laced with poison. I was fighting the urge to claw her fucking eyes out when it hit me that she'd done her research on me. Someone was obviously threatened, whether she acted like it or not.

"Unlike you, I'm not trying to marry Nick."

She forced out a laugh. "It doesn't matter, anyway. That would never happen. You won't last, and you won't be around for long. Nick will eventually get bored with a girl like you. If he's not already." She cast a glance in his direction. "And I'll be right here waiting. I always get what I want, sweetheart," she said with a small shrug and a smirk. "Always."

I glanced at Nick, whose eyes locked onto mine and then widened when he realized who I was talking to. He quickly grabbed the two bottles of beer and hurried in our direction.

I turned to Carla. "Not sure why you want someone who doesn't even like you. But—*goals?*" I used my fingers for air quotes.

"You really think that he doesn't like me? That our fathers haven't been planning this union for years?" She let out another evil-sounding laugh. "Nick won't have a choice in the matter. And either will you," she informed me before stalking away.

Nick won't have a choice in the matter? Her words rang in my ears as my stomach rolled.

"Jess, are you okay? You're pale. What the hell did she say to you?" Nick stepped in front of me, forcing my eyes to focus on his.

Rachel came up next to me and planted her hands on her hips. "What the hell was that?"

"Nothing," I said.

"Doesn't look like nothing. You're shaking, Jess." Rachel looked around the room. "You want me to go kick her *puta* ass?"

Smiling, I looked over at my roommate. "No. She'd probably sue you."

Rachel let out a sound somewhere between a frustrated scream and a growl. "You're right. I hate her, Nick. How are you friends with her?"

"I'm not," he said.

"Good." Rachel gave him a hard look before heading back to Trevor.

I swallowed hard. "Let's dance." I forced a smile as I grabbed my beer from his hand.

"Do you want me to go talk to her?" His voice was tight with anger as he scanned the room, searching for Carla. "I'll tell her to never speak to you again. To not even look in your direction."

I reached for his arm and squeezed. "She's not worth it, remember?" I exhaled before taking a long drink, loving the way he was protective over me.

"As long as you're sure you're all right . . ."

"I'm fine," I promised as I pulled him back onto the dance floor, holding him close to me as the music moved us.

The rest of the night was uneventful and—dare I say it?—a bit boring. A bunch of guys you'd normally see acting carefree and crazy at a party were suddenly all dressed up and on their somewhat best behavior. To be honest, I'd take the regular old frat party over this stuffy formal stuff any day.

"Had enough?" Nick whispered into my ear before kissing

my neck.

"Yes."

"Good," he replied before pulling me out of the ballroom without so much as a word to the people who still remained at the party.

A BETTER MAN

Nick

I'D WANTED THE night of formal to be when Jess and I had sex for the first time. But with all the drama over the radio interview and the scene at school, things got intense, and one thing had led to another. So by the time formal rolled around, we'd already done the deed.

Jess was different; she made me want things between us to be special. I actually cared about her feelings because I knew they were genuine. Maybe it was because of what happened at the frat party that one night, seeing her so vulnerable and scared. It sort of fucked me up for a while, to be honest, although I never admitted that to her, or to anyone other than my older brothers.

Before I knew it, I was falling in love with Jess. I think the spark was ignited the day I first talked to her in class, but now that spark was a blazing inferno that I couldn't imagine putting out. Something had been building between us, and the timing felt right after our restaurant date that night.

And thank God for that, because looking at the scene in front of me now, I was glad we hadn't waited. If we'd waited for tonight, our first time wouldn't have been special or romantic at all. It would have been a shit show, and I would have hated myself for it.

Three of my fraternity brothers were in the hotel room next to ours, drunk out of their minds, and shouting so loud it was like they were in the room with us. And when Jess and I walked through the front door of our suite after formal, one of the guys was screwing his girlfriend up against the wall like Spiderman.

I'd never seen Jess look so horrified as when she hauled ass into our bedroom and slammed the door. I followed quickly behind her as she went into the bathroom to get changed.

She turned to me, her eyes huge. "I can't believe he's just having sex with her and didn't even stop when we walked in," she said through a horrified sort of half laugh, half gasp.

I had no idea what to say. We were guys. We did whatever girls let us get away with.

I shrugged. "Actually, I was more shocked that she didn't stop."

Which was more or less the truth, although I knew those two had a reputation for doing it anywhere and everywhere. Another reason I was thankful to have my own master suite in the fraternity house. No one was fucking in my bathroom during our parties unless it was me.

"Did you have fun tonight?" I stepped up behind her, standing at the bathroom counter, and put my arms around her.

She leaned back against my chest. "Except for the girl who's lucky she still has a hand, I had a great time. It was different, but I liked it."

"I'm glad."

Jess turned around to face me. "Did you have fun? I know

you go to these things all the time, but do they ever get old?"

"Not when I'm with you." I leaned down, my lips grazing hers before I pulled back.

"Don't feed me lines, Nick."

I smiled. This girl was always cutting to the chase. "I'm not. Yeah, they get old, but not tonight. You let me wear a hat! No one has ever let me wear a hat before." I smiled as I grabbed the hat and tossed it off.

"Because you look hot in a hat. It was truly for my benefit."

When she winked at me, I picked her up, setting her ass on top of the bathroom counter.

"Wanna go somewhere with me?" I asked, catching her off guard.

"Where?"

"I want to take you somewhere. Come with me?"

"Of course." She smiled before wrapping her arms around my neck and pulling my mouth to hers.

"You probably want to change out of that dress, though."

I pulled on a pair of jeans and a snug graphic tee, then watched as Jess peeled off her dress and stepped into some skinny jeans and an off-the-shoulder shirt that was sexy as hell.

*

I OPENED THE passenger door for Jess and helped her into my truck, then drove us toward Santa Monica and my brothers' bar. It would still most likely be packed, even though it was almost closing time.

The closer we got to Sam's, the more excited I felt. My

brothers and I didn't get to spend nearly enough time together when I was growing up, or even now, so I loved visiting them at the bar. The minute I stepped inside, it felt like home. When something resonated so deeply inside you, you knew where you belonged. That's how I felt at Sam's with my family.

We got lucky as a car pulled out from in front of the bar just as we pulled up.

"We're seeing your brothers?" Jess asked, her eyes wide with what looked like equal parts awe and concern.

"Yeah, why? They'll love you, Jess."

"You could have warned me."

"Why? What would you have done differently?" I turned to study her.

"Nothing. But you know I'm not twenty-one yet." She frowned. "I don't want them to get in trouble."

I'd already thought ahead, knowing that I wanted to bring her here at some point. Reaching into the center console, I grabbed my wallet and pulled out an ID to hand to her.

"Bettina Fisher from North Carolina?" She read the name and state before scowling at me. "You named me after my dog?"

"I thought you'd laugh." I shrugged. "Plus, I knew you wouldn't forget your fake name if it was familiar," I said, hoping she picked up on the fact that I'd given her my last name.

"How'd you get this? It's got my picture and everything." She studied the ID, turning it over in her hands.

"I called in a favor. Come on." I turned off the ignition and stuffed the keys into my front pocket as she closed her fist around the card.

"I've never had a fake ID before," she whispered as we neared the security guard stationed at the front door.

"You're fine," I reassured her.

The security guard smiled as we approached. "Hey, Nick."

"Hey, Kyle, this is Jess. Jess, Kyle." I introduced the two and watched as she smiled at him, lighting up the whole damn street.

"Go on in," he said with a nod of his head, and I pulled the nondescript door open.

The sound of the crowd hit my ears immediately as I scanned the packed space. From the outside, you couldn't tell how many people were inside or what was going on.

My brothers both stood behind the bar, Ryan tossing bottles into the air and catching them effortlessly like some movie star while Frank looked on, his face changing from a grimace to a smile every few seconds.

"Those are your brothers?" Jess shouted above the noise, her eyes fixed on the two men behind the bar.

I couldn't stop the smile from taking over my whole face as I pulled her toward them. "Yup."

"I can tell you're related," she said, and I nodded.

My brothers and I definitely looked alike. Frank and I shared the same skin tone and jet-black hair, while Ryan and I had the same blue eyes. Other than that, Ryan had sun-bleached hair and a light dusting of freckles that neither Frank nor I had. Frank used to tease Ryan that he was adopted or that the mailman was his dad. When I was a kid, I didn't know what he meant, but I always laughed anyway.

Even with our differences, it was impossible to pretend we

weren't related. We resembled one another in build, stature, and mannerisms.

Jess looked at my brothers a little more before turning back to me. "You ever think about getting tattoos?"

My lips formed a devilish smile; I could feel it on my face. "Yeah. I want them but didn't think my old man would like it, so I haven't worked up the nerve yet."

Her face twisted a little as she tilted her head. "I dunno. I can't picture you with tattoos like him." She nodded her head in Frank's direction.

"Oh, you can't, can you?" I lifted her into the air and held her against me, slowly lowering her as I kissed her sweet lips.

"Brother!" I heard Ryan shout through my Jess-filled haze.

I lowered her to the floor and turned my head to find him.

"Everyone, this is our baby brother, Nick. Everyone say, 'Hi, Nick!'"

Hi, Nick rang out in unison from the crowd, and I offered a small wave before meeting Frank's eyes. He waved me over. I found the one empty seat at the bar and placed Jess in it.

"Don't move," I told her before hopping behind the bar with my brothers. "Hi there, sweetheart." I flirted with Jess as I handed her a menu. "What can I get for you?"

She laughed as she looked at the menu, the smile never leaving her lips as she read the names of some of the menu items out loud. "No Bad Days? Guy Hater? Adios Pantelones? What are these?"

I smirked. "They're the drinks."

"Hysterical." She grinned as she ran her finger down the ingredients listed for each drink.

"Great names, right?"

"They're awesome."

Pride soared within me. I'd not only designed the drink menu she was holding, but I'd also helped name the drinks.

I had to convince Frank that fun drink names would inspire conversation between customers, and would eventually lead to them ordering more and sticking around. He'd shaken his head, unable to believe the gimmick would actually work, but had promised to give it a try.

Ryan, on the other hand, was on board the second we'd started tossing out crazy names, even calling one "the Friendship Bracelet." I hated it, but Ryan and I had been right, the cocktails with the silly names were the most popular drinks in the bar, and did inspire lots of conversation and repeat clients.

"Which one do you think I'd like the best?" Jess squirmed on her bar stool as I leaned close to her, my elbows on the bar.

"Guy Hater is whiskey based," I said, and she winced. "And I don't think you're a whiskey girl, so that one's out. Adios Pantelones is obviously—"

"Tequila based!" she shouted, finishing my sentence, and I high-fived her. "I love that you have a drink called Good-bye Pants. Rachel will freaking die when I tell her."

"Well, you know what they say about tequila . . ."

"It makes your clothes fall off," we both said in unison, laughing.

"I don't really like tequila, to be honest," she said quietly, as if she might offend the tequila gods. "One bad tequila night and I was ruined forever. Can't even handle smelling the stuff."

"So I guess that leaves us with No Bad Days, which is vodka based, and honestly one of the best drinks in the bar.

You'll love it."

She bit at her bottom lip. "Okay. Do you know how to make it?"

I wanted to impress her so fucking bad, but knew that I'd probably ruin the damn drink if I tried making it myself.

"I want to tell you yes, Jess. But it's like a ten-step drink, so it's pretty complicated. Ryan makes them best, and I haven't practiced enough."

"Aw, you can practice on me," she suggested, and I smiled so big, I thought my face might split.

Ryan came to my side and tossed his arm around my shoulders. "She's way too pretty for you, baby brother."

I nodded in agreement as Jess's cheeks turned pink. "I'm well aware."

"I'm Ryan, sweetheart. Anytime you want to get rid of this guy and date someone more your caliber, you know where to find me." He reached for her hand and placed a kiss on top of it, and I thought for a second about knocking the baseball hat right off his head.

"I might be younger, but I will fight you," I said, staking my claim.

"And you'll lose," he teased. "What are you having?"

"I would like a No Bad Days, please," she said with a soft giggle.

"Coming right up." Ryan winked at her, and I growled under my breath.

I knew he was only flirting, turning on the charm even more to get a rise out of me and make Jess feel special, but I didn't like it. *Go flirt with the other thirty women in this damn bar*, I wanted to yell at him, but I didn't.

We both watched as Ryan grabbed ingredients, measuring

and pouring them into the chrome shaker. He put a lid on the canister and shook it with both hands, the muscles in his arms flexing as women at the bar swooned and took videos of him to post on social media sites. This kind of thing was gold, and I encouraged patrons to film us, talk us up, brag about the hot brothers at Sam's bar. Word of mouth was the best thing for any business, and a bar was no exception.

"You were right," Jess said to me, and I cocked an eyebrow at her.

"About?"

"He might be more charming than you are."

I narrowed my eyes, fighting off the urge to shove my brother for no other reason than I was an immature, competitive jackass sometimes. This was definitely one of those times.

"Only because he's had eight years longer than I have to practice. Just wait till you see me in eight years."

I gave her my best smile as Ryan stood in front of Jess, pouring her drink through a small strainer before peeling back the rind of an orange and running it around the rim of the glass.

Frank sauntered over, his hand extended toward Jess. "Anyone going to introduce me to this pretty thing, or are you both going to be rude assholes all night?"

"This is my girlfriend, Jess. Jess, this is my brother Frank."

Frank shot Ryan a look, and I knew it was due to my using the word *girlfriend*. I'd never called a girl that, let alone introduced one that way before.

"Nice to see you settle down with someone so respectable, Nick. And nice to meet you, Jess."

"Nice to meet you too," she said, her smile as big as mine.

MAIL CALL

Jess

NICK HAD INTRODUCED me to his brothers as his *girlfriend*. I knew that's what I was, but hearing it come out of his mouth when talking to his family made me feel even more special, if that was possible.

"All right, everyone. Last call!" Frank shouted from behind the bar as he rang the bell that hung from a rope, the tattoos on his right arm peeking out from underneath his gray shirt.

Ryan laughed and shouted, "You don't have to go home!" Then he waved at the crowd and they yelled in response, "But you can't stay here!"

Everyone in the bar cheered as I looked around, my eyes wide at the choreographed chaos that surrounded me.

"Here you go, sweetheart. I hope you like it." Ryan smirked before placing the light yellow drink in front of me and hustling down toward the other end of the crowded bar.

Nick watched as I tilted the glass toward my lips, taking the tiniest of sips without even smelling it first. "Ooh."

"Good?" he asked.

The citrus hit my throat, along with a few other flavors I couldn't even begin to place. "It's delicious," I said, taking a gulp.

"I thought you'd like it."

"Ryan!" the woman next to me shouted, and his head jerked toward the sound.

"Yes, m'lady?" Ryan said as he stopped in front of her.

"I'd like one last Adios," she shouted, and the rest of the girls in the bar yelled, "Pantelones" in unison with her.

Again, I had no idea what was going on, but Ryan winked at me, his sun-streaked hair falling in his eyes, before pulling his shirt off and tossing it near the register behind him.

Nick rolled his eyes, but the smile never left his face as he leaned toward me. "Every freaking night."

I cocked my head. "Every freaking night, what? He takes his shirt off? I don't get it?" I tried counting the well-defined abs that were now on display for everyone to enjoy.

"At the end of the night, if a woman orders an Adios Pantelones, Ryan takes his shirt off and makes the drink before he sends them home."

Confused, I said, "But the drink means take your pants off, not your shirt, right?"

Nick laughed. "Could you imagine if he took his pants off? Frank would kill him, and guys would stop coming here. The idiot takes off his shirt because it makes the girls go all swoony and dumb. And they always come back."

My jaw dropped open slightly. I could see how that might happen, but didn't want to admit that to Nick. If I weren't so into him, I'd definitely come here for the eye candy. The Fisher brothers—these guys should be gracing magazine covers and online websites the world over. They were that good looking.

And the swooning over them that was going on right now,

I completely understood it. I just happened to favor the youngest one. Thank God he didn't work at the bar.

*

A FEW DAYS after formal and meeting Nick's brothers, I believed nothing could stop the roll we were on. We felt solid, and I couldn't remember ever feeling so content with him as I felt now.

Rachel called out from the hallway, "Jess, you have a letter from Dean Corentha. Did you make his list again?" she asked, teasing me about making the dean's list last semester for my outstanding grades.

"Did you get one?" I narrowed my eyes at her. Letters from the dean were rare.

"Nope," she said before bouncing off into her room.

When I opened the letter, my heart started to race with the first sentence.

Dear Miss Michaelson,

It is with much regret that I must inform you that your major of Film Production will no longer being offered as part of our school curriculum after the spring semester of this current school year. We know that choosing a major is an extremely difficult and personal process, and apologize for the late notice in this matter. If you would like help choosing a new major that we offer, please schedule an appointment with your counselor at your earliest convenience.

Here at State, we pride ourselves on bringing our students diverse and useful majors that will help you in the real world. If this news means that State is no longer the right home for you, I encourage you to meet with your counselor as soon as possible to discuss your future options, as we may have recommendations and help that we can offer.

I apologize that this letter does not bring better news. I hope that you will continue your education here at State, but understand if that is no longer an option for you.

Sincerely,
Dean Samuel Corentha

Shit.

Shit.

Shit.

Nick had been right.

"Jess, you're pale. I mean, paler than normal for a white girl."

Rachel's voice entered my head as I handed the letter to her without saying a word. She gasped twice as she read it, only fueling my nausea.

"What are you going to do?"

"I guess I'll meet with my counselor and see what she thinks."

"This blows."

"The last thing I want to do is transfer, but I can't stay here if they don't have my major anymore." I headed for my room, wanting to curl up into a ball and wish the bad news away.

*

"MISS MICHAELSON, YOU have a couple options." My counselor brushed her long black hair back over her shoulder. "The first is you can switch majors and continue at State."

I shook my head. I refused to change my major. That wasn't an option.

"Or you can transfer and I can help. The professor who used to run the program here transferred to Northern a while back. It's up in Northern California; I'm sure you've heard of it. Anyway, he runs the program there now, and they're really good. They've won awards the last two years. I'm more than happy to give him a call and put you two in touch with each other if you'd like?"

"Are there any schools in Southern California that still offer my major?"

She cocked her head to the side. "There are. Although I don't believe that any of the programs are student-run, but you'd have to look that up yourself."

"What do you mean?"

"I mean that they have the equipment, but they're all run by outsiders. Most of them don't even have students involved at all. No college film program in California is a hundred percent student owned and operated anymore, aside from Northern."

"Do you at least have a list of the local schools?"

"I'm supposed to recommend you do all the legwork on your own, but since I feel like this is State's fault, I'll help you out."

Generous, I thought, keeping my sarcasm to myself.

She handed me a piece of paper where she had scribbled the names of three local schools for me to research.

"Thanks," I said before standing up. "Can I ask you something?"

"Of course, Miss Michaelson."

"Do you think any of the local schools are a smart choice for me?"

Her smile faded away. "I don't. Not for what you want to do. I honestly think that Northern is your best bet. You'll get a lot of hands-on experience there, and like I mentioned before, they've been winning awards for their program. They're kind of a big deal."

A scary thought hit me. "Will I be able to get in?" I asked, concerned that the best option wouldn't be an option at all.

"Yes. I will personally make sure that transferring isn't an issue, if that's what you choose to do."

My eyes burning, I sucked in a long breath and fought back the tears that threatened.

"I'm sorry I don't have better news," she said. "Would you like me to reach out to the professor running the program on your behalf?"

"Yes, please. That would be helpful, thanks."

She stood and extended her hand, and I shook it before turning and heading out the door.

I had no idea where I'd be going to school next year, but I knew for certain that it wouldn't be at State. And that meant leaving everything and everyone I loved behind for the sake of my future and my dreams.

I didn't know if I could do it, but I knew that I had to.

WEAK

Nick

WHEN JESS SAID we needed to talk, my stomach rolled and my shoulders instantly tightened. I had no idea what the news could be, but my instincts told me it couldn't be good. She had never "needed to talk" before. Heading over to her apartment for dinner, when I could barely stomach the thought of even eating, I carried half a dozen cupcakes from her favorite bakery on the slim chance that she might tell me something worth celebrating.

I realized that it was definitely not a cupcake-worthy moment as soon as I walked through the front door and caught sight of her face. She looked like she'd been crying, and I fucking hated it, couldn't stand the thought.

"What is it, baby?" I tossed the box on the counter, my concern only for the girl in front of me and not the cakes that had most likely just toppled over inside the box. I stepped close to her and traced the tearstains on her cheek with my thumb.

"Remember that day in the football stadium when you said they were canceling my major?"

I thought back to that afternoon. It seemed like a hundred years ago. I knew then that I had been right, but I had convinced her otherwise in an attempt to calm her fears. I'd all but forgotten about that conversation until this moment. Somehow in the midst of falling for Jess, I'd convinced myself that I had been wrong too.

"Yeah, I remember." My throat tightened.

"Well, you were right."

She shoved a piece of paper at me and I took it out of her shaking hands, the knots in my stomach twisting tighter with each word that I read.

"What does this mean?"

I hoped it only meant she'd switch majors and stay at State, but I knew better than that. Hell, I knew *Jess* better than that. She would never stay at a school that couldn't help her reach her career goals. I wouldn't either, if I were her.

"I have to . . . I have to transfer to another school." She stumbled on the words, clearly holding something back from me.

I struggled to swallow as I forced myself to calm down. Transferring wasn't necessarily a deal breaker. There were tons of other colleges in the area.

"Which school? You'll still be close, right?"

Surely she'd still be within a short driving distance after I graduated. Imagining Jess leaving my life wasn't something I was prepared for. And I sure as shit wasn't ready for the next six words that came out of her mouth.

She shifted her weight, looking past me before meeting my gaze and sadly shaking her head. "It's up north. In Northern California," she admitted as another tear slid down her cheek. Jess understood the gravity that her moving held for us as well as I did.

I took an involuntary step back and reached behind me, my hand searching for something for balance.

Ask her to stay. Beg her to stay. Make her promises. Give her money. Buy the fucking school. Do anything to make sure this girl doesn't leave your life.

"That's too far, Jess." *Nowhere is too far*, I thought, but refused to say the words out loud.

"I know, but it's the only school left in the entire state that has a student-run television station. Other schools have it, but they're run by other people. There aren't even students in some of the stations, can you believe that? What kind of college has a program with no college students involved?"

Her voice rose with her frustration as my mind still tried to process the fact that she was leaving me. Leaving us. When she continued, I swore I felt my heart crack.

"And this school has had the number-one television and radio stations in the nation two years in a row. In the nation, Nick! I have to go there. I have to. They're the best," she said, the passion for her future pouring out of her with every syllable.

On a gut level, I completely understood where she was coming from, and couldn't blame her a bit. But my heart ached with every breath I took as I tried to hold myself together.

Not feeling steady on my feet, I pulled out a chair at her kitchen table and sat down. I didn't want her to go. Hell, it was the last thing on earth I wanted, but I could never tell her that. Two seconds ago I was about to drop to my knees and beg her to stay, but I could never ask her that now. Not for me. Not for us. I'd never forgive myself if she compromised her dreams or her future for me. I wasn't worth that.

"Say something," she begged before sitting across from me.

"I get why you want to go there," I said with as little emotion as I could.

"That's it?" Her eyes implored me as she nervously twisted the silver ring on her finger.

"It's the best thing for your future. I get it."

She stared at me as if expecting something else, but I wasn't sure exactly what. The table between us felt like an ocean.

"I dunno, Jess. What the hell do you want me to say?"

"How about something along the lines of *we'll be okay*. Or that my leaving is no big deal, and we'll figure it out." She waved her hands in the air, her agitation rising. "I mean, I know it's obviously not ideal, but I was thinking—"

"No." My voice was firm, my resolute tone surprising even me.

Jess froze and dropped her hands. "No, what?"

Northern California was practically another world away. Hell, it should be considered another state with how far it was. And Jess still had two years left of school while I was on the verge of graduating. There was no way that I would allow her to split her attention between her classes and me. There was absolutely no way that I'd do to her what my old man had done to me, making me feel like I had no choice in my own life.

Girls were emotional—I knew that fact all too well—and if things got weird or bad between us, there was no doubt in my mind that Jess would put me first, before herself. She would put *us* first. I could practically see it in my head already, her hauling ass back here to fix whatever was wrong between us without giving it a second thought. And as much as I loved her for that, I could never let her do it. She'd skip classes, miss tests, do whatever it took to make us okay.

I'd never forgive myself if I was the reason Jess didn't get what she'd always dreamed of. She needed to be able to concentrate all her energy on her schooling, on her future, and the best thing I could do for her was to remove myself from the equation completely, no matter how badly it hurt either of us in the process.

This wasn't about me, and for once in my life when it came to a girl, I was making a decision that was the best one for her. She'd see that eventually. I knew she would.

"I don't do long-distance relationships," I said in a curt tone, ignoring the warning bells that rang in my head. My heart pounded, revolting against the lie that had just left my mouth.

"You don't *do* long-distance relationships?" She repeated my words back to me as her eyes filled with tears. "But I love you."

Her voice was so broken, so shattered, that I almost fell to my knees on the floor and begged for her forgiveness. It was the first time either of us had said those words to each other, and she was saying them now while I was breaking her heart.

I lowered my head, refusing to meet her questioning gaze, knowing it would kill me to look at her right now. "I can't do it, Jess. I'm sorry," I said, lying again.

I'd never dated anyone long-distance before, but I would have done it for her. I would have done anything for this girl if I thought it was the best thing for her. But one quick glimpse into the future and I was terrified. I was so damn scared that

I'd be the reason she moved back home or gave up her education, that it stopped all other reason from entering my brain.

Her face was anguished when I finally gained the balls to look at her. "Have you ever tried? Being with someone long-distance, I mean?"

"No, but I know myself. Hell, you know me. I can't date you long-distance. It won't fucking work, and you know it."

"I thought we were different," she said sadly.

I wanted to scream that we were. I wanted to remind her that every single thing about her was different, but I kept my mouth firmly shut.

Her eyes started to fill again, the blue of them turning a shade brighter with her tears, and the sight of it felt like a kick to the gut. "Nick, you're not even trying. We can talk every day on the phone, or we can video chat. I'll come down and see you every weekend that I can. I'll come back all the time for you. And you can come up."

See? She was already putting us before everything else, and I refused to be more important than her goals, no matter what my dad insisted the girl in my life should be like. I wouldn't take away her choices when I never had any. I wouldn't make her feel like she had to choose.

"I'm graduating this year, Jess. I'll be working for my dad in a month. I won't have any free time, and neither will you once you get up there. You'll see. This isn't a good idea."

"You won't even try?"

Fuck yes, I'd try. I'd do anything for you. "No. There's no point."

"But, Nick . . ."

The tears finally spilled down her cheeks. It killed me to be the one causing them, but I had to stay strong. I had to hurt us in the short term to make sure she had a successful long term. I'd had enough practice being an asshole to girls in the past, but it fucking murdered me to act this way toward her.

"Because it won't work, Jess. I can't do it. I can't have a girlfriend who's hundreds of miles away. I'm sorry. I wish I was a stronger guy, but I'm not. I'm not built for that kind of shit. I'd ruin everything we built in a week, and you'd never forgive me for it."

The words were bitter, tasting all wrong as they spilled from my lips. Part of me hoped she'd believe the lies, while the rest of me prayed she knew me better than that.

"What the hell are you saying? That you couldn't stay faithful if I wasn't here? Bullshit. That's bullshit, Nick, and you know it," she yelled.

I was so fucking relieved that she hadn't believed my crap, but I needed her to. I needed her to think I was weak.

"I honestly don't think I could," I said, doing my best to meet her eyes. *Lies. More lies.*

"You're a coward."

She was right. I was a coward.

I couldn't stand up to my dad. I couldn't fight for my future, or for the one person in the world who I wanted by my side. Even though I wanted to hold on tighter, to make her all kinds of promises about how I'd wait for her and stay faithful while she was away, I released her instead. I let her go, breaking my own heart in the process. I might not be able to be strong for myself, but for Jess, I'd do anything.

"I should probably go." I pushed up from the chair quickly, almost knocking it to the floor.

I needed to get the fuck out of that apartment before the walls closed in on me. I could barely breathe as it was with Jess leaving and taking my heart with her.

The worst part was she'd never even know she had it. She'd leave thinking I didn't want her anymore. She'd leave thinking I was perfectly intact, when the truth was I would never be whole again.

THE END

Jess

THE DOOR SHUT softly behind Nick as he left, and I let the tears fall.

I didn't understand at all how he could walk away from me like that, walk away from us. Stupidly, I had assumed he would at least want to try to stay together. The situation wasn't ideal, but it never occurred to me that he might freak out about staying faithful. In my heart, I knew he was lying, but I didn't know why.

How could I have been so wrong about everything?

"Did I hear Nick leave?"

Rachel's door opened, and she and Trevor peered out from behind it. I shook my head at them, sobbing, unable to say anything.

"Jess, what happened?"

"Are you okay?" Trevor asked, his concern genuine.

Pulling myself together, I choked out, "H-he broke up with me."

"No way." Trevor straightened up as if my words were hard to believe. "That's not possible."

"Obviously, it is possible." I hiccupped as I waved a hand at my face, which had to look like complete hell.

"What'd he say?" Rachel asked as she rubbed my back.

I plopped to the floor, burying my head in my hands. God, my heart hurt. Every breath hurt. My mind raced while I wished this was just a bad dream I'd wake up from.

"He said he couldn't do the long-distance thing, and he wouldn't even try." I looked up at my roommate and best friend. "I feel so stupid. I thought he loved me."

"He does love you. I don't believe for one second that he doesn't," Rachel said softly, trying to reassure me.

"He absolutely loves you, Jess. I can promise you that," Trevor added.

Their assurances should have made me feel marginally better, but they didn't. Nothing did. Nick had called it off, walked away, and taken my heart with him.

How would I ever get over him?

*

THE ONLY THING that saved my mental health was the fact that I was moving soon and had a ton of things to do. I still needed to choose my classes at a brand-new school, and I had to find a place to live ASAP.

For my own self-preservation, I buried myself in my upcoming relocation and did my best not to think about Nick. It wasn't easy. But as each day faded into night and I hadn't called or texted him, I gave myself a mental pat on the back for being strong enough to walk away, when all I wanted to do was call him and beg for answers.

I walked around in a daze the last few weeks of the semester, managing to avoid Nick completely, except for the single class we shared together. It was like a knife in the gut when he moved from his usual seat next to mine to the front row, sitting near the girl who'd clamored for his attention on the first day of class. It took every ounce of my willpower to stay seated the entire lecture and not bolt or throw up.

I hated not being near him, watching him effectively ignore me as if I didn't exist. How could I have meant so little to him when he meant so much to me?

I forced Rachel to tell me repeatedly that I hadn't made up my relationship with Nick in my head, that I didn't see things that weren't really there. Somewhere between our beginning and our end, I had convinced myself that it wasn't real, that it was just the plot of some bad romance novel.

And every time I asked, Rachel would say the same thing. "You didn't make anything up. It was real. He loved you. Hell, he probably still does."

The entire campus seemed to know that we had broken up, but no one knew why. The rumor mill spun about our demise, but Rachel ran interference like an NFL linebacker so efficiently that I rarely had to deal with any of it. Most of the lies that spread were generally spoken behind my back and not to my face, and for that I was grateful. When I found the courage to make eye contact with other girls, half of them gave me sympathetic looks while the other half sneered at me, clearly excited that Nick was on the market again.

On the last day of class, Nick stopped in mid-step as he was passing by my seat. He turned, staring right into my eyes. I held my breath as I waited for him to speak, dying to hear his voice, no matter what he might say, but instead he shook his head and rushed out the door.

I jumped up from my seat, determined to confront him, but when I got outside, he was gone. It was like he had vanished into thin air, nowhere to be seen.

I couldn't believe that *that* would be the last time I would ever see him. School was over and I was moving. I couldn't wrap my head around how well I thought I knew him, and how little I truly must have. I couldn't comprehend any of it.

"We all knew it was coming. I'm just shocked it took as long as it did," a familiar voice said, and I came to a sudden halt.

I told myself not to look up, not to give her the time of day, but my eyes didn't listen to my pleading. Carla Crawford stood in front of me, her hip jutted out so that she looked like she was posing for a magazine cover.

"What do you want?" I asked breathlessly before gathering something that resembled gumption. "To rub it in my face? You want to hear that you were right?"

She raised a perfect eyebrow. "I already know I was right."

"Then what do you want?" I asked again, tired of her games.

She leaned in close to my ear, the smell of her perfume overwhelming, and I fought off the urge to wave my hands in the air. "I wanted to tell you in person that I'll be taking your place now. And unlike you, I won't be going anywhere. Ever. Nick and I are a sure thing, and nothing and no one is going to stand in our way."

I bristled with her words, and as much as I didn't want to give them any weight or value, something inside me did. "I'm not sure who you're trying to convince," I said, hoping my words sounded stronger than I currently felt. "Me or *you*."

She made an annoyed sound before straightening, her height advantage making her seem to tower over me. "I don't owe you anything, Jess. I was simply trying to be courteous by giving you a heads-up. I won't make that mistake again." She deliberately bumped her shoulder against mine as she strode away, leaving me standing there alone as other students filed out around us.

I dropped my sunglasses over my eyes and forced the tears to stay at bay as I walked across campus, staring straight ahead to avoid any further confrontations. If anyone else approached me, I knew I wouldn't be able to keep my composure.

To be honest, I wasn't sure how I'd held it together for so long in the first place.

*

My half of the apartment was in boxes as Rachel watched me pack. "I can't believe this is really happening," she said for the fiftieth time that afternoon.

I stopped sealing up the box that I had just filled and looked up at her from my spot on the floor. "I know. It's not fair."

"I just figured we'd be here the whole time together," she said wistfully. "That we'd graduate together and throw some stupid party for the two of us."

I swallowed around the lump in my throat. "I know. I did too."

I had never once thought that I'd have to leave State. When I had gotten accepted, it was one of the best days of my life. Now I was sitting on my apartment floor, packing up my life so I could start my junior year at a brand-new school in a brand-new city where I knew no one and had no friends.

Rachel plopped down in front of me and took my hands in hers. "Stay. Don't go. Who cares about your major and your goals? Your dreams are dumb. Make new dreams and stay here with me, Jess," she said seriously with a slight laugh.

Pouting, I said, "I can't."

"I know."

Hit with inspiration, I perked up. "But you can come visit."

"And don't think I won't. That's only an hour flight, or one super-boring six-hour-long road trip, but don't think that I'm not coming there. You do not get to have a new best friend. I won't stand for it, *gringa*."

I laughed. "I can't even imagine anyone taking your place." I blew out a soft breath. "My life is going to be so boring without you."

"And don't you forget it," she said, her accent coming out a little stronger as she wagged her finger in my direction.

A knock at the door startled both of us, and we turned to stare at it as if we could figure out who was behind it if we looked hard enough.

"Trevor?" I asked.

Rachel shook her head. "He's at work until eight."

She pushed up off the floor and headed into the living room. When she opened the front door, my heart slammed against my chest as the sound of his voice filled the room.

Nick.

Nick is here.

Rachel stepped back into my room, sounding uncharacteristically nervous as she said, "Um, *chica?*"

I swallowed hard. "It's really him?" I asked, my voice barely above a whisper.

She nodded. "Should I let him in or stomp on his nuts?"

I glanced around at my room as her options echoed in my mind. It looked like a tornado had torn through it.

Giving her a slight smile, I said, "I guess you can leave his nuts alone for now."

"So I'm sending him in?" When I nodded, Rachel disappeared.

Nick stood in my doorway a minute later, wearing an odd expression I couldn't quite place. "Hey."

He looked tired, defeated even, but I wasn't sure that it had anything to do with me. Maybe he looked that way because his reality after graduation had sunk in. Nick had to go to work for his dad's company instead of following his heart and working with his brothers at Sam's. I knew how that prospect tore him up, and it made me hurt for him.

Remembering that he'd addressed me, I offered a nonchalant "hey" in response.

He stood there, his hulking frame casting a shadow over me. When he didn't say anything else, I returned to my packing, not knowing exactly what he wanted from me and half afraid to look him in the eyes. They'd be my undoing.

A moment later, he sat down directly across from me. He said nothing, his silence stabbing me a little more in my gut with each moment that passed between us.

"Why are you here?" I finally asked him, my broken heart desperate to know why he had shown up to destroy what was left of it.

"I wanted to see you," he said, his voice sounding pained.

"I'm really going to miss you, Jess."

I finally raised my eyes to meet his, praying that I wouldn't get emotional when I looked into their depths. The eyes of the man I had fallen in love with, still loved, but didn't want me anymore.

"You're going to miss me?" I managed to ask through my surprise.

"You find that hard to believe?"

I shook my head, not sure what I believed anymore. "Don't say that, Nick. Don't say things like that to me right now." Swallowing hard, I gathered my courage and added, "Unless it's followed up with something about you not letting me go, or you wanting us to get back together because you realized you made a huge mistake. If you're not here to tell me any of those things, then don't say you're going to miss me. It's not fair." I bit my lip, still determined to keep it together.

"I'm sorry. I mean it, though. I am going to miss you."

He winced, looking at the floor for a moment as my stomach tightened. It was so hard to be this close to him and not be a part of his life. After all, I had wrapped myself up in all things Nick Fisher so tightly that not being with him when he was this near seemed foreign. Looking at him from a distance seemed wrong—it all felt wrong. Why didn't he feel it too?

"Then why are you giving up on us? I hate you for that." My eyes filled with tears as my inner strength failed me.

"I know. I know you do. I just—" He squeezed his eyes shut for a second before giving me an intense look.

"You just what? Can walk away like we never mattered? Like I never mattered?"

His jaw tightened. "You know that's not true."

"I really don't," I said, fighting to keep my voice steady as the tears threatened.

He pushed up to his feet. "I shouldn't have come. I'm sorry, Jess. I just wanted to say good-bye to you in person."

Everything inside me fell to pieces at those words. Good-bye seemed so final, so resolute, like something we could never overcome. Part of me had held out hope that Nick was here to seal the cracks he had inflicted on my heart, but he wasn't. I was moving, and he was letting me go without even trying to keep us together.

He didn't want me. Why I needed to constantly remind myself of that fact was beyond irritating.

"Good-bye, Nick."

He reached out a hand, and I only hesitated a moment before accepting it and launching myself into his arms. I hated the way I still wanted to be touched by him, but I loved him. I couldn't shut off my feelings as easily as he had.

I breathed him in, my hands finding their way to the back of his neck as I committed him to memory—the curve of his neck, the warmth of his skin, the stubble on his cheek. His lips found my cheek and I closed my eyes, knowing it would be the last time that I would feel them on my skin. I wanted to remember how they felt, how soft they were, how gentle he was with me.

When he released me and stepped back, I almost gasped at the distance. It felt like I was losing him all over again. I had finally gotten to a place where I didn't feel the pain of his loss with every breath, but now I felt like I would have to start rehab all over again to kick my Nick addiction.

He reached into his pocket and pulled out a small box

before handing it to me. "Open it later. After I'm gone, okay?"

I stared at it a second, trying to figure out what could possibly be inside. "Okay."

"You'll do great up north, Jess. You'll be great. Go be great."

He leaned down and placed another kiss on my forehead, his lips lingering too long, but I refused to complain. With a small squeeze of my shoulder, he hurried toward the door before turning back one last time.

"You don't need the luck, Jess, but I wanted you to have it."

Confused, I frowned as he disappeared from my sight. I wanted to chase after him, but chasing a man who didn't want you was pointless. Even my broken heart knew that much.

The door slammed, and I stood there with the box in my hand, my heart in my hand, my pride in my hands . . . feeling overwhelmed and emotional.

"Jess?" Rachel said in a small voice, and I looked up to see her standing in the doorway. "Is he gone?"

I nodded, afraid that if I tried to speak, I wouldn't be able to find my voice.

"What's in your hand?" she asked, and I shrugged. "Open it. Open it right this instant!"

I removed the top, and when my gaze landed on the red-and-white-striped poker chip nestled on the cotton inside, I almost dropped the box. He'd given me his grandfather's lucky poker chip?

"Why the hell did he give you a poker chip?" Rachel asked, her expression as confused as my heart and mind.

"I don't know," I admitted.

"But does it mean something?" She reached for it but I pulled the box away. "Is it an inside joke between you two? I don't get it."

"It was his grandfather's," I said and then shook my head, not wanting to give away any more details of a story that wasn't mine to share.

"Are you going to thank him for it?"

"Thank him for it? Thank him for what exactly? Coming over here, confusing the living shit out of me by giving me this gift that supposedly means the world to him when he refuses to stay with me because I'm moving four hundred miles away? No, I'm not going to thank him for it, Rachel."

She threw up her hands in defeat. "Easy, tiger. I was only asking."

"I know. Sorry. I just don't understand him at all. I can't take this." I shoved the box into Rachel's hand.

"What do you want me to do with it?" She pulled out the chip and flipped it back and forth in her palm, studying it like it held magical powers.

"Give it back to him. Please."

"What if he won't take it?"

"I don't care. Throw it at him. Tell him it's not mine to keep. Just tell him I couldn't keep it, that it means too much to him and it shouldn't be with someone else."

She drew in a loud, dramatic breath. "He won't like that, Jess."

"I know. So you'll do it, right?"

A wicked smile crept over her face. "Of course I'll do it."

I smiled back at my little spitfire roommate, feeling more conflicted than ever as I finished packing.

She was right—Nick wouldn't like it—but I couldn't care about that right now. Right now I needed to finish packing and start my new life without Nick, without Rachel, without State.

A new life I never saw coming.

LEAVING HOME

Jess

LEAVING RACHEL HAD been hard. The day my dad came to help me move out of our apartment, I couldn't stop crying. I knew it was a combination of leaving behind my best friend, a school I genuinely loved, and allowing the emotions of everything regarding Nick to finally bubble up to the surface. Transferring to Northern was the best thing for my future, and I never questioned that decision, but it still hurt to say good-bye when I didn't really want to leave.

"I'll miss you so much. As soon as you get settled, I'm coming up," Rachel said.

"You better," I said fiercely.

"You can't get rid of me that easily, *chica*. You're *my* white girl," she said with a smile before delivering a rapid-fire Spanish-filled rant she knew I wouldn't be able to understand. When I rolled my eyes dramatically, she just talked faster, gesturing with her hands as she spoke.

"Stop!" I laughed through my tears. "You know I don't know what the hell you're saying."

"I know. That's why it's so fun for me. I was just threatening anyone who tried to think that they could take my best friend from me." She stuck out her tongue before wrapping me in a tight hug. "Text me every day."

"Of course."

I squeezed her hard before walking out of our apartment for the last time. Refusing to look back, I put one foot in front of the other and headed toward my dad's truck, now full of all my belongings.

"You okay, sweetheart?" he asked when I buckled myself in.

I nodded as I swiped at my cheek. "I will be."

"That's my strong girl," he said, then put the truck in gear and drove us back home for the summer, away from my old life.

*

THE SUMMER FLEW by. I found an apartment to share next semester with another student with the help of the Film Production department head at Northern. He had given me his personal e-mail address after my counselor at State had reached out to him, and had been helping me in every step of my transfer journey. I knew he didn't have to be so kind, but I was beyond thankful for the way he went out of his way for me. My classes were scheduled, I had a new place to live come fall, and I hadn't even visited the campus yet.

Feeling like my upcoming journey was pretty much set-tled, I started working with my parents at their deli to occupy my time. Any moments that weren't crazy busy were the emotional death of me. I needed all the help I could get to keep my mind and thoughts occupied so I wouldn't focus on Nick's silence, but it didn't usually work. He was a force to be reckoned with. His memory refused to be pushed aside, even though he had easily dismissed me.

The moments when I really started to miss him, I reminded myself that he had looked me in the eye at my old apartment and told me he couldn't stay faithful. I also reminded myself that he hadn't called or texted me the entire summer. I knew he was busy working with his dad, but no excuse truly lessened the sting. I felt rejected, cast aside, discarded.

I was so mad that he could go day in and day out without reaching out to me, showing me with every twenty-four hours that passed how little he truly cared. But then I was so happy he didn't reach out to me, terrified of how my heart and mind would react to any attention from him.

I was nothing if not a woman of extremes and contradictions.

One second I was so pissed at him for not asking me to stay. The next, I was so thankful that he hadn't. My heart ached when I thought about him not fighting for me, for us. Just as quickly, my heart beat in relief that he had let us go.

"If he would have asked you to stay, what would you have said?" Rachel asked one night over the phone.

I planted the heels of my feet against my wall as I leaned back onto my mattress. "I would have stayed," I said with a long sigh. "At least, I really would have wanted to."

"Maybe that's exactly why he didn't ask."

"Or maybe he was happy to see me go?" I said it like a question, but the words tasted wrong in my mouth. My heart knew they were lies, but my bitter mind wanted them said anyway.

Rachel laughed. "You're being stupid."

"I know. How's Trevor? Tell me something good, please, and not Nick related."

"He's great. I've got nothing to report except we're really happy. It's sick, right?"

"No, it's sweet. You deserve it."

"Thanks, *chica*."

"It's true," I said through a yawn. "Hey, did you ever give Nick back the poker chip?"

I'd pretended to have forgotten about Nick's gift, but the truth was that that poker chip was on my mind almost as much as he was. What had it meant? Why had he given it to me?

She let out an uncomfortable laugh. "Not yet. I haven't seen him since he started working for his dad. But I will, okay?"

"Okay. Maybe wait until I move up north so that I'm really far away when he gets pissed off about getting it back," I suggested, hoping that the additional distance would lessen whatever reaction Nick had about it. If he had a reaction at all.

"I probably won't see him before you leave anyway, but I'll wait."

"Thanks."

"You'll be okay, Jess. You know that, right?" Rachel's tone softened as she lowered the protective wall she always maintained, and allowed her sensitive side to come through.

"I do know that. Honestly, I think I've been doing okay considering I feel like my heart beats in broken pieces now." A piece of my heart felt like it had lodged in my throat, and I was thankful to be alone and having this conversation on the phone instead of in person.

"You've been doing more than okay. You've been really great. I just know you're hurting, even if you don't say it all the time. I know what Nick did really messed with you, and I'm sorry. I wish I knew what he was thinking or why he did it."

"He told me what he was thinking and why he did it, Rach. He was thinking that I wasn't worth staying faithful for, that he could never date someone long-distance. He spelled it out for me. I don't know what more you think there is to know."

She groaned. "You know I think that's all bullshit. Every word of it."

"Well, it doesn't matter," I said with attitude. Because it didn't. What Rachel thought, what I thought, none of it made a difference if Nick refused to change his mind.

"You're right. I just want to see you happy again. Maybe you'll meet someone super hot at your new school."

"I think I'm done with guys for a while." I let out a small giggle.

"Ha! And that's when you find one. What will Nick do if he finds out you're dating someone? Oh my God, I can't even imagine. It's going to be epic."

I groaned, wondering when every single thing would stop revolving around Nick, or be associated with him. "First of all, I'm nowhere near ready for that. I really just want to focus on my classes."

It was true, I did want to focus on my classes, to make contacts and hopefully score an incredible internship this semester. But even more true was the fact that my heart wasn't ready to date, and neither was the rest of me. I wasn't over Nick, and I wasn't sure when I would be. Dating someone new hadn't even factored into my mind until Rachel brought it up.

"Okay. Shit, Trevor's here. I'll talk to you tomorrow."

"Night. Tell him I said hi."

Once we'd hung up, I dropped my phone on the bed and allowed myself to be flooded with emotions.

I was excited to move to a brand-new place where I didn't know anyone.

I was terrified to leave everyone I'd ever known for a brand-new place where I didn't know anyone.

But mostly I felt sad and confused, and my heart ached in all the places where Nick had once lived. Apparently he'd permeated every part of me, because I currently hurt all over.

*

I SETTLED INTO Northern California pretty easily. Sure, it was a completely different environment and atmosphere than what I was used to, but I was the one who decided to move, so I was determined to make the best of it.

My new roommate, Brooke, was really nice, but also a little socially awkward. When I walked into our apartment the first time, located conveniently across the street from campus, she barely glanced up from her computer to give me a smile, her light brown hair pulled back into a messy ponytail. As soon as I started bringing my things inside, she disappeared into her room and closed the door.

At first I thought she was rude, but soon learned that she was painfully shy. I wondered briefly how she would make it in a major like television production, but my reservations disappeared when she showed me an editing project she was working on for her YouTube channel. She was talented, smart, and creative, all things I wouldn't have guessed simply by looking at her and observing her body language. Brooke was completely focused on her classes and I appreciated that, figuring she would help me stay focused too, instead of distracted with things I didn't need, like guys.

I had to admit that even though the weather in Northern California was far colder than it was back home—which sucked—and the people were completely different, my classes were awesome. The school had state-of-the-art equipment, and I started working at the campus television station within my first month of arriving, getting the most hands-on training I'd ever had. I was completely enthralled and totally captivated, convinced I'd made the right decision to move, even when things outside of school didn't always feel right.

I was more homesick than I ever thought possible, as the feeling of not belonging and being in the wrong place nagged at me, but knew I needed to stay. I made sure that the positives outweighed the negatives in my mind; otherwise, I'd probably pack up my car and leave in the middle of the night.

Rachel never believed me when I told her that the people up north were far less friendly than the ones in LA. Whenever I had walked through campus at State and said hi to people I didn't know, they all responded or at least smiled back.

Not here.

When I said hi to a stranger, they looked at me like I had two heads and continued walking, never once responding to me or doing something as simple as smiling. I wasn't acknowledged in the slightest, but Rachel didn't believe me. She insisted that I was exaggerating. I couldn't wait to prove her wrong the first time she came to visit.

As I was sitting on my bed, thinking about all the things I missed from home, my cell phone sang out its familiar ringtone for Rachel, pulling me from my pity party.

"I was just thinking about how much I missed you," I told her.

"Come back."

"Stop. It hurts me when you say that. Being away sucks. It's so different up here."

"You like it though, right?"

"Not really," I admitted before pulling open the sliding glass door in my room. Stepping onto the oversized balcony, I sat down on the old couch we'd placed outside, and propped my feet on the balcony railing. "But I love my classes. And the TV station is unbelievable."

"That was the whole point right?"

I swallowed. "Right."

"How's your roommate?"

I thought about Brooke and how different she was from Rachel in every single way. "She's . . ." I paused, unsure of how to describe her exactly.

"She's what?"

"She's really nice, but she's super shy and doesn't like to leave the apartment unless she's going to the library or class."

Rachel burst out laughing. "I'm so glad your roommate sucks," she said between more fits of laughter.

"She doesn't suck!" I whisper-shouted. "She's just not you."

"To be honest, Jess, I'm relieved. I was going to hate having to off your new roomie when I come visit."

My ears perked up at her words. "Please tell me you're not messing with me."

"Why would I mess with you?"

"So you're coming up here?" I asked hopefully.

"Are you coming down anytime soon?"

Her question made me want to pack a bag and leave the second we hung up.

"I want to, but probably not." My class schedule wasn't heavy enough to keep me away from home, but the extra nights I spent at the television station were a problem.

"Yes, I'm coming up."

I squealed into the phone and slammed my feet up and down on the balcony floor in my excitement. "Thank God. I can't wait to have you here!"

"Me either," she said, sounding happy and upbeat before her tone changed. "So, I ran into Nick last night."

My heart lurched straight into my throat. The simple mention of his name still affected me, made me feel . . . something. Even though I wished I didn't, I missed him. It was easier trying to pretend I was fine than accept the reality that I wasn't when I really wanted to be.

"Where?"

"At the bar near campus. He was so drunk, Jess. God, he wouldn't shut up about you. He asked me a thousand questions. And he looked like hell."

"Good," I said, then immediately regretted it. "I don't mean that."

"Sure you do."

I sighed. "It's sick that I want him to hurt, but I'm hurting too, Rach. Still. And I want him to want me back. Why doesn't he want me back?" I squeezed my eyes shut as a breeze blew over me.

"He had a one-track mind last night, and it was all you. I'm convinced he's not over you. He asked if you were happy, how you liked your classes, if you were dating anyone, when you were coming back. God, he wouldn't shut up, and I stopped answering him and told him if he wanted to know so bad, he could call you himself and ask. That shut him up real quick."

I bit back a laugh. This wasn't funny. My broken heart was no laughing matter. "Did he say he'd call?"

"No. He walked away."

"I don't understand him at all," I admitted, feeling defeated.

"Me either sometimes."

"Trying to figure him out gives me a headache."

Despite that, I loved hearing all of this. Knowing that Nick had asked about me filled me with hope. Maybe we weren't doomed. Maybe there was a future for us somewhere down the line.

"Before he walked away, though, Jess, he was crazy. Relentless. He forced me to answer one question, and he wouldn't let go of my arm until I did."

"What question?" I asked, on pins and needles waiting for her answer.

Rachel huffed into the phone. "He wanted to know if you were happy."

I clutched my free hand against my chest. "What'd you tell

him?"

"I told him you hated it and it sucked, but you were doing what you had to for your future."

Pursing my lips, I nodded in agreement, even though she couldn't see me. "What'd he say to that?"

"Nothing. That's when he dropped my arm and walked away. But I chased after him."

My heart raced inside my chest. "What? You did? Why?"

"Because I had that stupid poker chip in my purse, and I remembered only after he started practically running away. I pulled it out and gave it to him."

My heart stopped racing, stopped beating completely. I held my breath, pain stabbing me in the gut. "What'd he say?"

"Nothing, but the expression on his face almost made *me* throw up. He looked like I'd kicked his puppy into oncoming traffic or something."

"But he didn't say anything?"

"No. He shoved it in his pocket and left. But I swear, Jess, he looked like he was about to fucking cry."

"Yeah, right. Nick Fisher cry?" I fought back a sick laugh as my heart allowed the familiar ache of his loss to return. I honestly hated that we weren't together. "I don't believe it."

Rachel let out a sad sigh. "I wouldn't believe it either if I hadn't seen it."

I sat there with conflicted emotions swirling around inside me like the sea, pulling me under. I didn't know which way was up, or how to break through to the surface. I was engulfed in an ocean of Nick, and assumed I probably always would be.

There was no getting over this guy.

BROKEN SILENCE

Jess

A FTER HANGING UP with Rachel, I sucked in a long breath and headed back inside, wondering if my new roommate would want to actually leave the apartment for once and grab some food with me. I had to get the hell away from my own thoughts, and needed a distraction.

"Brooke?" I yelled from behind her closed door. I waited, expecting to hear her shout back at me, but her door opened instead.

"Hey, Jess."

"I was wondering if you wanted to grab some dinner or something?" I almost suggested going to a bar to drown my misery, but figured she'd never agree to that.

When she stayed silent for a beat longer, I added, "I really need to get out of here, and I could use the company." It was more than I'd intended to say, but if I didn't do a little extra prodding, I'd be eating alone. Again.

"Are you okay?" She tilted her head to the side, causing her long bangs to fall into her eyes.

I nodded. "I will be. Are you hungry?"

A soft smile lit up her face. "Yeah. Let me grab a sweat-shirt."

Relieved, I ran into my room to grab my own sweatshirt before meeting her in the living room. The evenings in Northern California got pretty cold. Even if it was eighty degrees during the day, which it rarely was, a chilly wind kicked up out of nowhere each night, making the need to cover up a necessity.

"Where should we go?" she asked as she tucked her hands into her front pockets.

"Um . . ." Shit. I hadn't really thought that far ahead since I'd assumed she'd say no. "Craving anything in particular?"

She shook her head.

"We can just go somewhere close, so we don't have to drive and worry about parking," I suggested, knowing that we had plenty of restaurant options within walking distance of our apartment.

"How about Sparks?"

I smiled at her suggestion. "Oh my gosh, yes. Barbecue sounds perfect." I practically drooled, wondering why I hadn't thought of it myself.

It was a quick five-minute walk to get there, and I silently thanked the food gods for the lack of a wait. No line was practically unheard of for a Saturday evening, but I wasn't complaining.

When our hostess seated us, Brooke craned her neck, looking around as if she was searching for someone.

"Who are you looking for?" I asked, and her cheeks turned pink.

"Huh? Me? No one, why?"

She was a horrible liar.

"Oh my gosh, Brooke. You like someone who works here.

Who is he, and how do I not know this?"

Brooke's cheeks reddened even more as she reached across the high-top table and covered my mouth with her hand. "Jess, please be quiet."

I let out a muffled laugh as she pulled her hand away. "Okay, okay. But you have to tell me everything."

"There's nothing to tell. I have a crush, but he doesn't know I exist." She rolled her brown eyes. "Typical, right? I'm such a stereotype."

I glanced around at the guys working, wondering who it could be. I wasn't sure why it surprised me so much that Brooke would be interested in someone. Even shy workaholics paid attention to their hearts sometimes.

When my gaze fell on a waiter with wavy blond hair, I glanced at Brooke to see where she was looking. Just as I had suspected, her eyes were glued to the back of this guy's head.

"That him?" I asked with a subtle nod in his direction.

Her eyes snapped to mine. "Please don't say anything, Jess. Please," she begged, shifting in her seat.

"Why would I say anything? I don't want to embarrass you."

Her shoulders relaxed slightly, and I wondered exactly what kind of person Brooke thought I was. It was clear that she didn't really know me, but to be fair, I didn't know her very well either. We had gone out to dinner a total of two times since I moved in, and this was our third.

I narrowed my eyes at the guy, wondering if I could place him. "Is he in our major?" I asked, and she shook her head.

"No, but he works here and at the campus library."

Choking back a laugh, I felt things click into place in my

mind. "And I thought you spent all your time at the library because you were such a good student."

She gave me a sheepish look. "I am a good student. But I might spend more time there than is really necessary."

"I would too," I admitted with a smile.

"It's not stupid, right?"

"I'm probably not the best person to ask, but if I liked someone who worked on campus, I'd spend all my time there stalking him. I'd never come home," I said, half serious, half joking.

A waitress stopped at our table to take our order, and dropped off two glasses of water. Brooke relaxed a little more, probably because she was relieved that the cute guy wasn't waiting on us.

Giving me a curious look, Brooke asked, "So, why aren't you the best person to ask?" When I narrowed my eyes in confusion, she added, "About this kind of stuff. Do you have a boyfriend back in LA? I kind of assumed you did."

My heart sank. I wasn't sure where the hell it thought it was heading, but thoughts of Nick made it plummet without my consent.

"Really? Why would you assume that?"

She shrugged. "Because you don't go to any of the fraternity parties. It doesn't seem like you're trying to meet anyone, so I thought you had someone back home."

Emotions swirled through me. Talking about Nick with Rachel was one thing. It was easier, somehow, since she had gone through it all with me. But talk about him with Brooke? I didn't even know where to begin, or how.

"It's complicated," I said before taking a gulp of my water.

"Shit, it's not complicated. I don't know what it is." That wasn't entirely true. "It's nothing. I don't have a boyfriend back home. I did, but he broke up with me before I moved here."

"He broke up with you? Why?" She leaned forward, seeming genuinely interested.

"I really don't know. He said that he didn't want to date long-distance. That it would never work." I tried to say these things with as little emotion as possible, but knew I was failing when I felt that telltale burn behind my eyes. *Dammit.* I fucking hated that Nick still affected me this way, that he could still affect me at all.

Brooke leaned back, studying me a moment before stating, "He broke your heart."

I couldn't disagree. "He did."

"And it's still broken."

My eyes began to fill. Furious with myself, I swiped a finger under my eyes and steadied myself. I wanted to argue with her. I wanted to convince her that she was wrong, that I was fine, that I was over it. Over him. But every aspect of that would have been a lie, and I wasn't a liar. "It's in a million pieces."

She reached across the table and laid her hand on mine for a moment before she gave it a squeeze and pulled back. "I've never had a broken heart, so I don't know what it feels like, but I'm really sorry he did that. And I'm sorry you're hurt."

"Thanks." Sniffling, I grabbed my napkin and wiped away the tears that had escaped without my permission.

"Can I ask you something else?" she asked, and I nodded. "Have you talked to him since you moved up here?"

"I haven't talked to him since I moved out of my apartment at State."

"Not even a drunk text or a drunk anything?" she asked innocently, unable to hide her surprise.

A choked laugh escaped me at her question. "No. Not even a drunk anything."

"Does that shock you? I mean, I've never had a boyfriend, so I really don't know how any of this works other than what I see in movies or on TV, or and read in books. But I feel like he shouldn't be able to go all this time without talking to you."

Brushing her question aside for a second, I said, "First of all, I can't believe you've never had a boyfriend. We need to fix that."

Brooke admitting she'd never had a boyfriend didn't surprise me half as much as I pretended it had. She was a pretty girl, crazy smart, and had a lot to offer, but I knew it was her shyness that kept her single more than anything else.

"Second, does it shock me that he can go day in and day out without ever saying a single word to me or seeing how I am?" My heart seemed to stutter and stumble over itself. "Yes. Incredibly. Every day that passes, it hurts a little less, though. The shock is a little less jarring. I've come to expect that he won't reach out, you know?"

"Have you reached out to him since you left? A drunk text or a drunk anything?" She smirked as our waitress came back to deliver our food.

I waited until our waitress disappeared to wherever it was that waitresses went when they weren't doting on you. "No. I haven't. He broke up with me, and I didn't want to be that pathetic girl who couldn't accept it. Even though half the time

I feel exactly like that on the inside."

Brooke frowned at me. "You're not pathetic. You moved hundreds of miles away to come to a school you'd never even set eyes on before. You left behind everything and everyone that you loved to chase your dreams. That's not pathetic, that's brave."

I'd never thought about my move in quite those terms before, but Brooke framing it that way made me think. I didn't feel like I was being brave by deciding to move. It honestly felt like I had no other choice. That wasn't bravery; that was doing what was necessary to get ahead.

"Thank you, Brooke. I appreciate it."

We finished our dinner mostly in silence, except for a few moans from each of us as we ate the best barbecue in town. Once we'd finished and moved toward the door to leave, Brooke's crush suddenly appeared, holding the door open for us.

"Good night, Brooke," he said as he looked right into her eyes.

She fumbled a moment before saying, "Oh. Good night, Kenny. Thank you."

Thrilled for her, I wanted to jump up and down, but I tamped down my enthusiasm until we were outside on the sidewalk.

"I guess he does know you exist," I said before bumping her shoulder with mine, and grinned as a smile took over her face.

The night air had grown even colder, so we both walked quickly, as if we were in a race to get home. We couldn't get there fast enough.

"Thanks again for coming to dinner. I needed that," I said to Brooke once we walked into our chilly apartment and I flipped on the heat.

"It was nice," she said, beaming. "We should do that more often."

It was my turn to smile. "Yes, please."

"Well, I have some work to finish, so I'm going to my room."

"Okay. I'll see you later," I said as she closed her bedroom door.

I'd just walked into my own room when my cell phone started ringing, and I glanced down to check the caller ID.

When I saw Nick's name, I wanted to throw up. What incredible timing. Had he sensed that I was just talking about him? That I'd just been saying how much it hurt that he could go all this time without reaching out to me?

My surprise faded as I remembered what Rachel had told me earlier about running into him last night. Half of me had expected this call, whether I'd admit it or not, especially after learning that Rachel had finally returned the poker chip to him.

The IGNORE CALL button flashed, tempting me to press it, but in the end I couldn't bring myself to ignore him. I wasn't sure if I'd ever be able to.

"Hello?" I tried to sound as composed as possible, but my heart was racing and I couldn't feel my legs as I walked over to my bed and climbed on.

"Jess."

Just the sound of him breathing my name over the phone line instantly sent flutters through me.

"Nick."

"I gave the poker chip to you, Jess. It was for you. Why would you do that?"

My stomach clenched at how broken his voice sounded. "It didn't seem right for me to keep it."

"I wanted you to have it. I needed you to take a part of me with you when you left."

He what? God, he was so confusing. This was so confusing. I didn't know what to say in response to that, so I sat still, listening to him breathe into the line.

"Why are you so far away? Why did you leave? Fuck, Jess, why did you leave me?" His voice slurred, telling me he'd been drinking.

"Are you drunk?" I pretended to sound annoyed, but I wasn't. I wasn't annoyed or irritated at all.

This was Nick, my Nick. And even though he broke my heart when he told me he didn't want to even try to be together, I couldn't help the way I felt when it came to him. I still wanted him, and I was too surprised by his call to hate myself for it.

"A little," he said. "God, why aren't you here right now? I need you. I need you here."

His words stopped my heart, and the south of his voice silenced the thundering in my chest. I was certain he would always affect me this way.

"Listen to me, Jess—" He stopped for a second to yell at someone, and then spoke to me again. "Sorry. Listen to me. You don't belong up there. You don't belong where you're at. You belong with me, and I'm coming to get you. Me and Dan are going to head up there tomorrow to pick you up, throw you over my shoulder, and bring you home. Do you hear me? I'm coming to get you and bring you home."

Nerves surged through me as I struggled to not only think, but to breathe. Nick wanted to come get me? God, nothing sounded more appealing in this moment than him going all caveman on me, but I knew I couldn't let him. I couldn't leave here—this was my school now, and I couldn't just leave in the middle of the semester.

"I can't leave," I said in a whisper.

"Yes, you can. Listen, Jess. For once, just listen."

For once? I thought, then focused on what he was saying.

"I hate that you're up there. I can't fucking handle how far away you are from me. Do you understand that? Do you know how crazy I'm going every day without you? And besides, you don't even like it up there. I know for a fact you don't," he said so convincingly, obviously believing what he was saying. "Rachel said you were miserable. She said you hate it up there. And it's not where you belong, anyway. I'm coming to get you tomorrow, so start packing."

My jaw fell open. Stunned, I felt torn in two. One side of me loved his utterly crazy, insane words, and wanted him to come up here and get me away from this place.

But the other side of me knew that what he was saying was impossible, unreasonable, and unrealistic. My parents would flip out, not to mention that the whole reason I had moved here in the first place was for my degree, and ultimately, my career. I was thriving at the TV station.

"Nick—"

"Don't fight me on this."

"You can't come up here. I can't go home with you."

"Yes, I can. And yes, you can."

"No, I can't."

"We can do this all night."

"Don't come up here. I'm begging you. Stay home." *What am I saying?*

"I'm coming. I miss you so damn much. I can't do this without you anymore. You need to come home. I need you. I love you."

He . . . what?

He loves me? Since fucking when?

"That's not fair," I said as tears filled my eyes, torn between hating him for confessing these things in his inebriated state, and hoping he'd tell me more.

"What's not?"

"You can't tell me you love me now." Trembling, I clenched the comforter with my free hand and pulled it around me.

"Well, I do, Jess. I should have told you months ago. I fell in love with you the night of the fraternity party, but I was too stupid to admit it."

"Why are you doing this?"

"I told you already. I need you. You belong with me. We belong together. I need you to come home. Just be ready. I'll be there tomorrow."

With that demand, he ended the call, and my complete and utter freak-out began.

Was he really going to come up here and expect to be able to drag me home? He sounded pretty drunk—maybe he wouldn't even remember calling me in the morning.

Nick said he loves me . . .

What an asshole. He couldn't say it when we were together, but now that we were apart, and after months of not talking, this was when he decided to tell me that?

Love. He clearly didn't even know what the word meant.

What the hell was I supposed to do if he showed up here tomorrow? I fought the urge to call Rachel, not knowing what I'd say or how I'd explain anything to her.

I decided to sleep on it and see what the morning would bring. My stomach knotted as I curled up in a ball on my bed and tried to force myself to sleep.

WAITING

Jess

M Y NIGHT WAS filled with fitful dreams that kept me from sleeping soundly. I woke up feeling anxious, paranoid, and sick to my stomach. Would Nick really show up here and try to bring me home? What the hell would I do if he came to my door?

And what the hell would I do if he didn't?

Sure, I'd told him not to come. Begged him, actually, but he ended the call saying he was coming anyway. I considered texting him, just to see where his head was at now that he was probably sober, but I was too scared to do it, too terrified of what his answer might be. Logically, I knew him showing up here was a long shot, but somewhere deep down, I think I genuinely wanted him to.

That caveman inclination to come rescue the girl who didn't need rescuing turned parts of me to silk. I would have never expected that a girl like me would like the things that he said last night, but I did. I wanted Nick to want me enough that he would do something crazy for me, to love me like he couldn't live without me. Lord only knew how "well" I was living without him.

The hours passed as I stared between my bedside clock and

my cell phone, refusing to move from my room. I kept the television playing in the background in an attempt to drown out the quiet, but I wasn't paying any attention to it.

Instead, my mind churned with a million questions. Would he show up? How far away was he right now? Did he really love me?

My stomach rolled as the questions refused to stop. Questions that I could easily have the answers to if I dialed Nick's number or sent him a text. But I was too scared to hear that he was still in So Cal, or that he didn't remember calling me the night before. Too scared to hear it confirmed that he wasn't on his way. My heart couldn't take that reality. So I sat alone in my room and waited, like the coward I was.

By four in the afternoon, the realization that he wasn't coming started to set in. The disappointment was far greater than I ever expected it to be, and I leaned back on my bed and reached for my phone.

"*Chica*," Rachel shouted into my ear as music blared in the background.

"Rach?" I said softly.

"Jess? What's wrong?" she asked, and the music stopped suddenly.

"Are you busy? Can you talk?"

"I can talk. I was just rocking out while I was cleaning. What's up?"

I wasn't sure what to say or where to start, so I decided to start at the beginning. "Nick called me last night."

"Last night? And you're just telling me this now? It's after four, Jess! The hell?"

"I know. I wanted to call you, but I was so confused."

She breathed a laugh into the phone. "What'd he do now? Oh, was it about the poker chip? I bet it was about the chip, wasn't it? How pissed was he?" She started talking a mile a minute the way she always did, and it made me miss her even more than usual.

"He mentioned the chip, but that wasn't really why he called."

"Jess, you're being weird and cryptic, and I need you to get to the point because I'm literally dying here. I can feel myself withering away while I wait for you to tell me *what the hell Nick Fisher said to you last night!*" She yelled this last part so loudly, I had to move the phone away from my ear.

I waited a beat before blurting, "He said he was coming up here to take me home."

"He *what?*" she asked, her tone completely incredulous.

"He said he was bringing me home, that he knew I wasn't happy. He said I didn't belong up here. That I belonged with him."

For once, Rachel was quiet on the other end of the line.

Too quiet. For too long.

"Rach?"

"I'm here. I'm processing."

Shit. If Rachel needed time to process, then how the hell was I supposed to feel?

"I can't believe he called you and said that," she finally said.

"I know. And I'm just sitting here like an idiot, waiting for him to show up at my front door so I can jump into his arms like some fairy-tale princess."

"Tell me you didn't start packing," she said in a sarcastic

tone, and I let out a small laugh.

"Yeah, right. I haven't packed a thing. I can't move home in the middle of the semester—" I started to say before correcting myself. "I can't move back home at all until I graduate."

"I know. Trust me, I know." She sucked in a breath and released it slowly. "Okay, so, what else did he say? He said he was coming up today and bringing you home?"

I nodded, even though she couldn't see me. "Uh-huh. He might have also said he loved me."

"Jess, stop. This is too much craziness for one phone call. My little Latin heart can't take anymore."

This caused a real laugh to escape from my chest. "*Your* heart can't take it? How do you think mine feels right now, knowing that he isn't coming?"

"You wanted him to come?"

"Of course I don't want him to come. But he called and said he was, and I got all confused about that. I mean, it would have been a nice gesture, right? Him showing up here, all knight in shining armor, to take me home."

"It would have been something, all right," she said in a tight voice.

"What's wrong?"

"I'm getting pissed, Jess. Which is what you should be."

"Did I mention he was drunk?"

"No, you didn't mention that." She sighed. "Still, he shouldn't have said those things to you."

"Will you think less of me if I tell you that I liked hearing them?"

"No. Because if it were me and Nick Fisher, I would have

liked hearing them too."

"Really?" Her admission made me feel a thousand times better about my reaction, made me feel less weak.

"Really. But I don't like that he did all that. It's not fair to you."

"Ha! I said the same thing."

"I'm sure he really cared," she said with a groan.

"Like I said." I paused. "Drunk."

"Like I always say." She mimicked my dramatic pause. "Selfish prickface."

I laughed. "Since when do you always say that about Nick?"

"Since now. Since right fucking now."

She was pissed, and no one was safe when Rachel got truly angry. She would lash out at the cause of her fury until they apologized or righted their wrongs.

Nerves suddenly shot through me. "Don't talk to him, Rachel. Don't say anything. This isn't your battle, okay?" When she didn't respond, I said, "I'm asking you nicely. Please. This isn't on you."

The last thing I wanted was Rachel chasing Nick down and giving him a piece of her mind. It wasn't her place. Plus, if anyone was going to yell at Nick, it should be me.

A loud huff sounded in my ear. "Fine, *chica*. I will do my best."

We stayed on the phone a little longer, neither of us saying much, but her presence helped calm me down.

I looked at the clock. It was past five. "He's definitely not coming. What do I do?"

"You move on. Get over him. Instead of it being one hell

of a grand gesture, it was the asshole move of the century."

I nodded in agreement with my best friend's assessment. "I know it wasn't realistic. It's not like I could have left with him. But I'm so fucking disappointed, Rachel. Why am I so disappointed? Why am I like this when it comes to him?"

"Because you still love him. And you want him to fight for you. But instead of fighting, he's giving up. And that's twice now."

I sniffed and tried to swallow the bitter truth in her words. She was right. That was twice now. And I did want the fight . . . I wanted to be worth it. And Nick not showing up only proved to me once more how much I wasn't.

"Are you going to call him?" she asked, breaking through my thoughts.

"No."

"Really?"

"I can't. What if he says he doesn't remember calling me last night? Or that it was a mistake, that he was drunk and didn't mean anything that he said? I can't handle hearing that from him. I can't handle hearing him take it all back," I admitted as my emotions started to get the best of me.

"Then can I offer you a terrible suggestion?"

I laughed. "Yes. I expect nothing less."

"They always say that the best way to get over a guy is to get under a new one. Go sleep with some random hottie."

"You know I can't do that." I wasn't a one-night-stand kind of girl, and I didn't hook up with guys I wasn't at least interested in.

"I know you're not, but it was worth a shot. Promise me you'll try and meet someone else. Please. Go out. Drag Brooke to some frat parties. You need to try to get over Nick once and for all."

I sat there shaking my head, the very idea seeming impossible. "I'm not ready," I said honestly. "I will be. Hopefully soon. But right now I'm just not ready."

And I wasn't. No matter how hard I wanted Nick to be a part of my past so I could move on without thinking about him, I simply wasn't there yet. I still woke up thinking about him every morning. My heart still ached when I thought of him. Memories of us were still the last thing that played in my mind each night before I fell asleep.

She sighed into the phone. "I know, *chica*. You still need more time. I get that."

I was thankful for her understanding. Rachel made me feel less alone and a little less crazy.

"Thanks. I'm gonna go."

"Okay. And for the record? I'm sorry."

When we ended the call, I sat there with my phone in my hand, debating whether to shoot Nick a text.

In the end, I couldn't bring myself to do it. The fear of what he might say was far greater than my need to know where he was. It was obvious he wasn't coming up here. And the rational part of me knew that was for the best, even if my heart didn't agree.

My heart would eventually get on board with the rest of me. I was sure of it.

CONTINUALLY SCREWED

Nick

MY BROTHERS' BAR was closed for the night, but I had no intention of leaving. It was the only place where I found any sort of solace lately. Their bar had become my escape, my sole place of peace.

"Have you talked to Jess?" Ryan asked from behind the bar where he was washing and hand-drying glasses. I would have thought that he knew something about my call to her last night if he didn't ask me that question every time I saw him.

Because he did ask. Every fucking time. And the answer was always the same as the last time he'd asked.

No.

"I might have called her last night. I was drunk out of my mind," I said, and both my brothers stopped what they were doing to give me shocked looks.

"Classy," Frank said with an eye roll from across the room.

"It's the only time I have even half a ball to dial her number, okay?" I admitted, and it was the truth.

I had wanted to call Jess every second of every single day, no matter how busy I was at work, but I couldn't do that to her. Not if I couldn't offer her a relationship or tell her I wanted to get back together. Calling her would only hurt her, and up until last night, I'd been trying my best not to do that anymore. I knew I'd already hurt her enough. Hell, I'd hurt us both enough.

"I don't understand why you let her go in the first place. Explain that to me, little brother."

Strange that the question came from Frank; I would have expected it from Ryan. He was definitely the more romantic of two of them, whereas Frank was stuck in some relationship he couldn't seem to get out of. That aside, I'd already told both of them this a thousand times.

I groaned and lifted my beer for a sip. "You already know why."

"We just like to hear how stupid it sounds when it comes out of your mouth," Ryan said with a laugh.

"Yeah. And we're hoping one of these times it will sound stupid to you too. Idiot," Frank added.

I moved my stool back to stand up and face off with my brothers. "You're supposed to fucking help me. Not make me feel worse."

Ryan stepped in front of me, his eyes meeting mine. "Sit back down. You're right. We're just giving you shit."

"I can't take it right now, okay? Between Dad and the pressure to take over the company one day, and he keeps pushing me to date Carla so our families can merge and be this superpower entertainment giant—"

"Wait. What?" Frank and Ryan said at the same time. Ryan dropped a glass, its shattering on the tile floor deafening in the quiet bar, but neither of them paid it any mind.

"What are you talking about?" Frank asked, his green eyes narrowing as he leveled a hard look at me.

"Which part?" I took another sip of beer, wishing it were something stronger.

Frank and Ryan looked at each other before looking back at me. "All of it?" they both said. You'd almost think they were twins sometimes with the way their minds were so in sync.

When I just shrugged, Frank walked over and snatched my almost empty glass of beer away from me.

"Hey!" I shouted.

"You'll get it back after you start talking."

I looked to Ryan for support, but he crossed his arms and raised his eyebrows, clearly on Team Frank. I really hated them sometimes.

Sighing, I said, "What do you want to know?"

"Start with Dad and the company," Ryan said.

"How is this surprising you guys right now? You both know he's been grooming me to take over the company since I was thirteen."

Ryan leaned back against the counter. "Right," he said, dragging out the word. "But you don't want to. When are you going to stop doing what he wants you to and live your own life?"

I bristled. "That's not fair. You didn't have to deal with any of this shit. You didn't have this version of Dad, but I do. He didn't expect either of you to come back and run the company, but he pounded it into my head nearly every day."

Frank pulled up a stool next to mine and sat down. "But you hate it."

I shook my head. "I don't hate it; I'm actually really fucking good at it. I just don't want to do it forever. And I want to work here with you guys."

He placed a hand on my shoulder and squeezed. "And we want you here. But mostly, we want you to be happy."

"And we want you to live your life for *you*," Ryan added. "It's not right that Dad does that to you. We can talk to him, if you want."

"No. It'll only make things worse."

"How?" Frank asked.

Clearly, neither of them understood how drastically our father had changed since becoming successful.

"He has a temper. I guess that's a new thing, according to Mom, but I've always been privy to it."

Frank's jaw clenched, and Ryan cocked his head to one side hard enough that I heard his neck crack.

"He hit you?" Ryan asked.

"No, no. God. No. Nothing like that. He just gets really angry. He likes to threaten the things I care about. He's manipulative. The man doesn't like to lose, and I really fucking hate disappointing him."

Frank handed my beer back to me, his face pinched as if he were in pain. "I'm sorry you've had to go through all that alone. I had no idea things were that bad."

I downed the rest of my beer and pushed my glass away. "It's not your fault."

"It's not yours either," Ryan said. "Now, what about this whole dating-Carla thing?"

Frustrated, I closed my eyes for a minute. I'd hoped they'd forgotten that part. "Dad wants me to date Carla Crawford."

"Why? Why does he give a shit who you date?" Ryan asked as he drew himself a beer. "And who is Carla Crawford?"

"Her dad owns half the TV stations in Southern California. That's a lot of marketing Dad would get access to if I were dating her."

Frank and Ryan shared a confused look, then Frank shook his head. "It's like we don't even know the man you're talking about."

"I can't even imagine him being so cold, so heartless." Ryan scowled. "Caring about the business over the family?"

I didn't know what to say in response. Dad being cold was all I had ever known. Him controlling my life, telling me what to do in every aspect of it was part of the deal.

"I don't know what you want me to say."

Ryan raked his hands through his hair, as if the idea of reconciling the man he knew with the one I talked about was almost impossible. "Okay. I can't—I just can't deal with this right now. It's beyond fucking crazy to me. It's crazy. You do know that, right, Nick?"

My throat was tight as I tried to swallow. "It's all I've ever known, really. I'm used to it."

Frank slammed his hand down on the bar top. "No! You're not used to it. You don't get to be used to it, Nick. It's fucked up. This whole thing," he said, his eyes a little wild, "everything you're saying . . . it's so fucked up."

I threw up my hands in defeat. "Bro, I don't know what you want from me."

Ryan and Frank shared another quiet look that told me everything. They'd be discussing this later without me present. They didn't like the things I was telling them, and that both terrified and excited me. I'd never had anyone stand up for me before, and God only knew I needed all the help I could get. I'd never been able to stand up to Dad on my own. When I was a kid, I was too young, and by the time I got old enough, it seemed too hard to change. It was easier to just roll with it, especially with how intense and angry he got when he even thought I was challenging him.

Ryan downed his beer before he turned to pour three shots. "Enough of that. Let's get back to Jess. What did you say to her last? What happened?"

"Yeah, little brother. I want to hear this."

Frank took over the bar stool next to mine. Ryan passed each of us a shot, and we downed them without question.

"I might have told her I was coming up there to get her and bring her home." I couldn't look them in the eye when I said the words, too afraid of the judgment I'd see there.

Ryan burst out laughing. "Oh, that's rich. Are you kidding?"

Frank leaned toward me, forcing me to meet his gaze. "You told her you were coming up there to bring her home?"

"Yeah."

"Why would you say that exactly?" he asked as Ryan propped his elbows on the bar and rested his chin on his hand.

"Because her old roommate said she hated it. She told me that Jess was miserable up there. And I'm fucking miserable down here without her," I said, hoping my reasoning sounded as logical as it seemed to me.

Frank glanced around us at the empty bar, then met my gaze. "So if you're supposed to be up there bringing her home, why the hell are you here with us?" He frowned at me, apparently not too thrilled with me at the moment.

"She told me not to come, okay?"

"Wait." Ryan squinted at me. "Did she say those words

exactly . . . 'Nick, don't come up here?' Or what did she say? Gimme more info."

Frank groaned and leaned his head back in frustration. "Sometimes, Ryan, I swear to God. You're such a fucking chick."

Ryan gave him a shit-eating grin. "For your information, I'm romantic. The ladies love romance."

"Then why don't you have a lady in your life?" Frank fired back, and Ryan grabbed his heart, pretending to be wounded.

"Because I haven't found the right woman yet, okay?"

"Lord knows you try." Frank scoffed and exchanged a glance with me, hinting at Ryan's serial-dater ways.

"I'd rather try and find the right one than be stuck in a relationship I can't get out of," Ryan shot back before sucking in a breath. "Shit, dude, I'm sorry. Too far."

A muscle jumped in Frank's jaw. "It's fine."

He had moved his live-in girlfriend, Shelby, here to LA with him when he relocated from Arizona to open the bar, rather than breaking up with her like both Ryan and I told him to do. Apparently he'd felt obligated somehow, as if he owed it to her to bring her along for this transition. We both knew that Frank felt stuck, but he hated talking about it. He was too nice a guy to break Shelby's heart, so he stayed miserable instead. And he kept it all in.

"Let's get back to harassing Nick. It's much more fun," Ryan said with a laugh. "Tell me what happened on this call."

Grimacing, I pushed my shot glass in his direction. "I might need another shot."

Ryan turned his back to fill our shot glasses one last time. I downed mine quickly, letting the burn course through my throat all the way to my stomach before starting.

"I called her and told her I wanted to come get her and bring her home where she belongs."

"Did she like that caveman crap?" Frank said, interrupting.

"Obviously not, since I'm sitting here with you two idiots."

"For fuck's sake, Frank, stop interrupting. Go on," Ryan said, glaring between me and my oldest brother.

"She told me not to come. Said she couldn't leave, but she told me *not* to come get her." I winced a little, as reliving the sound of her voice and her words forced the pain to slice through me.

Ryan cleared his throat. "Little brother, of course she said that. What was she supposed to do, pack up her shit and move home with you? She's still in school."

"Yeah," Frank added. "What were you thinking?"

"I was thinking that she was miserable up there. I was thinking that she'd want to see me and that I could save her. I wanted to be the one to save her. To make her happy again instead of sad. I wasn't thinking she'd tell me no."

"She can't possibly tell you yes." Frank rolled his eyes, as if I was the world's biggest idiot for thinking otherwise.

"Well, she didn't have to say that she didn't want me to come up there at all. She told me to stay home. She begged me to stay here." Scowling at them, I willed them to see my side of things, but they didn't budge.

"You're being unrealistic. You can't be her knight in shining armor when she doesn't need rescuing," Ryan said with a smug smile.

"You think this is funny?" I leaned into his space, looking

for a fight. Anything that would let me get my aggression out.

"A little," he said, baiting me.

"Keep it in your pants," Frank growled. "Have you called her since your epic fail last night?"

"No."

"No?" he bellowed into the empty bar.

"Did I stutter?" I was getting real sick and tired of them picking apart my every move. Maybe confiding in my brothers wasn't the best idea.

"Oh my God, Nick. How did you get so stupid? Is this because we were gone by the time you started to grow up? You can't be related to me and be this bad at love." Ryan groaned as if my ineptness at romance was somehow a reflection on him.

"What? She told me *not* to come. She told me to *stay here*. I didn't think that warranted a phone call the next day just so she could say it to me again. I can't take it from her. I can't hear her tell me she doesn't want to see me."

"She still thought you'd come," Ryan said, shaking his head. But he was wrong. There was no way in hell Jess thought I'd show up.

"Not possible," I argued.

Ryan sighed, then spoke slowly as if I were the stupidest guy in the world. "She's a chick. They want the fairy tale. She might have told you not to come, but you planted one hell of a fucked-up seed in her head, and then you left it there to rot."

"You only think that because you don't know her," I said, waving him off. "She told me to stay here, and I listened. I listen to the things she says she wants from me. That's what you do when you love someone."

It wasn't entirely true. Jess had wanted to stay together and I told her no, but that had been different. She wasn't thinking clearly when she asked me that. I knew it would be disastrous, us trying to date long-distance, and I couldn't do that to her. Jess thought she wanted us to stay together, but I knew the best thing for her future was to be apart.

Ryan shook his head sadly, as if he was some expert on the subject, even though he hadn't had a serious girlfriend in the last five years. "No, you idiot. You read between the lines when you love someone. You learn when to listen to them and when to call them on their bullshit. And you learn the difference between when to fight and when to walk away."

"Says the serial dater," I shot back.

"I'm a serial dater because I know right away that the woman isn't right for me, and I don't string them along. That doesn't mean that I haven't learned to read women. Hell, I'm probably better at reading women than the two of you combined." He waved a finger between Frank and me.

Frank let out an annoyed huff. "I think you should call her. You owe her an apology. And as much as I hate to admit it, knucklehead over here is probably right. Even though she told you not to come, she was probably still hoping you would."

Ryan whipped out his cell phone and pressed a button. "Shit, Frank. Can you say that again? Nice and slow for the camera."

Frank shoved away from the bar stool and flipped off the camera as he headed into the back office.

"Great. You made him leave," I said, and Ryan turned the camera on me.

"Wave hi to the camera, Nick," Ryan said with a laugh, and I flipped him off before spinning around, turning my back to the camera.

"Neither of you are any fun," he grumbled. "I need to finish cleaning up the bar. We good here?"

I spun back around to face him. "Yeah, we're good."

Ryan headed back behind the bar as I flipped and turned the poker chip in my pocket, his words and my thoughts warring in my head.

Had Jess really wanted me to show up, even though she'd told me not to? Was Ryan right? I liked to think that I knew Jess's heart far better than my brother did. There was no way she hadn't meant what she said to me last night. The tone of her voice was way too serious, not playing around at all. And it wasn't like she had called me today either. She knew I wasn't coming, and she didn't want me to.

I should have never called. Jess probably never wanted to hear from me again, and I didn't blame her.

I'd never want to hear from me again either.

GETTING OVER HIM
Jess

I'D HALF EXPECTED time to slow to a crawl, for it to feel like it was barely moving at all after Nick's call that night. But it hadn't. If anything, time felt like it moved at warp speed, the days and weeks passing by in quick succession until they became months. I became more involved at the television station at school, picking up shifts when people were sick, and volunteered to work at all the fundraisers.

I loved how busy and productive my life had become, leaving me little time to think of Nick, even though he still lurked somewhere in the back of my mind. I wasn't sure if he'd ever not be a part of me, even if only a small part. I'd noticed that when I gave his memory an inch, it took a mile, but thankfully even that seemed to be fading.

I'd even agreed to go on a date with a guy from the TV station who I thought was cute, but when I found there was less than zero chemistry between us, I didn't encourage him further. Honestly, I was grateful that it was the lack of chemistry and not the abundance of Nick Fisher on the brain that had stopped me from seeing him again. At this rate, Nick would be a thing of the past in no time.

My courses were a breeze. I wasn't sure if it was because

the subjects came naturally to me or because I was so intrigued and invested in them, but I was thankful I wasn't on the dean's shit list at this school the way I had been down at State. One less thing to worry about was a good thing in my book.

Rachel came up twice to visit, and both times, she insisted we go to frat parties. When she complained the entire time about how much they sucked, I wanted to yell at her for being rude, but couldn't find the willpower. Comparing these parties to those Nick's fraternity used to throw was a joke. There was no comparison. It was sad, really. I mean, how hard was it to throw a good party for a bunch of underage, sex-crazed college students?

Apparently, Rachel and I were "frat party elitists," as Brooke had dubbed us tonight after we decided to call it quits well before midnight and left the party. She wasn't wrong. Nick's parties had ruined us for all others.

Rachel and I walked home, our arms wrapped around our midsections. Brooke had stayed at the party to spend time with Kenny, who was surprisingly in the very fraternity whose party we were attending. I never would have pegged him as the frat-boy type.

"It's freezing up here," Rachel complained as she sped up her pace.

"Preaching to the choir." I still wasn't used to the weather change myself, and doubted I would ever get used to it. I pulled out my keys and raced to the front door, thankful I lived so close to campus.

"I'm kinda hungry," Rachel said as soon as the door closed, and I laughed and pointed her in the direction of the kitchen.

"Make whatever you want."

She searched the cupboards and the fridge before settling on a bag of microwave popcorn. I'd already started getting ready for bed by the time Rachel joined me in the bathroom, the two of us sharing one sink as we washed our faces. Even when we lived together, we didn't have to share a bathroom, so this was a little more togetherness than we were used to.

The microwave beeped, and Rachel rushed out to grab the popcorn. "Meet you in your room."

Once I'd dried my face and put on moisturizer, I hopped on top of my bed and joined Rachel, who'd already claimed a spot and turned on the TV, then snagged a fistful of popcorn.

"You never really told me about your date," she mumbled through a mouthful of popcorn.

"Yes, I did," I argued, remembering the text messages I sent her immediately following.

"You just said there was no chemistry."

I narrowed my eyes at her. "What more did you need to know? There literally couldn't have been less chemistry than if I was on a date with an alien."

She shrugged, giving me a sidelong look. "So it had nothing to do with Nick?"

I choked out a laugh. Nick and I were clearly over. We had been for weeks, if not months. Somewhere between him never showing up that day or calling me to apologize, I'd accepted that fact and was finally ready to move on.

"That's what you've thought this whole time?"

"Can't blame me for wondering,'" she said with a shrug.

She was right. I couldn't blame her.

"It had nothing to do with Nick, I swear," I said, throwing

up a hand. "Scout's honor. Not that I was a scout, but still."

"So you're totally over him?"

Am I? "For the most part, yes," I answered honestly.

"What does that even mean, for the most part?"

I chewed on my bottom lip as I wondered how to put the thoughts buried deep inside me into words. "I know that Nick and I are over. For now," I added.

"For now?" That line apparently piqued her curiosity. She stopped chewing and stared right through me.

"As long as I'm up here, there's no hope for us. I'm fine with that. I've accepted it. But I'd be lying to you, and myself, if I didn't admit that I thought there was still hope for us one day in the future."

"So you think you guys will get back together when you move back?"

"I have no idea," I said, not sure if she thought my train of thought was crazy, or if she was on board with it. "I'm just saying that I realize we can't be together now. That the timing is wrong and we don't work, I guess. But that doesn't mean the timing will always be wrong, does it?"

"I guess not." She agreed way too easily and fidgeted a moment, not meeting my eyes. "So, I'd been putting off telling you this because I wasn't sure how you'd take it. But you seem so much better."

I sat up straight, tucking my legs underneath me, and turned to face her. "What is it?" I sensed instantly that it had to do with Nick. Much to my surprise, my stomach didn't dip or knot up like I expected it to.

She waved a hand in the air. "It could totally be nothing."

I squeezed my eyes closed for a moment. "Spit it out.

Whatever it is, I'm sure it won't faze me," I lied, hoping I was convincing.

She narrowed her dark eyes at me. "I wish that were true."

I wondered for a moment what she could possibly be wary of confessing to me after everything I'd just said to her. Then a sudden dark thought ripped through my mind.

"Wait. Nick's okay, right? Like, there's nothing physically wrong with him. He isn't dying or anything?"

Rachel hunched over with laughter. "Seriously? That's where your white-girl mind goes? You think I'd be scared to tell you Nick was dying?"

I cocked my head, studying her. "You wouldn't be? How sick and twisted are you?"

Shrugging, she grabbed another handful of popcorn. "Pretty sick and twisted."

"If he's not dying, then what could it possibly be?" I asked, my curiosity piqued.

"I heard that he's dating Carla Crawford," she said quickly, her tone quieter than it had been a moment earlier.

Carla Crawford. The girl who told me she'd end up with Nick. The girl Nick swore to me he wasn't interested in, and never would be.

My stomach, which moments before had been just fine, flipped and began a slow churn. Rachel had been right. I guessed there were some things I wasn't ready to handle or hear when it came to Nick.

"Are you sure?" I squeaked out, feeling like I'd been stabbed in the back by the only guy I'd ever really loved.

"Like I said, I could be wrong." She gave me a small smile, but it faded. "But I know I'm not."

My head nodded on its own, without my willing it to. "This doesn't make sense."

"I know, right? I thought he hated her."

Her words snapped me out of my momentary trance, and my stomach stopped its gyrations.

"He does hate her! I mean, I don't know if he *hates* her, but I know he doesn't like her. Not like that, anyway." Another thought hit me, and I muttered, "This has his dad written all over it."

"I actually thought the same thing. But you know what, Jess?" Rachel waited for me to meet her gaze before she continued. "It's pretty pathetic that he does whatever his dad tells him to. Why doesn't he just tell him to fuck off? Is he going to follow his dad's orders for the rest of his life?"

I shrugged. "It's not that easy for him. I'm sure he's just trying to get his dad off his back. But, God, why her, of all people? Why won't she just go away already?"

"I know. It's like he's dating your nemesis."

My nemesis. I groaned. "He has to be doing it for his dad. He has to be," I said firmly, not sure who I was trying to convince at this point.

"I hope you're right. Because I'd really hate to see her win," Rachel added.

My thoughts churning furiously, I glared at the wall. If my eyes had any sort of superpower, they would have burned a hole straight through it.

"Hey." Her hand grazed my shoulder. "You okay?"

I nodded. "Yeah, I'm fine. There's no way this is real. There's no way he's not doing this for his dad."

Rachel agreed with me; I could tell by the look in her eyes.

Even if she hadn't, she didn't know Nick and his relationship with his father the way I did. I knew how hard it was for him to stand up to his dad. Even though I hated even thinking about Nick with Carla, I knew there had to be a reason for it.

Nick wouldn't date her on his own. I was convinced of that.

"You sure you're all right?" Rachel asked, drawing my attention back to her.

"I'm sure. It's not like he loves her. I'd bet money on that."

"I would too," she said with a confident nod. "I didn't just set you back, did I?"

"No, I'm fine. Promise."

"Are you sure you didn't get under someone else?" Rachel asked with a grin.

I rolled my eyes. "I'm sure. I did it the good old-fashioned way. I used Father Time. He's super helpful."

She scooped up some popcorn that I'd all but forgotten about, and popped it into her mouth.

I stared absentmindedly at the TV show playing, my mind lost in thoughts of Nick with Carla, my heart aching for him and the position he must be in. I wanted to hug him and punch him at the same time. It felt like now would have been the perfect time to stand up to his dad once and for all and tell him no, but I wondered if Nick would ever be able to do that. He probably wouldn't, but I acknowledged to myself that that was Nick's battle to fight and not mine.

"I'm sorry for telling you, but I had to, you know?" Rachel said, her eyes pleading for my forgiveness.

"Don't apologize. I want to know stuff like that. Thank

you."

"I feel bad because you've made so much progress."

"I would have hated finding this out somewhere down the road, and then learning that you knew the whole time and didn't tell me."

"I didn't even think of it like that," she said, scrunching up her face. "So we're good?"

I reared back a little in surprise. "Of course we're good."

We watched a few more shows before calling it a night. If I was being honest with myself, I was slightly concerned what that night's sleep might have in store for me, but I woke up in the morning relieved to have had a dreamless night. Rachel was already packing her things when I opened my eyes.

"It takes forever to get back, especially on Sundays."

"I know," I said through a stretch as I worked my way out of bed. "Thank you for coming. It's always better when you're here."

"I miss you too." She smiled and hauled her bag over her shoulder before disappearing through my door. "Call you when I get home. Go back to sleep."

Falling back into my bed, I did as she asked, still somewhat surprised by how calm I was about this. Of course I didn't like the idea of Nick with Carla, of all people, but I couldn't bring myself to give it any real weight. Even after our time apart, I still felt confident that I knew Nick's heart better than most people did.

It was the only way I could process this crazy information without going crazy myself.

*

TIME CONTINUED TO fly by. I was acing my classes and still picking up extra hours at the station. I'd even gotten an internship at a local news channel. I had been up against a lot of other applicants, but somehow I had gotten the job.

Things felt like they were falling into place easily, and I wondered if that's how things happened when they were meant to be. It made me question everything else that had been such a colossal struggle in my life. Maybe when you were on the right path, things simply worked out without the fight.

My phone vibrated where it lay on my mattress, and I reached for it before casting a casual glance at the screen.

Nick. Holy shit. How long has it been since we last talked?

Chills raced down my spine. Nick didn't call for no reason. Hell, Nick didn't call anymore at all. It had been three months since our last conversation. Three months since he told me to start packing. Three months since I'd heard his voice. Almost seven months since I'd seen his face.

Seven months without Nick . . .

If you would have asked me a year ago, I would have insisted that I'd never last that long without him. Funny the things your heart is capable of handling without your knowledge. We are so much stronger than we realize.

"Hey." I tried to sound nonchalant as I answered, pretending that hearing from him wasn't sending me into an emotional tailspin. I thought about him and Carla, and suddenly wanted to throw up. That was a first.

"Jess," he said, his voice thick, deep, and instantly recognizable.

"Nick. How are you?"

"Good, I'm good. How are you?" The fact that he sounded

calm—too calm, too relaxed—rattled my every last nerve.

"Good. Just doing some required reading." I closed my textbook and set it aside.

He paused, sucking in a breath before he spoke. "I need to tell you something."

"What is it?" I pushed myself up until I was sitting straight up, preparing myself, but for what?

"Well, first off, I'm dating someone," he said, his voice barely above a whisper, and I knew there was more to this phone call than that tidbit of information I already knew.

"So? Why would you call me to tell me you're dating someone? Good for you, Nick. I'm dating someone too," I lied. "So what?" Anger swirled in my gut, mixing with regret, fear, and sadness. In that order.

"We're getting married."

What?

If I had ever thought that my world had crashed around me before, I had been wrong. Dead wrong. Because in that moment, the sun dropped from the sky and fell into the sea, leaving the world shrouded in the darkest shade of black.

"You're getting married? Are you kidding?" I prayed quickly to God that this was all a joke. I even looked at the calendar on my wall to make sure it wasn't April first. This couldn't be real.

"I wanted to be the one to tell you. It would kill me if you heard from someone else," he said, as if that somehow made this all okay.

"How noble of you. So, who is it? Who the hell are you marrying, Nick?" I tried to sound like I didn't care, but the shakiness in my voice gave me away. Not to mention the anger.

He stayed quiet for a heartbeat. Then two. I wasn't sure he'd ever speak when he sucked in a breath and said, "Carla," his words like knives.

Thud.

"Carla?"

Tears fell without warning, blurring my vision until my surroundings turned into a watercolor painting where things mixed together with no distinction, everything all blurred. I wanted to scream into the phone, *What are you doing?* but I refrained, although that sentence repeated itself over and over again inside my mind.

He was planning on marrying Carla.

Nick planned to marry someone who wasn't me.

I never realized until that moment how much hope I'd still held out for us. Apparently I'd buried the sliver of hope somewhere deep inside me, but here it was, making itself known, feeling less like a sliver and more like a redwood tree.

He cleared his throat, and I realized I'd been sitting silently on the line with no clue how long it had been.

"Is it your dad? Is he making you do this?" I had to know, because none of this made any kind of sense.

"No. It has nothing to do with him. I got to know her and we have a lot in common," he said, his tone unconvincing.

"You're joking, right? You have nothing in common with that horrible person."

"Jess," he growled, telling me I'd crossed a line. "It just seems right, you know?"

I shook my head. No, I didn't know. I didn't know anything anymore. "Bullshit. That's total bullshit. You can lie to everyone else, but you don't get to lie to me. This has your dad written all over it. How is he possibly getting you to do this, of all things, for him?"

His silence told me everything I needed to know, so I continued. "Remember when we talked that one day about the things he asked of you?" I waited for his confirmation, but he still stayed quiet. "I told you that one day he'd ask you to do something that would be a turning point. That if you did it, there would be no going back. This is it, Nick. This is *so* it."

He sighed, sounding utterly exasperated. "You don't understand, Jess."

"Then enlighten me!" I yelled, my emotions overwhelming me.

"I can't," he said, sounding so broken, and I got pissed.

"Of course you can't. Have a nice life, Nick. You're a fucking idiot."

I ended the call, expecting to cry hysterically, but the tears had stopped falling. I was too angry, too disappointed, too pissed off to cry.

There would be no coming back from this for us. There would never be an *us* again if he went through with this.

It was supposed to be me—it was *always* supposed to be me. Nick and I were supposed to be together.

I never planned to stay away forever. Once I graduated, I intended to move back home to Southern California. I'd stupidly assumed Nick and I would pick up where we left off, like I'd told Rachel that night. No matter what he said or how much time had passed, I always figured we'd find our way back to each other. I never once thought that I'd lose Nick forever.

How could he give up on us like this? It was like I truly didn't know him at all.

And maybe I really never did.

BREAKING HEARTS

Nick

I COULD HAVE never imagined how badly it would hurt telling Jess about Carla. And it did. It hurt something awful. Hearing the pain in her voice when I spilled my news slayed me. My heart bled out in my chest in response to her tone.

Jess was pissed, but mostly she was devastated. I heard every ounce of pain that she tried to hide behind her anger. I honestly figured that I was doing the right thing by being the one who told her about the wedding, but fuck, maybe I should have let Rachel tell her? Maybe I shouldn't have told her at all, kept her in the dark.

No. See? That's even more fucked up.

Jess deserved to know what I had done, and she deserved to hear it from me. But now I felt like a complete asshole, even more than I already did. If there was a way to feel lower than the dirt on the bottom of someone's shoe, I achieved it. I was currently living it.

I still loved Jess. Goddamn, I still loved her more than anything, but I couldn't tell her that.

She called it right away too. Jess knew my dad was responsible for this entire fiasco, but I couldn't admit that to her without giving her the rest of the details. If I gave that girl a morsel of information, she'd hammer at me until I gave it all up. And if she knew the whole story, she'd come unglued, take the first flight back here, and try to talk me out of it.

I knew at least that much, and I couldn't let her do that. I'd protect Jess's future the only way I knew how—by marrying Carla.

Jesus. Just putting the words *Carla* and *marry* in the same sentence made me want to throw up.

Honestly, I never thought I'd marry anyone other than Jess. Even through all the crap of my letting her go and move away from me, I had always planned to win her back. As soon as she had that damn diploma in her hands, I intended to make her mine again.

I couldn't have cared less if she was dating some guy or what other obstacle stood in my way when it came to getting her back in my arms. I never planned on stopping until she gave in. I'd apologize, tell her how much of an idiot I was, and fight for however long it took to win back her trust and her heart. We belonged together, and we both knew it. Living my entire life without Jess wasn't a thought I had ever entertained.

Until now.

Now I had to accept the fact that I'd be living my whole life without her, because there'd be no winning her back after this. Even Jess had a limit, and this engagement had pushed her too far over it. Eventually she would learn the truth, that I'd done all this for her. And maybe one day, she'd actually forgive me for it, or at least understand. If there was a god, I hoped like hell he'd help her.

Hopping into my truck, I headed toward Santa Monica. My brothers and their bar still served as my only place of refuge, and I wasn't sure that would ever change. Especially now.

When I walked inside, I was thankful to see only a handful of customers. It shouldn't have surprised me, considering that it was the middle of the day and Sam's didn't usually start hopping until sundown.

"Little brother," Frank called out, greeting me as soon as I stepped inside and removed my sunglasses.

As I made my way to the bar, I briefly considered heading into the private office. Instead, I sat down on an empty bar stool at the opposite end of the bar, as far from the other patrons as possible.

"You look like shit, sweetheart," Ryan's voice boomed as he rounded a corner and came into view.

"Appreciate it," I mumbled, knowing I probably looked as devastated as I felt.

"Aw, baby brother. Why so glum?" he teased, his bottom lip jutting out in a pout as he crossed his arms over his chest.

"Just in a shit mood is all."

"You're always in a shit mood," Ryan said, and I wished like hell it wasn't the truth, but it was. He turned his back to me and started mixing a drink while I watched, eyeing the ingredients carefully.

"What's that?" I asked, pretty familiar with all the drinks they served, but I hadn't seen this one before.

"Something new I whipped up last night. Frank thinks it tastes like piss, but the ladies who tried it last night loved it." He grinned.

"They were so drunk, they would have told you that anything tasted good enough to be on the menu," Frank grumbled.

I laughed for the first time that day, watching as he walked down to the other end of the bar to check on his customers.

Ryan shoved the rose-colored concoction toward me, and I sniffed it before bringing it to my lips and taking a slow sip. Pulling back, I shoved the glass back toward my brother.

"Girls said they liked this?"

"Be helpful or get out," Ryan said as he pointed toward the door, clearly butt-hurt.

He was good at creating new cocktails, but his ego was easily bruised at first when it came to the feedback. He was typically defensive before he set about correcting things, making it better than any of us could have ever thought.

"First of all, it has too much lime. And whatever the juice is? God, it's hard to swallow, like an unbalanced sweet and bitter. Needs more rum or less juice, something so it goes down easier. What is the juice? It's so light, I can't place it."

"Watermelon." Ryan grimaced before taking a sip, and I grinned. "Hell. You're right." He dumped it down the sink and set about remaking it.

As he worked, I tilted my head back, concentrating on the flavors that lingered. "Was that a hint of cinnamon I tasted?"

"Yeah."

"That was brilliant. It only hit after," I said with a smile. My brother was seriously a cocktail genius.

"Yeah, that's the plan. I think I'll use it as a garnish, maybe toss a cinnamon stick on top at the end." He grinned as he measured and mixed ingredients, and my brain reeled as I tried to come up with a name for it.

Frank joined us, and automatically hand-washed and dried

the glass that Ryan had just tossed into the sink before looking at me. "So, are you going to tell us what's got you so wound up?"

I stared between my brothers, who were both giving me the side eye while I decided how much to admit to them. As if Ryan knew the only way to get me to open up was to ply me with alcohol, he set two shots of tequila in front of me, then one each in front of himself and Frank.

"Why do I get two?" I asked, already knowing damn well the answer to that question.

"Because you clearly need it," Frank said, then tipped his in a toast to me before knocking it back.

"And we know how much you run your mouth after you've had some liquid courage, brother," Ryan said with a laugh. "So drink up." He nudged mine closer to me and waited for me to shoot them.

The first went down with a wince, burning my throat before coating my insides with warmth that made me feel like a rookie. I took a few steadying breaths before downing the second without another thought.

When I slammed the empty on the bar and announced, "I'm getting married," they both started choking. Simultaneously, as if their lungs were connected.

"Married?" Frank asked, his voice shooting an octave higher.

"To who?" Ryan leaned forward, his brows pinched together.

"Carla." God, her name was as bitter on my tongue as Ryan's watermelon drink.

I stared past my brothers, fixing my gaze on the liquor

bottles that lined the wall. I was afraid to see the level of disappointment in their eyes.

"Carla? The chick whose dad owns the TV stations?" Ryan said, putting it all together quicker than I'd expected. I'd only barely told them I was dating her.

"The one you started dating just to get Dad off your back?" Frank added.

I nodded, tapping the empty shot glass against the top of the bar. Ryan returned with the bottle and filled all three of our empty glasses.

"You can't do this," Frank said as he tipped back another shot.

"Yeah, this is crazy. Why the hell would you marry this girl?" Ryan frowned and ran a hand through his hair, making it stick out in every direction.

I downed another shot before reaching for the bottle and doling out the shots myself, filling them to brim until some of the liquid spilled over.

"I don't have a choice," I confessed, realizing that I needed someone in my life to know the truth. The whole truth.

"What does that even mean?" Frank bit out. "How do you not have a choice?"

"I thought you loved Jess?" Ryan said.

I bristled. "I do love Jess."

Ryan scowled at me. "You have a funny way of showing it."

Agitated, I threw my hands out wide. "Why the fuck do I keep coming here when all you two do is give me shit instead of help me?"

Ryan laughed. He fucking laughed. "You come here because you know what you're telling us is completely crazy, and we're the only ones who will call you out on it."

"I don't need to be called out on it."

"Then what do you need, brother, a swift kick in the ass? Because this is insane. It's fucking nuts," Frank practically growled. "Look, I saw you with Jess. I'd never seen you so happy or proud to be with a girl before."

I narrowed my eyes. "You'd never seen me with a girl, period."

"True, but I've seen plenty of pictures. You didn't look half as happy in any of those as you did the night you brought Jess in here. Plus, you don't see your face when you talk about that girl."

"This isn't about my feelings for Jess, okay?"

"Then what the hell is it about?" Ryan asked.

Before I could answer, Frank quickly added, "Because things aren't adding up."

I gripped the edge of the bar, feeling the effects of the tequila swimming in my head. "He threatened her. He threatened Jess."

Ryan and Frank both froze and exchanged a glance.

"*Who* threatened Jess?" Frank balled his hand into a fist that made the tattoos on his forearm dance.

"Carla's father, Mr. Crawford. He threatened her future in the entertainment industry. Said he'd make sure she never got a job or worked anywhere in this town if I didn't do what he wanted." My shoulders unknotted a fraction, relaxing as I confessed this to my brothers.

Ryan gave me a confused look. "And what he wanted was for you to marry his daughter?"

"Yeah."

I knew it didn't make any sense, wasn't at all logical. I had no idea how I'd gotten in the middle of it, but I'd panicked, straight up nearly lost my shit when Mr. Crawford not only said he knew about Jess, but then threatened her future. I would have agreed to almost anything he asked if it meant he wouldn't hurt my girl.

"But why that? Why the hell would Mr. Crawford want you to marry his daughter that badly? What's in it for him?"

I shrugged. Their guess was as good as mine. "I can only assume it's because that's what Carla wants. She's been after me since State. She's always told me that we'd end up together one way or another."

"And let me guess." Ryan rolled his eyes. "Whatever Daddy's little angel wants, Daddy's little angel gets?"

"She is his only child," Frank muttered, and held up his phone. "Just doing some quick recon. She's an only child. Her mom was killed in a car accident when she was eight. Apparently Carla was in the car. She's very popular on social media. Traveled all over the world, and lives the life of a socialite. It looks like she wants for nothing, and in an interview back a couple of years ago, her dad mentioned that she was his only weakness. *'If Carla isn't happy, I'm not happy. I will always do anything in my power to keep a smile on her face, no matter what it takes, no matter the cost.'*"

"She's a grade-A pain in the ass is what she is," I said with a snarl. "She's the most spoiled rotten, vapid person I've ever known."

"Then you can't do this, Nick. My God, you can't tie yourself to that," Ryan said, shaking his head.

"I told you. I don't have a choice." I pulled at my hair,

feeling no better.

"Does Dad know?" Frank asked.

"He knows. He's the one who keeps pushing me to go through with it."

Frank's fist met the top of the bar, and I almost jumped out of my seat. I'd rarely seen him this angry.

"None of this makes any sense, Nick. None of it."

Ryan nodded his head in agreement. "Yeah. This is insane. This is like a damn movie you watch, not something that happens in real life."

Looking away from both of their glares, I stared at the lights of the bar, letting my focus go in and out. "Look, I don't have any of the answers. And I don't know why Dad is so hell bent on making this union happen either, except that he really wants that partnership. He always has."

"So this is all about money?" Frank's mouth twisted in disgust.

"Dad has enough money." Ryan's expression still looked more confused than anything else.

I groaned, wishing I knew exactly what the hell it really was about for our old man so I could fill them in. "Maybe it's about power? Control? I don't know, you guys. Greed is an ugly thing. And success changes people."

Frank glanced at Ryan, his disgust only deepening. "It hasn't changed us."

"It's changed me a little," Ryan offered with a shrug before signaling to us that he'd be right back. The bar had all but cleared out by this point, except for the two stragglers who'd finished off their beer and were ready to pay their tab.

Frank and I waited in silence for Ryan to return before we

started talking again. Blinding sunlight filtered through the open door for a second as the customers left.

"What do you mean, it's changed you a little?" Frank asked the moment Ryan was within speaking distance.

"I just meant that I like the success we've had with the bar. And I want more of it. Not at any cost, and I don't want to hurt anyone, but it's definitely made me more motivated."

Frank nodded in quiet agreement. "I totally get that. I want more too. I'm really proud of what we've built."

I looked between them, my heart aching, wishing so badly that I was a part of their team, at the bar every day. But I refused to let my ego take anything away from them. They had built the most popular bar in Santa Monica from nothing, and were constantly featured in online reviews.

"I'm really proud of you guys too."

"We couldn't have done it without you," Frank said with a small smile, and I shrugged off his praise. "I mean it. The drink names, the marketing . . . you're a big part of our success, Nick."

"He's right," Ryan added. "Neither of us could have done half the marketing you did. You're responsible for the success of our launch, and keeping us relevant in those early days when we weren't."

"Thanks," I said in almost a whisper.

His jaw still clenched, Frank said, "Back to the matter at hand, Nick, this is too far. Dating is one thing—"

"Still stupid."

"Dating is one thing," Frank continued, glaring at Ryan for interrupting, "but getting married is a whole different ball game. It's crossing a line you can't come back from."

"Jess said the same thing," I admitted.

"She knows?" Ryan perked up at the mention of her name.

"I called and told her before I drove over here."

Ryan clapped me on the shoulder. "They're both right, Nick. If you do this, when will it stop?"

"I don't know," I said with a slight shrug, feeling about a foot tall.

"Never. It will never stop. They'll both own you, Mr. Crawford and Dad. Nothing in your life will be yours, Nick. Nothing."

Frank spoke the words with such certainty and fury that I couldn't help but wonder if he was projecting his own shit onto me. I knew he felt out of control when it came to his own life and decisions, making them for his girlfriend's well-being instead of his own, but I let it slide. I was too caught up in everything I was currently losing, too overwhelmed with the state of my life and wondering when the hell I'd become such a fucking victim.

"I'm calling Dad," Frank said before anyone could argue, and pulled out his cell phone.

My jaw dropped open slightly before I closed it, clenching my teeth as I waited for the hell this would bring.

"Hey, Dad," Frank said, then pressed the speaker button.

The sound of our father's voice filled the empty bar. "Hello, Frank. How's the bar?"

I was shocked at how chipper Dad sounded. He never talked to me like that. When he spoke with me, his tone was always disappointed or demanding.

"The bar's great. You'd know that if you ever came down here and saw it for yourself." Frank tried to hide his own disappointment, but failed. I hadn't realized that he was upset at our dad for that.

"You know how busy I am. I can't take time off to come hang out at some bar, Frank. Jesus, I'd think as a successful business owner, you'd understand that," my dad fired back.

I had to bite back a grin. There was the asshole I knew and hated to let down.

"Nick told us what's going on. You're basically pushing him to marry some girl?"

Dad growled, "Butt out, Frank. You don't know anything."

"So, tell me then. Why would you possibly do this to him?"

Frank wasn't intimidated by our dad the way I was. He didn't care if he pushed him too far, cornered him, or asked the hard questions. I never seemed to be able to do any of that shit.

"I'm doing what's best for him. Nick wouldn't know the right thing to do if it hit him in the face."

Both Ryan and Frank's eyes met mine in that instant, and I swallowed hard around the lump in my throat. Maybe now they'd understand how little our dad thought of me, how he treated me, and why I was a complete pussy when it came to defending myself.

A disgusted laugh escaped from deep within Frank's throat. "You clearly don't know your son at all. He's one of the smartest and most talented people I've ever met. I'm pretty sure he could make a decision or two on his own, especially when it comes to who he should or shouldn't marry."

"Frank," Dad said, his voice firm, "I'm warning you. Butt

out of this and mind your own damn business."

"Warning me? What are you gonna do, make me marry Carla's sister?" Frank said, and Ryan laughed before quickly covering his mouth with his hand.

"She doesn't have a sister, smartass. Stay out of this and leave Nick alone. He's marrying that girl, and that's final. I don't have to explain myself or my reasons to you or your brother."

"So that's it then? No discussion, no conversation like two rational adults." Frank pushed a little harder, willing my dad to break, but I knew it was no use. My dad refused to crack.

"We aren't two adults, Frank. You are my child and I am your father. Now, get back to running your bar before Ryan burns it down being an idiot."

When the call disconnected with a click, Ryan stood there with a shocked look on his face.

"He thinks I'm an idiot?" he asked, looking genuinely hurt.

Frank put his phone back in his pocket and stared at me. "I'm really sorry you had to grow up with that man. That isn't the father we grew up with. I don't know who that is."

I shrugged, unable to find the words because we'd been through all this before. "I know it sucked, but I'm thankful you got to see that side of him. It's the only side I've ever known."

"An idiot?" Ryan was still fixated on the name our dad had called him before snapping out of it. "Who was that man?"

"Apparently that's Nick's dad," Frank bit out.

I had to laugh. They didn't want to claim the asshole any more than I did.

"Do you guys understand now that I don't have a choice?" I asked, hoping for at least their understanding if the situation couldn't be fixed.

"There has to be something we can do," Frank said, refusing to be defeated. "Marrying the wrong person isn't something I'd wish on my worst enemy."

"I don't know how to fix this. I just don't see any other way."

I laid my arm on the bar and dropped my head onto it, praying for one of my brothers to disagree with me, to say anything. When I was only met with silence, I accepted my future and my fate.

DAY FROM HELL

Jess

ALL THE PROGRESS I'd made with being over Nick came crashing to a halt when he called and told me about him and Carla. Since then I'd been sick over the news, even going so far as to look up his dad's office number. More times than I could count, I pressed every digit of it but the last one on my phone, then chickened out every time. I was devastated and wanted answers, and needed more than anything to ask him why he was doing this. Nick marrying this awful person didn't just affect Nick, it affected me too, and I wanted his father to know that.

When Rachel e-mailed me the online announcement about their engagement, with the wedding planned for only three months away, all the oxygen left my lungs in a single whoosh.

Three months. I had no idea why everything was so damned urgent, but I'd given up trying to make sense of it. The only silver lining was Rachel informing me that she'd be spending the "wedding weekend from Hades" with me so I wouldn't have to go through it alone. I had no choice in the matter, and to be honest, I was grateful. There was no way I'd be able to get through that day on my own.

To my surprise, my sadness eventually dissipated as time passed, and anger took its place. I no longer blamed Nick's dad for everything—I blamed Nick. He had the power to end this madness, to walk away from it, to stand up for himself once and for all. But he didn't. He never did. And I refused to blame anyone else for what boiled down to being Nick's actions, or inactions really.

I finally realized one day as I was eating with Brooke in the commissary on campus that this was Nick's life, and mine was no longer tied to it. He'd willingly cut the cord that bound us together, freeing me. His choices and decisions had no longer had anything to do with me, and I needed to stop acting like they did.

"Maybe I will get under someone else," I blurted during our lunch, and Brooke stopped eating her salad to stare at me.

"Huh?"

I laughed. "Just hearing Rachel in my head is all. Sorry. She told me to get over Nick by sleeping with someone else."

Brooke contemplated what I'd just said, squinting up at the ceiling for a moment before she looked back at me. "I guess that could work. But probably not, since you'd just be covering up your pain instead of truly letting it heal."

I laughed again, truly amused that Brooke had taken my statement and dissected it like a scientist. "You're probably right. Plus, it's really not my style. I'm just so pissed all the time. I'm pissed at Nick. Pissed at myself."

"Why are you pissed at yourself?" She placed her fork down and really focused on me.

"For not being able to deal with this better. I'm so disappointed in him, and I shouldn't care. At this point, after all we've been through, I shouldn't care what he does with his stupid life."

Brooke grabbed her drink and took a sip. "It's because of everything you two have been through that you do care."

"How are you so smart?" I asked as her words resonated deep within me.

"Because I'm logical," she answered with a straight face.

I chuckled at her response, then had a sudden thought. "If you were in my shoes, what would you do?"

Brooke straightened in her chair, her gaze roaming from the ceiling to something far off in the distance before landing on mine. "I don't know. I've never been in your situation before. But I think I'd cry. Probably a lot."

"Brooke!" I all but shouted before cracking up.

"What? Whenever you tell me about him, I get mad because I think he's stupid, but my heart also always hurts for you."

It was honest. Too honest.

"I've cried enough over Nick Fisher. I'm done with that," I said firmly, then sucked in a quick breath. "Except for on the wedding day. I might cry one last time then." I winced with my admission.

Brook sighed with a small shrug. "I would too," she said before picking up her fork and attacking her salad again.

*

TIME CONTINUED TO speed past like we were in some kind of unspoken race.

My anger at Nick had taken hold, and anytime I felt myself slipping and starting to feel bad for him, I simply reminded myself that he had the power to change his situation. That simple notion set my anger raging every single time. I also found myself reminding my heart that his decisions didn't affect me anymore. This had nothing to do with me, it wasn't about me, and it never would be again.

The majority of the time, I was fine with it. I honestly felt that I had moved on, settled into a place where I was okay with where our paths had taken us. But as the wedding date neared, my strength and resolve slipped further and further away.

Rachel had arrived late Friday night before Nick's wedding, full of ideas for ways to keep my mind off of him. We both knew it was a losing battle.

"Brooke, come in here," Rachel shouted from where we were sitting on my bedroom floor.

Brooke came to the doorway and eyed Rachel. "Hi."

"Are you coming out with us tomorrow?" Rachel asked.

Surprised, I cocked my head to look at her. I had assumed Brooke would be with us, but had never officially asked.

Brooke grinned. "I'm yours all weekend."

"No Kenny?" I asked, and she shook her head.

"I told him that I was having a girls' weekend. I've never had one of those before."

Her smile broadened, and it was infectious. Before I knew it, I was smiling too.

"Perfect!" Rachel said. "Let's go to the store and have a girls' night in tonight. We'll get ice cream and watch a movie, because tomorrow night, we're going out and getting fucked up."

I looked at Rachel warily before agreeing. "I'd like to drink tomorrow right off of the calendar."

"What?" Rachel said with a laugh.

"If I get so drunk that I don't remember anything, then the day will go *poof.* It'll be like it never happened." I clasped my hands together like it was the most brilliant idea ever.

Brooke's smile fell. "I think we should get stuff at the store for hangovers. Not that I know what we need, but we should be prepared."

"Great idea. You're so smart with all your thinking ahead." Rachel pointed at Brooke. "Who's driving?"

The trip to the store was ridiculously eventful, despite the fact that it was late at night and the workers were in the aisles stocking the shelves. Rachel flirted unabashedly with every single one of the guys, no doubt just trying to make their night. Brooke darted away from her quickly, her cheeks flaming.

When I looked at Rachel and shook my head, she laughed. "What? I'm having fun. I'll never see these guys again."

With our arms filled with ice cream, brownie mix, graham crackers, soup, orange juice, coffee, eggs, and bacon, enough provisions for our girls' night in and for our "hangover breakfast" in the morning, we headed toward checkout.

"You sure you have ibuprofen at home?" Brooke asked one last time, scanning the shelves before grabbing a pack of gum and tossing it onto our pile.

"I have literally every kind of pain reliever they make," I said confidently. "My mom sent me away with a crazy care package. It had everything in it from aspirin to Tums to Cliff bars and Gatorade. They're all still in there."

"Your mom's so dope," Rachel said. "She totally packed

you a hangover-cure box, and you didn't even know it."

I smiled, suddenly missing my mom a little. "And I haven't ever needed it."

"This is going to be fun," Brooke said with a giggle that sent us into a fit of laughter.

And it was. We spent the night baking brownies and eating ice cream until our stomachs hurt and I was forced to break into my care package to grab the Tums and Pepto-Bismol. None of us brought up Nick, and my mind wasn't even fully focused on him. Girlfriends were the cure for everything, I decided.

*

WHEN I WOKE up the next morning, dread consumed me. Nick was getting married today—to someone who wasn't me. And to make matters worse, he was marrying a person I couldn't stand. My stomach felt like it was carrying a lead balloon inside it, and my feet felt like they were encased in concrete.

"I will not fall apart. I will not apart," I chanted softly to myself. I had decided last night before falling asleep that it would be my mantra today. I'd fake it till I made it, or however the saying went.

Or at least I'd try.

But how was I supposed to be okay with this when I wasn't? My mind rewound to when Nick and I were just starting out, our relationship a thing of envy for all the girls at school who weren't me, Carla included. Everyone who assumed I was just another one-month date fest for Nick realized quickly how wrong they were, and all the girls who used to wait on the sidelines for their chance with him, stopped waiting. What we had wasn't perfect, by any means, but it was ours.

How had we fallen so far from where we once were?

How the hell had this happened to us?

I will not fall apart. I will not fall apart. Nick did this. Nick happened to us.

Nick's a pussy. The thought came out of nowhere, and I started laughing uncontrollably. I laughed and couldn't stop, eventually waking Rachel up.

"The hell are you laughing at?" She sat up from the couch, rubbing at her eyes. The three of us had decided to sleep in the living room last night, like a good old-fashioned slumber party.

"I don't know." In a heartbeat, my laughter turned to tears, and I muttered, "Shit." I'd been laughing so I wouldn't cry. Now it was too late to stop—the tears were falling.

"Oh, *chica*, come here." Rachel pushed up and held out her arms, pulling me in for a hug.

"I don't want to cry. He doesn't deserve my tears anymore," I said as my mind ran through a gamut of emotions.

"I don't think these tears are for him," she said as she rubbed my back.

I pulled away and wiped at my face. "Who are they for then?"

"I think they're for you."

Brooke nodded. "You're grieving. You haven't really grieved the loss of your relationship because in the back of your mind, you were always holding on to the possibility of there being a future for the two of you. You let that go when you heard about his engagement, but today is the end."

"It's the nail in your guy's coffin," Rachel said, and their words only made the tears fall harder.

"I'll be fine. After today I'll be fine. I just need to get this out, I guess," I said, my body shaking.

After a few minutes of silence, I pulled myself together and looked between them. "What time do bars open, anyway?" When Rachel laughed and Brooke instantly looked worried, I said, "I'm kidding, Brooke."

She looked to the ceiling and let out a sigh. "Thank goodness."

As the day dragged on, I found myself staring at the clock on my phone more than usual. Nick's wedding started at four thirty, and the lead balloon in my stomach grew heavier with each hour that passed.

"We have to be drinking by the time the wedding starts. I can't be here. I have to be drowning in alcohol by then. Please. Promise me?" I begged, knowing how pathetic I sounded.

Rachel placed a hand on my shoulder. "We'll head to the bar whenever you're ready. But we'll definitely be there by four, okay?"

"Okay." I let out a long breath, feeling somewhat relieved. Apparently the cure for my broken heart was not only my girlfriends, but alcohol. Lots and lots of alcohol. And I wasn't even that much of a drinker.

We got ready together in the bathroom, and Brooke begrudgingly let Rachel do her hair and makeup. When she was done, Brooke looked gorgeous, but nothing like herself, and even though I knew she was uncomfortable, but I could tell she also felt pretty.

"Thanks, Rachel," she said as she stared at her reflection in the mirror.

"You have gorgeous skin and cheekbones, girl. All I did was accent them a little," Rachel said with a wink.

Brooke touched a finger to her cheeks, running along the contour line. "I'd never be able to recreate this look. Ever." Then she took out her cell phone and snapped a few selfies.

"I can," I said from behind her. "I'll help you anytime you want."

"Thanks, Jess."

Several bars were lined up only a few blocks away from our apartment, so the decision to walk there was easy. But that didn't stop Rachel from complaining the entire time about the weather (too chilly) and her shoes (hurt already).

I gave her an exasperated look. "No one told you to wear four-inch heels. It's a college bar, Rachel."

She stuck out her tongue. "Don't make fun of the fact that I like to look gorgeous at all times."

She did look gorgeous, but the shoes were ridiculous.

I glanced at the time on my cell phone once more, noting that it was almost four. All the air in my lungs expelled as if I'd been punched in the stomach, and I stopped walking, bending over at the waist to catch my breath. Squeezing my eyes closed, I demanded the tears not fall.

I will not fall apart. I will not fall apart.

Both girls were at my side in an instant. "You okay?" Rachel asked, and I nodded.

"Come on. Let's get you drunk!"

The fact that those words came out of Brooke's mouth and not Rachel's had me standing up and putting one foot in front of the other instantly.

"You can do this. We're right here with you," Rachel

reassured me as we walked arm in arm.

"Yeah. And Nick's the stupidest guy I've never met. I may not really know him, but I hate him anyway," Brooke said.

Glancing at her, I couldn't stop myself from laughing. The girl was comedic gold today.

Our first stop was at the biggest and rowdiest bar on the row. Even though it was still early, plenty of people were already there.

Brooke and Rachel were both already twenty-one, but I still needed to use the fake ID Nick had gotten for me. Nerves shot through me as we approached the beefy security guard manning the door, even though I knew I had no reason to be nervous. The picture on the ID was me, even if the name wasn't, but this would only be my third time using it.

When we got in easily, I glanced at Rachel, my eyes wide like it had been a close call, and she laughed.

"That's literally the best fake I've ever seen. Stop stressing."

"Nick got it for you, right?" Brooke asked, even though I'd told her that the other time we'd gone out together.

"Yeah."

She cocked her head, giving me a serious look. "At least he was good for something."

"I think you're responsible for this," I said to Rachel, jerking my chin toward Brooke. "All that makeup and hair has given her sass."

The three of us headed straight to the round bar in the center of the room and sat down on the stools. When the bartender asked us what we wanted, I felt like a complete rookie, having no idea what the hell to order.

I couldn't ask for a No Bad Days because I didn't even

know if it was a real drink, or what was in it. So I grumbled, "I need to get drunk quick. So probably a shot."

"What kind of shot," he asked, already irritated by my indecision.

"Just give us three kamikaze shots, please," Rachel said, and the bartender turned his back.

Brooke frowned. "He's not very nice."

"I think I made him mad."

"So sue us for not knowing what we want to drink. I'm so sorry we aren't professional alcoholics," Brooke spat out, and I couldn't help but laugh at her.

"You're killing me tonight," I told her as the bright drinks appeared in front of us.

"Are we making a toast?" Rachel asked as she picked up her drink.

I grimaced. "To forgetting? To moving on? To assholes?"

"Or how about to good friends. They're much better than guys nine times out of ten," Brooke said.

We toasted each other, clinking our glasses together before downing the sweet drink.

"That's not gonna do," I admitted. "I definitely need something stronger.

DRINKING IT ALL AWAY

Jess

ONE STRAIGHT SHOT of vodka turned into two, and my head already felt fuzzy. Why people drank this stuff straight was beyond me, but here I was, doing the same damned thing.

"I think I need some cranberry juice in the next one. I can't just drink this shit straight. It's awful," I admitted as I sneaked a glance at the time on my phone. It was well past five now.

"Let's pace ourselves, or we'll be carrying you home in an hour. And I did not drive all the way up here to be in bed by six o'clock, Jess Michaelson," Rachel demanded.

"You're right. I don't want to be in bed by six either. Six is for losers. Losers who are getting married right now. Or who are already married, probably dancing at their stupid reception or cutting a stupid cake," I babbled as a hiccup tore through me, hurting my chest. "Ow."

"Can I get a water, please?" Brooke asked the bartender, her sass level down a notch. Apparently normal Brooke was back in full effect.

At some point, I stopped keeping track of the time and counting how many drinks I'd poured down my throat. The world was soft and I felt good, happy even. I looked at my two girlfriends as we bopped around on the makeshift dance floor.

"Alcohol is my new best friend. No offense, girls."

They laughed and asked if I was ready to go home yet. Rachel's feet hurt, and Brooke could only take the bar scene for so long. I nodded, content with my buzz. I'd have agreed to just about anything in that moment.

We ended up staying out until nine, which didn't sound very impressive, but when you started partying at four in the afternoon, making it until nine seemed like something you should win an award for.

"Can we order pizza when we get back?" I asked. "Say yes. Please say yes, or I might punch you."

"When you put it that way, you leave us no choice," Rachel said, guiding me by the arm down the street.

"I bet her dress was pretty. Do you think it was pretty? Probably custom made," I babbled as we walked home, my thoughts returning to Nick and Carla. I swore my mind hadn't been there just five minutes earlier, but now they were all I could think about.

"It was probably gaudy, trashy, and over the top, just like her," Rachel snapped.

"I hope she tripped walking down the aisle," Brooke added with a wicked grin, coming to a halt as we rounded the corner to our apartment. "What the hell is that? Is that someone at our door?" She squinted at a dark figure that sat slumped against our door, as if that would help her see more clearly.

Rachel and I both stopped walking, and I gasped. I'd recognize that shape, that shadowed figure anywhere, even in my drunken state.

Nick.

He was here.

"Oh my God," Rachel whispered before letting my arm go.

"What is it?" Brooke asked before it dawned on her. "Wait, is that him?" When Rachel nodded, Brooke's gaze pinged between Nick and me. "Is he dead? He's not moving."

My heart jumped. "Don't say that," I demanded as I rushed toward him. He sat against the door, his arms crossed over his chest as he slept. Lord only knew how long he'd been waiting there.

It had been so long since I'd seen him. Too long. If I thought time would be bad to him, I was wrong. Nick Fisher looked better than ever, and it had nothing to do with the tux he was wearing.

"Are you gonna wake him up, or do I get to do it?" Rachel asked wickedly, and I felt like a wild animal, willing to tear her arm off if she even touched him.

I bent down, my face inches from his as I studied him. As my heart pounded inside my chest, the weight in my stomach disappeared. This was Nick, my Nick, and I still loved him. After all this time—God, I still loved him.

Placing my hand on his shoulder, I gently shook his sleeping frame.

His eyes opened slowly and his wary gaze instantly softened as recognition dawned. "Jess."

"What are you doing here?" My eyes filled with tears, my entire body hopeful after so many months of feeling anything but hope.

"I couldn't do it," he said as he reached for my face, and I leaned into his touch, craving it. "I couldn't fucking do it,

Jess."

When someone cleared their throat behind us, alerting Nick to the fact that we weren't alone, he looked up and pushed himself up from the ground with a crooked smile on his lips. "Rachel."

She grinned back at him. "This better be good. I swear to God, Nick Fisher, this better be the story to end all stories," she said, but her threat lacked any real force behind it.

Nick looked at me, his eyes locking on mine as he said, "I'll let you know how it ends."

"I'm Brooke, by the way," my roommate said as she moved past him, reaching for her keys.

"Pleasure to meet you. I'm Nick."

"Oh, I know who you are. And yeah, what Rachel said." Brooke tried to sound tough before unlocking the door and disappearing inside, dragging a reluctant Rachel with her.

"How long have you been out here?" I asked. The alcohol that only minutes ago was fogging my mind had seemingly evaporated, leaving me acutely aware of every detail of what was happening now.

He shrugged. "A couple hours, maybe."

"Why didn't you call?"

"I don't have my phone. I had your address on a napkin in my glove compartment. It's been there for months. I could never bring myself to throw it out. Thank God I didn't, although I would have found you anyway."

I pursed my lips, a million questions on the tip of my tongue, but I stopped them all and waited for Nick to take the lead. He stared at me, his eyes looking into mine like he was searching for answers somewhere in their depths.

"I am so sorry, Jess. For everything." He reached for my hand, and I let him take it. "I messed up when it came to you, over and over again. It's like the only thing I could get right was doing you wrong." His eyes narrowed, his expression pained.

I sucked in a shaky breath, hoping he would go on before I was required to say anything in response. I craved more from him, needed more than just a simple apology. As I waited, his thumb drew lazy circles across my fingers.

"I know it's not enough to tell you how sorry I am. I know they're just words. But I walked out of that wedding today for you," he said before adding, "and for me."

I gasped, already knowing that his being here most likely meant that there had been no wedding today, but I didn't know the details. And I suddenly found myself wanting them. Every single last one.

"You walked out?" I asked through my surprise and shock.

"I wanted to run." He smirked, and I returned his smile as he dropped my hand. "Can we go inside? It's freezing out here."

"Yeah, of course," I said, feeling silly for not suggesting it myself as I opened the door and stepped inside. Both Rachel and Brooke were on the couch with the television on, graham crackers in their hands.

"We ordered that pizza, by the way," Rachel announced as soon as Nick closed the door behind him.

"Pizza?" His ears perked up.

"Not for you," Rachel snapped. "Unless we decide you deserve it. We might want you to starve."

I smiled, so grateful for my friends. "We're going to talk in my room. Do you need anything out of there?" I asked Rachel, and she made a face.

"Nope. Just don't do anything gross on any of my stuff."

"Always nice to see you, Rachel," Nick said.

As he followed me down the hall, I waited for a smartass response from my best friend, but it never came.

There was nowhere really to sit in my room, no couch or chair, so our choices were either my bed or the floor. Without much thought, I hopped onto my bed and scooted until my back was against the wall.

Nick stood in the doorway until I told him that he was allowed to join me. Avoiding my eyes, he made sure not to sit too close or crowd my personal space, even though I wasn't sure how much distance between us in that moment. He had just walked out of his wedding, after all.

"Okay, so where was I?" he asked.

Nervous, I played with my bottom lip until I noticed he had shifted. When I saw where his gaze had landed, I let go of my mouth.

"You were telling me about the wedding," I said, refusing to call it *his* wedding.

He sucked in a deep breath, his chest expanding, and now my eyes were the ones that couldn't get there fill.

"I couldn't do it, Jess. I just couldn't bring myself to walk down that aisle to marry someone who wasn't you. I kept hearing your voice in my head, telling me that there would be a moment that was too far, and I realized this was that moment. Frank said the same thing. Ryan too. But there were bigger things at play here, Jess. It wasn't just the fact that I hated letting my old man down. It was different this time, a lot more at stake."

Frustrated and confused, I demanded, "Just tell me. Please. Tell me everything."

"Carla's dad threatened to blackball you in the entertainment industry if I didn't marry his daughter. I believed him, Jess. Hell, I still believe him, but I won't let him do it. I don't know how, but I'll make sure he has no say in your future."

I wasn't even the least bit prepared for that. Nick didn't hold back, though, and I was grateful for it. I didn't want him to protect my feelings or keep things from me. I wanted to be in the loop, completely clued in, no matter what. But this sucked.

Fear ripped through me as I thought about losing everything I'd worked so hard for. "Could he really do that?"

"He has a lot of power and tons of contacts." Nick shrugged. "But I don't really know how your industry works."

It worked like that; it definitely worked like that. My fears were pushed to the side, though, as another realization sank in. It had taken a minute for me to put together the fact that Nick had done all this to protect me.

"You were going to marry her for me?"

Nick nodded vigorously. "I thought it was the only way. I didn't know what else to do. But I was sitting in that room this afternoon, so fucking torn over which way was up. I would do anything to protect you, but marrying her felt so wrong."

I scooted closer to him. He was too far away.

"So, what happened today? Did you just leave or did you say something?" I asked, wondering if he had caused a scene, fought with his dad, or quietly slipped out a back door without anyone's knowledge.

"Ryan and Frank stopped by the room I was waiting in until the service started, and noticed how I was losing my shit. I told them I couldn't do this, that I would do anything for you, but this seemed like going against you somehow."

"What did they say?" I asked with a small smile. I really liked his brothers.

"If Ryan had pom-poms, he would have turned into a cheerleader in that moment. He's always been Team Jess," Nick said with a laugh. "And Frank was as tough as usual, promising me that we'd figure this out and make sure no one messed with your career."

"But they were on board with you walking out?"

"They couldn't have been more on board. The only thing they asked me to do was tell our dad before I took off."

My heart plummeted. "Oh my gosh. Did you?" I could only imagine how awful that conversation must have been.

"I didn't have a choice. He walked in at that exact moment, like he sensed that I was about to bolt."

GET THE GIRL

Nick

J ESS GASPED AGAIN, and I wanted to take her pretty mouth and make sure the only sound coming from it was from the pleasure I was giving her. But I was jumping ahead of myself, and I knew it.

"Dad took one look at me and knew what I was about to do. He told me to sit down, then asked Frank and Ryan to leave."

Her gorgeous eyes widened. "Did they?"

"Hell no. They both leaned against the wall and crossed their arms, refusing to budge."

That got a giggle out of her. I loved that laugh. I fucking missed it something fierce.

"Go on. I'm dying here," she admitted with a grin, and it made me smile back like a lovesick fool.

"Dad asked me what was going on. For once, he actually looked and sounded concerned for my well-being."

"Shocking."

"I know, right? Anyway, I told him that I couldn't do it, and then I apologized, Jess. Can you believe that? I fucking apologized to the man. But I told him I wouldn't do it, that this was asking too much of me. Told him it wasn't fair and it wasn't right. And then I quit. And I told him if he ever threatened you or your future again, that I'd kill him."

Her eyes grew wide again and she whispered, "You said that? To your father?"

"It was like once I started talking and stood my ground, I couldn't stop. I told him I had to go. That I didn't care what he did to me, but I was leaving. And you know what he said, Jess?" Her head tilted as waited for me to continue. "He told me to go. He told me to get out of there before anyone saw me. That he would handle things."

Her hand flew to her mouth, covering what I was certain was another gasp of surprise. "I can't believe this."

"He also apologized to me as I was walking out the door. He told *me* he was sorry. That almost stopped me in my tracks so I could turn around and acknowledge what he was giving me. But it wasn't enough. Not when I compared it to you." I touched her cheek for only a moment. "I couldn't get here fast enough, Jess. I got into my truck and drove straight here. It pissed me off every time I had stop for gas, which was only once, but it was one time too many."

Her expression softened, her eyes brightening with the tears that were forming. "I can't believe you quit. I'm so proud of you." She beamed. "So you'll work at the bar then?"

"I haven't talked to Frank and Ryan about it yet, but that's the plan."

"What does this mean? For us?" Her expression fell slightly, and I hated the doubt I was responsible for putting into her heart.

"I thought that was pretty self-explanatory. I want you, I'll always want you, I never stopped wanting you. You're my future. I just hope I'm still yours."

"I still have another year left up here," she said, her tone a little colder than it had been a moment ago.

I nodded. "I know exactly how much time you have left. I don't care, and I never did. I shouldn't have broken up with you, Jess. I was just so worried that you'd put me first, and I didn't want you to end up hating me, or resent me somewhere down the line because of it."

"Why couldn't you just tell me that? You let me think you didn't want me. You let me believe you didn't care about us at all. My God, Nick, you let me think you couldn't stay faithful."

My insides twisted. I hated how much I'd continually hurt the one person that I loved. I had a lot of making up to do if she'd let me, and I sat there praying that she would.

"I know." I grimaced. "I know what I did. I know every single lie that I told you and made you to believe. I shouldn't have done it. I should have just been honest with you, but I knew you wouldn't see reason."

Shit. That wasn't the right thing to say, and I realized it immediately.

Jess glared at me. "See reason? You didn't even let me try. You just decided for both of us."

I threw my hands up in surrender. "Wrong word choice, sorry. I knew that you wouldn't let me end things, even if my reasons made sense. Even if it was the last thing I wanted to do, I knew you would tell me no."

She glared at me for a moment too long, making my heart plummet at the thought that there would be no getting her back. I'd waited too long, pushed her too far.

"You should have been honest."

"I know. I've regretted it every moment of every day since. Please believe that, even if you believe nothing else," I begged her, not knowing where her head or heart were at.

"What's your game plan?"

"My what?"

"You had six hours in the car by yourself, Nick. What'd you come up with?"

"Jess." I shifted around so that I was facing her head on. "I know I've done a lot of things that hurt you. I know I've waited too long to try to win you back. I've pushed you over the edge time and time again, let you down and disappointed you in more ways than I want to count right now."

My voice tightened with emotion, and I struggled to control it. "But if you'll forgive me, or at least tell me that you'll try, then my game plan includes never doing anything to hurt you ever again. I'll never let you down. I'll never disappoint you. I'll include you in every decision I make, and I won't keep things from you, no matter what. We'll be a team, you and me, us against the world, and God help anyone who tries to break us apart or stand in our way."

"Yeah?" she said, her tone so flat, I couldn't read her at all.

"Yeah."

"You really hurt me."

"I know."

"You made me think I couldn't trust you. You made me feel lower than I'd ever felt in my life," she said.

Her words only twisted the knife in my heart even more. I didn't blame her, though. I'd never blame her for how she felt when it came to me, to us. I had done this.

"Have to be honest, Jess, that I really hate hearing that. It fucking kills me, okay? It tears me up inside, knowing how I made you feel. But I can't fix the things I've already done. I can only promise you to be a better man going forward. And I am promising you that. I'll do whatever it takes. Whatever you need me to do. Just tell me."

I wasn't above falling to the floor and getting on my knees, my hands in a prayer position, if that's what it took. I'd do anything. *Anything* to make this right.

Jess stared at her hands, not meeting my eyes. "I don't know."

"Do you still love me? Hell, do you still have any feelings for me at all?"

That got to her. I saw it all over her face.

"Yes," she said, not specifying which question she was answering, but it didn't matter.

"Do you want me to leave and never come back?"

Her face fell, and when she met my gaze, her eyes glistened. "No."

"I've suffered, Jess. I know you probably don't think I have, because you haven't been the one dishing it out to me, but I swear to you that I've suffered on a daily basis without you. Please don't make me suffer any more if it's not what you really want. Don't try to prove a point here. It's only wasting time, and I don't want to waste any more time without you."

Tears rolled down her cheeks at my words.

I was scared to touch her without permission, even though every part of me wanted to claim every part of her again. When I reached toward her, she all but dived into my arms, throwing her arms around my neck and pulling me tight.

"I just don't want to be stupid," she mumbled into my shirt. "You hurt me so much, but I still love you. I always thought we'd end up together, but then you got engaged, and I knew there would never be an *us* again. I hated that the most."

I pulled back far enough to look her in the eyes. "I promise that if you choose to forgive me, it will be the least stupid thing you ever do in your life."

She giggled against my chest. "Of course you're going to say that. You're your biggest fan."

"And my worst enemy," I added. "Forgive me, Jess? Please say you'll try."

When she said she would, my heart skipped a beat. I'd take it.

"Can I kiss you?" I wanted to tell her I was going to kiss her, give her no option, but it didn't feel like the right time to go all alpha male on her while I was still on shaky ground.

"If you don't, I might never forgive you," she said before pressing her lips to mine.

I opened my mouth, begging her to do the same, and she did. Our tongues met in the middle, touching softly before pulling away. Kissing her was pure joy, like tasting heaven.

But more importantly, kissing her reminded me where I belonged and with whom.

LIFE IS UNEXPECTED

Jess

NICK HAD CONFESSED so much to me tonight, filling in all the gaps of the past year, and all I offered him was a simple *I'll try* when it came to forgiving him. After he'd walked out of his wedding today and come straight here.

For me.

For us.

I wanted to do more than try. My past hurts couldn't be erased in the minutes it took him to apologize, but Nick's intentions had been good. I couldn't overlook the fact that he had been making decisions he thought were in my best interest, no matter how much they might have frustrated me. He'd also tried to keep me safe, and I'd never known anyone, aside from my parents, who would go that far for me.

I had no idea how I would have reacted if put into a similar situation, but I'd like to assume that I would have done whatever it took to keep Nick safe as well. I couldn't hold that against him, and to be honest, I didn't want to. That kind of character trait was rare in people, especially in guys. And here Nick was, willingly throwing away a guaranteed future to make sure I got to keep mine.

I believed him when he said he was sorry. And all the

promises he'd made to me tonight while we sat on top of my bed? I believed those too. The moment his lips touched mine, I was a goner. When you shared a connection like we had, it wasn't something that was easily brushed off or ignored. You couldn't pretend it didn't exist.

A knock on my bedroom door caused us both to turn and stare at it, even though whoever was behind it couldn't see us.

"Pizza's here," Rachel said. "I mean, you've probably worked up an appetite with how long you two have been in there, and to be honest, I'm dying out here not knowing what's going on in there, so *come out right now*!" she yelled at the end.

I laughed. "We'll be right there."

"Do I get some?" Nick asked.

His gaze on me was gentle, but I hated that he didn't look completely relaxed. I knew it was because I hadn't given him cause to.

"You definitely get some." When Nick laughed, my cheeks burned as I quickly added, "Pizza. You definitely get some pizza."

He pushed himself off my bed first before giving me a hand. "Come here," he said, pulling my body against his and holding me tight. "I thought I was never going to get to do this again." His grip on me tightened.

"Me too," I agreed as I tightened my hold on him as well.

"We're going to be okay, right?" he asked, his breath warm against my neck.

I nodded, not wanting to make him think otherwise anymore. "I think we're going to be better than just okay."

He pulled back, his blue eyes filled with so much hope.

"Yeah?"

"Yeah."

"I love you. I never stopped," he said, and there was no doubting his sincerity.

I smiled as I pulled him toward my door and opened it. When we walked out of my room holding hands, Rachel noticed immediately.

"Thank the Lord, finally. Here!" Rachel shoved two plates holding pizza slices at us before hesitating. "Wait, does he get some or not?"

"He gets some," I said with another laugh, and watched as Rachel handed it over. Nick and I sat on the couch, our thighs touching.

"Hurry up and fill us in. Brooke and I are just making shit up out here, and we know we're all wrong."

"I'm pretty sure Nick isn't in the mob and was only marrying Carla to keep the opposing mob boss from killing everyone he ever loved," Brooke said, waving her pizza around. "That one was Rachel's guess, by the way."

Rachel rolled her eyes and leaned toward us. "Just tell us if you're back together. That's really all I need to know. And if he groveled. And, oh my gosh, please tell me that you left Carla at the altar! I hope that bitch cried all over her stupid dress and ruined her makeup."

I didn't know what to say, so I looked at Nick. "You can take that one."

"Thanks." He grinned before nodding at my best friend. "I don't want anyone but your girl, Jess, here. So as far as us being back together, I'm working on it. But I don't plan on stopping until that answer is a firm yes." He glanced at me before continuing. "I'm not sure if I groveled enough, but I tried." He turned to face me again. "If it wasn't enough, let me know. I'll do it again. I'll do more. I'll do whatever it takes."

"My goodness." Brooke's mouth fell open. "Sorry, I've just never seen something like this in real life. You're good." She pointed at Nick with her free hand. "He's good," she repeated, looking between me and Rachel.

"He knows," Rachel said. "Now, tell me about the wedding."

Nick shrugged. "I left before it started. I never even saw Carla, so I'm not sure what she did or how she reacted."

"Hasn't anyone filled you in?" Rachel demanded, looking shocked. "What kind of friends do you have?"

"I left my phone at the ceremony site. Ran out so fast, I completely forgot it."

"Shit, Nick. Who has it?" Rachel asked, suddenly concerned. "Call his number, Jess. I mean it. What if that crazy *puta* has his phone?"

"What if she does?" I shrugged.

Rachel shot up from her seat and bolted into my room, reappearing seconds later with my phone pressed to her ear.

"Who's this?" she snarled, and I thought for a moment that Carla did have Nick's phone. "Oh, hey. No, I'm Rachel, Jess's best friend . . . Yes, as a matter of fact, he is . . . Uh-huh . . . Right? Who leaves their phone behind and drives six hours without one?" She laughed. "No way, buddy, that's on you. He's not my brother . . . Sure, hold on."

She tossed Nick's phone into the air and he caught it easily, pressing it to his ear.

When I looked at Rachel with wide eyes, she smiled.

"His brother."

"I gathered that much. Which one?"

"Oh. Ryan, the flirty one." She giggled and I shook my head, imagining the trouble the two of them could get into together.

"Don't even think about it, Rachel."

"Think about what?" She batted her eyelashes innocently.

Brooke squinted at her. "I thought you had a boyfriend."

"She does. Thank you, Brooke."

"You two are no fun." Rachel faked a pout just as Nick hung up the phone. He had done a lot of listening and not a lot of talking.

"Everything okay?" I asked.

He smiled. "You'll love this," he said, and Rachel sat up straighter.

"Please tell me. Please let it be awesome." She clasped her hands together and glanced up at the ceiling.

"Well," Nick said, "apparently Carla refused to believe that I had really left for good. She claimed that I would never put Jess's future in jeopardy like that, and she insisted that I had to be coming back."

When both Rachel and Brooke's faces twisted in confusion, I held up a hand to interrupt as I explained. "I'll fill you guys in on that tidbit later."

Nick continued. "Right. Sorry. Jess will tell you. Word spread to the guests that the wedding was off, but Carla ran out there and stood at the altar, screaming for everyone to remain seated. She said it was all a misunderstanding, and that no one was allowed to leave."

"Denial much?" Brooke asked with a surprised expression.

Rachel laughed. "This is too rich."

"Anytime someone tried to move, she would yell at them to sit back down. Ryan said he couldn't stop laughing. So I guess my dad sought hers out at some point after I left to help avoid any embarrassment to Carla, but that clearly didn't work. Ryan said she broke everything in her bridal room. Smashed the mirrors, threw vases out windows, and destroyed all of her bridesmaids' flower arrangements with her shoes. Went total bridezilla-psycho crazy."

"Are you kidding?" I asked, overcome with horrified amazement.

"No, and apparently it's all over social media. Someone filmed the entire thing and posted it online. They even made a dub mix," he added, but Rachel had already snatched up her phone and started swiping at the screen.

"Holy crap, it's trending on Twitter, and it's the first search term on YouTube." She couldn't stop laughing. "She deserves this, Nick. She deserves this and so much more. I have never hated another person as much as I hate her."

"Is she really that bad?" Brooke asked, and the rest of us shouted "Yes!" in unison.

"I feel like maybe I should feel sorry for her, but I don't. I don't at all." I looked at Nick. "Does that make me a bad person?"

His hand cupped my cheek. "After everything she's done, you're asking if you're the bad person? This is why you could never be bad, babe. But there's more."

Rachel clapped her hands together joyfully. "What else could there be?"

"Apparently, Mr. Crawford was threatening my dad as

well. Basically, ladies," he said, addressing Rachel and Brooke, "he told me that Jess would never work in Hollywood if I didn't do what he wanted."

"He what?" Rachel's fiery temper appeared as she jumped to her feet, fury replacing her joy, and Nick threw up his hand to stop her.

"He threatened me, but I guess he also threatened my dad."

"What could he possibly threaten your dad with?" I asked, wondering how this situation could get even more insane than it already was.

"He said he'd close down the bar. That he'd bog it down with so many code violations and fines that Frank and Ryan would never be able to reopen. At least, not before becoming irrelevant and losing their entire customer base. My dad apparently thought he had the means to go through with it, the same way I felt about his threats to you."

"Is that why your dad pushed you to agree to the wedding?"

Nick ran his hand through his hair while he nodded. "Yeah. So while I was trying to protect you from threats to your future, my dad was trying to protect my brothers from threats to theirs."

It was all so messed up. Everything Nick was saying was beyond the level of crazy that anyone should be forced to deal with.

"This is not normal. You guys know that, right?" Brooke's eyes were even wider, and she almost sounded scared.

"We know." Rachel grimaced. "So, why would Mr. Crawford do all of this? Because his daughter wanted you?"

Nick looked at me. "In a nutshell, yes. She said that I embarrassed her. That once I started dating Jess, I'd blown her off and done it publicly more than once, and she couldn't handle that. She was mad and hurt, and claimed that she wanted you to suffer the same way she had."

"By getting you to marry her?" The whole thing was way too ridiculous for me to comprehend.

"She wanted to win, and she wanted to hurt you doing it."

"Why would her dad go along with something like that? I don't get it," I asked, still trying to wrap my head around all the craziness.

"She's all he has. His wife was killed in a car accident, and he never remarried. He said his whole goal in life is to keep Carla happy and give her whatever she wants," Nick explained, like this was typical father-daughter behavior.

Rachel blinked hard at that. "No matter what she wants or asks for?"

"Apparently, there's no limit to what he'd do for her," Nick said, then looked at me. "And there's no limit to what I'd do for you."

He placed a soft kiss on my forehead and apologized once more. I melted against his touch, knowing that I never wanted to be without it again.

"I forgive you," I whispered. "For everything."

"Really?"

"Yes." I nodded because I had. I did. And I didn't want him thinking for a second longer that I didn't.

"I forgive you too," Rachel said, wearing her smart-aleck grin when I glanced at her. "Yeah, I heard you."

"Brooke?" Nick said. "While we're doling out forgiveness

here, how about you?"

Brooke took a few seconds to think. "Two hours ago, I hated you. But I've never heard a guy say the kind of things you said to Jess tonight, unless it was in a movie. If Jess and Rachel forgive you, then so do I."

Nick smiled bigger than I'd seen in a long time as he pulled something from his pocket and flipped it in the air. I grinned, knowing exactly what it was. His grandfather's lucky poker chip landed in his palm, and he brought it to his lips and kissed it.

"Thank you," he said to the chip before putting it back into his pocket. "I knew it would bring me luck. I just didn't know it would bring me this much."

"You two are grossing me out. Get a room," Rachel said before recanting. "No. No. Do not get a room. Because then I won't have anywhere to sleep, and I need a good night's sleep before that hellish drive tomorrow. Dammit, Nick!" she yelled, switching gears. "Why the hell couldn't you have done this yesterday so we could have carpooled? Now we both have to drive back to LA separately, and it's awful. Trust me. The drive sucks. And you don't even have your phone," she added, laughing.

"It's kind of nice, actually," he said before grabbing my legs and throwing them on top of his. "I like being unreachable right now."

As I finished off another slice of pizza, Rachel said, "Can I ask something obvious?" When no one said anything, she asked, "You both realize that you're going to date long-distance, right? Is that what's happening here? Because I thought your dick would fall off if you did that, Nick."

Nick choked on his pizza as he punched at his chest. "My dick will be just fine, Rachel, but it appreciates your concern."

"You forget that I was there when you broke her heart and told her you couldn't date anyone long-distance without cheating."

"I lied," he deadpanned.

Rachel spit out a laugh. "I knew it. We both did. Hell, we all did."

"Yeah?" Nick cocked a brow in my direction.

"We assumed," I said, clarifying, "but I believed that you meant what you said."

"I'm sorry. Again." He kissed my cheek.

"I know you are." I offered him a small smile. That day when he broke up with me no longer felt like a moment that had just happened, but more like something that happened eons ago.

"Will you be my girlfriend, Jess Michaelson?" Nick asked loud enough for the girls to hear without straining.

"I thought I already was?" Annoyed, I narrowed my eyes on him. I had assumed that my forgiving him and him being here meant that we were back together, no questions needed.

"You were, but I still wanted to ask you. Officially."

"You two are going to ruin me, I think," Brooke said as she reached for another slice of pizza. "How can any relationship compare to this?"

Rachel rolled her eyes. "Be thankful you weren't there when they were at State together. You dodged a bullet, my friend." Looking at Nick and me, she said, "Although I couldn't be happier for the two of you. Really. I mean it."

I smiled at my best friend, knowing that her words were

sincere. I didn't care if Nick and I made people sick. I'd never care about what people thought about us ever again.

Like Nick said, it was us against the world, and God help anyone who got in our way or tried to break us apart ever again.

EPILOGUE

Jess

Fifteen months later

IF NICK AND I had any qualms about being in a long-distance relationship, you'd never know it. He came to visit me every chance he got, even if it was only for a day. I thought it was sweet but not necessary, considering how busy we both were. I tried to tell him to stay home, but Nick refused to listen, claiming that he wanted to spend all of his free time with me. He said it didn't matter where I lived—he was going there.

After he left that weekend, he had gone straight to the bar to pick up his phone from Ryan and fill his brothers in on what had happened between us. Nick's dad was sitting in the bar drinking a beer when he arrived. Apparently, Nick had been surprised but thankful to see everyone in one place, hoping to mend any broken fences once and for all.

When his dad presented him with paperwork releasing him from his contract at the company, and then Frank tossed him a partnership agreement offering him a one-third ownership in the bar, Nick couldn't sign each one fast enough. The day he called to tell me *that* news was something I'll remember until I die. I'd never heard him so happy, relieved, and excited before. Everything was finally falling into place for my guy, and that thrilled me to no end.

I parked my car in the bar's small reserved lot and hopped out with a smile on my face, wondering for a moment if I'd ever stop smiling. When I graduated with honors this past spring, I moved back to Southern California the very next day, not wanting to delay my life with Nick another minute. Seeing him sitting in the crowd at graduation with my parents was one thing, but coming back home to him where I belonged was another.

"Hey, Jess," Kyle said from his perch handling security outside the door.

"Hi, Kyle." I greeted him with a bear hug as the bar noise from indoors filtered out. "Busy night?"

Shaking his head, he shot me a look. "What do you think?" he said sarcastically, and I laughed.

It didn't seem possible that Sam's could get even more popular, but after Nick bought in and started working there, that's exactly what happened. Word spread that there was a third Fisher brother, and that brought in even more customers and all kinds of publicity.

Women had their bachelorette parties there, posting clips and pictures all over social media, thanks to Nick. He had created a special filter for Snapchat you could only use when you were inside the bar, as well as a clever backdrop for posting pictures only to Instagram. He really was brilliant, using popular social media sites to his advantage.

Local news channels featured the brothers at least once a week, and every type of reality television show wanted to film scenes at the bar, claiming to love the vibe there. But we knew the truth—it was the three gorgeous brothers the cameras loved, not to mention the audience. Tourists insisted on visiting the "bar hotties with the bodies," a new catch phrase that came out of one of those reality shows.

Pulling the door open, I stepped inside the packed room, searching for my guy. I spotted him behind the bar with Ryan at his side as they mixed drinks with big smiles on their faces. Frank was at the other end, craning his neck so he could hear someone shouting their order to him.

There wasn't anywhere to sit at the bar, so I hung out in the back while I waited for Rachel to show up.

"I see the love of my life," Nick shouted, his voice rising above the bar noise, and I glanced up to see him making a beeline straight for me.

When he reached me, he slid one arm around my waist and pulled me into a deep kiss, our bodies connected. The crowd cheered, and some girls groaned their disappointment. I was used to it.

"Glad you're here," Nick said with a wink. "But I have to get back to work." He planted a quick kiss on my cheek before turning to run off.

I smacked his ass as he hustled away, thanking every single star in the night sky that this guy was mine as Rachel walked in.

"Holy shit, this place is a madhouse!" she yelled before pulling me into a hug.

"Summer," I answered with a shrug. The summer months were always the busiest time of year at the bar.

"I saw him kiss you." Rachel shook her head. "I can't believe he did that in front of everyone."

I ran a finger across my bottom lip, still feeling his lips there, and smiled. "He does it all the time."

Nick often advertised the fact that he wasn't single, definitely wasn't available, and he never pretended otherwise. Whenever I walked into the bar, he pointed me out to everyone, sometimes introduced me, but he *always* greeted me with a kiss.

I tried to explain to him one night that I knew how important the illusion of being available was to a lot of bartenders, especially when your clientele was mostly women. It made good business sense to want to keep the women happy, to keep them coming back for more. To do that, you sometimes flirted, acted single, or pretended that the women had a shot in hell in dating you someday.

But Nick didn't want any part of that. "I won't pretend to be something I'm not, Jess. And I absolutely refuse to let women think they have a chance with me. It's not happening. If they want a Fisher brother, they can flirt with Ryan," he'd argued one night, and I let it go because I loved his answer. Absolutely *loved* it.

"Where are we going to sit? Can we sit? Is there anywhere to sit?" Rachel shot rapid-fire questions my way, her head swiveling as she looked for seats.

"It will clear out soon. They have to close."

"I need a drink," she shouted to me over the noise.

As she spoke, Nick reappeared carrying two No Bad Days. He handed us each a drink, greeted Rachel, pressed a quick kiss to my cheek, and hurried back to the bar.

"What's this?"

I smiled. "Just try it. You'll love it. It's my favorite drink here."

"Really?" She took a sip and her face lit up. "Dear God, this is amazing."

"Ryan's a cocktail genius."

"I love that man," Rachel said with a sigh, and I narrowed my eyes.

"No, Rachel." I felt like I was scolding a bad puppy.

"I know, I know." She waved me off, but her eyes told me otherwise. She'd take a chance with Ryan in a heartbeat, and I knew it. But so would most women, so I couldn't blame her for it.

"He's just so delicious," she said dreamily. "I mean, look at him."

I turned my head, but my eyes sought out Nick instead of Ryan. He was the only Fisher brother I could see, the only one I wanted, the only one I needed. Nick's eyes met mine, and he paused for a second before giving me a wink. My insides melted at the gesture. Everything he did went straight to the core of me.

Eventually, the bar cleared out, leaving Rachel and me alone with the guys as they cleaned up.

"I heard a rumor the other day," Ryan said over the music that played in the background.

"What kind of rumor?" I asked.

He laughed. "That your best friend moved to London and was being wooed by a prince, or something to that effect."

I turned to Rachel, wondering why she was sitting next to me if she was supposed to be in London.

"Not your real best friend." Ryan gave Rachel a nod. "Carla."

"Oh." My eyes widened when everything clicked. "Shut up. A prince?"

"He's not a real prince, but she's playing like he is, posting all over social media with him."

"As long as she's over Nick, that's really all I care about." I practically groaned as I remembered the hell she'd put us through. Nick and I had come so far since then, our relationship so solid, so beautiful, so completely fulfilling.

"I hope he's a prince who lives in some small-dick country, and she marries him and has to live there forever," Rachel blurted.

When she downed the rest of her third cocktail, Frank doled out five shot glasses that were only partially filled.

"To small-dick countries and staying there forever." He lifted his shot glass in the air, and we all repeated the toast before downing whatever he had poured us without question.

"Speaking of other countries, Dad called today," Nick said, drawing everyone's attention. "He said he loves Italy and he's never coming back."

The brothers' relationship with their father was better than ever. He'd apologized profusely, to me as well, seeming truly remorseful for his behavior. We had family dinners when we could get everyone in the same room, but more often than not, Mr. Fisher could be found sitting here at the bar, tossing one back with his sons. It warmed my heart to see that relationship mended.

"Hell, can you blame him?" Ryan said with a laugh. "Next time I go there, I might not come back either."

Frank scowled at him. "You're not going anywhere."

"I might, Frank. You never know," Ryan said, trying to

goad him.

"I've always wanted to see Italy," I said with a grin. "I'll go with you, Ryan."

Ryan leaned across the bar and placed his hand on my arm. "We'd have the best time, sweetheart," he said.

"Hands off my woman," Nick said in a threatening growl. "I don't care who you are."

Ryan removed his hand slowly, his fingers lingering as he dragged them away, and I fought off a laugh.

Rachel squeezed my thigh under the bar. "That was hot. A little crazy, but totally hot," she whispered.

"You like crazy." I rolled my eyes, and she nodded.

"I'd better go," Rachel said almost an hour later. "I'm exhausted, and I have to work tomorrow. 'Bye, guys," she shouted before they each stopped to tell her good night and to drive safe.

Rachel hadn't found the job of her dreams yet, so she was currently working at an upscale boutique. But working in retail meant that she worked on weekends and most nights. It was part of the reason why we didn't get to see each other as often as we wanted. Our schedules tended to clash more than they meshed, even though my job was Monday through Friday and normal business hours, for the most part.

I'd gotten an entry-level position at one of the big studios in town. It wasn't my dream job, by any means, but it was in my dream department, movie production. I had my foot in the door and was able to meet people I'd otherwise never get the chance to. I was grateful and I worked hard, putting in overtime without complaint whenever they asked.

"You have to work? Why didn't you say anything?" I

whined before pulling her into a hug, not wanting to let her go.

"Because I wanted to see you. I miss you," she said with a pout. "And it's always fun to hang out here." She smiled as she walked out the back door, and I found myself missing her already.

I agreed wholeheartedly. It was fun. My life, my relationship, the bar, it was all perfect.

Nick walked over, his hand extended as he waited for me to hand over my car keys. This was our routine whenever I came to the bar and stayed until closing. I'd drive here, let loose and have some drinks, and he'd drive us home, completely sober.

"Let's go, babe." He wrapped his arm around my midsection and pulled me tight against his side.

"Wait!" Ryan called out, and we both stopped walking. "You're not even going to give me a hug good-bye?"

I laughed before wiggling out of Nick's grip, which had tightened the second Ryan started teasing him.

"Night, Ryan!" When I squeezed his broad shoulders, he picked me up and twirled me around, just to get a rise out of Nick.

"Night, Frank," I said before giving his giant body a hug as well. It was far less dramatic hugging Frank than it was hugging Ryan.

I was back in Nick's arms within seconds, my body melding to his because that was where it belonged, that was where I fit.

"You ready to go home now?" Nick asked. "I'm tired."

I nodded, practically drooling at the thought of crawling

into our bed with him and closing my eyes, snuggled in his arms.

Home was where Nick was, where we lived together. And I never wanted it any other way.

The End

Thank you for reading! I hope you enjoyed the story as much as I enjoyed writing it.

Please join my mailing list to be notified as soon as Frank Fisher's story, *Guy Hater*, is set to release!

http://tinyurl.com/SterlingNewsletter

ACKNOWLEDGMENTS

This book was a lot of fun to write. Don't get me wrong, it took a toll on my emotions as well, and I might have been a mess on more than one occasion, but I hope that you enjoyed reading and getting to know Nick and Jess (not to mention the other boys). I might sort of be in love with them, and I hope you are too. :)

I based Sam's bar and the drinks in the book off of my favorite local bar, Mario & John's in Petaluma, California. The owners Micah and Nick (no relation to the real Nick Fisher- lol) were kind enough to let me borrow their drink names for not only the story, but for all 3 book titles as well. If you're ever near Petaluma, make sure you stop by the bar, find Danny or Franco and order up a No Bad Days (you won't be sorry), and tell the guys I sent you.

I want to thank every blogger who takes the time to read my books, promote them, and tell people to read them. This job is so very hard when you do it all alone, so I am very appreciative of all your tireless effort and hard work. You don't have to do it—but you choose to—and I am so thankful. Thank you.

Thank you to my #Squad, and to the Kittens in my private Facebook group (come join us). Thanks also to Krista Arnold, Jillian Dodd, Tarryn Fisher, Colleen Hoover, Tara Sivec, Claire Contreras, and Corinne Michaels. To Josh for being just what I needed for this cover. To Michelle Warren for once again designing something I can't stop looking at. To Pam for taking my words and making them far better than they were before you read them. To Cat and Becky for always being there, cheering me on and not judging my heart. And to Brina and Stephanie for your friendship, especially right now. To Blake for being the best thing in my life. To Peter for being the best dog to ever grace Snapchat (LOL).

And to you. Yes, you.

OTHER BOOKS BY J. STERLING

In Dreams
Chance Encounters
10 Years Later – A Second Chance Romance
Heartless
Dear Heart, I Hate You

THE GAME SERIES
The Perfect Game – Book One
The Game Changer – Book Two
The Sweetest Game – Book Three
The Other Game (Dean Carter) – Book Four

THE CELEBRITY SERIES
Seeing Stars – Madison & Walker
Breaking Stars – Paige & Tatum
Losing Stars – Quinn & Ryson (Coming Soon)

THE FISHER BROTHERS SERIES
No Bad Days – Nick Fisher
Guy Hater – Frank Fisher (Coming Soon)
Adios Pantelones – Ryan Fisher (Coming Soon)

ABOUT THE AUTHOR

Jenn Sterling is a Southern California native who loves writing stories from the heart. Every story she tells has pieces of her truth in it, as well as her life experience. She has her bachelor's degree in Radio/TV/Film and has worked in the entertainment industry the majority of her life.

Jenn loves hearing from her readers and can be found online at:

Blog & Website:
www.j-sterling.com

Twitter:
twitter.com/RealJSterling

Facebook:
facebook.com/TheRealJSterling

Facebook Reader Group:
facebook.com/groups/ThePerfectGameChangerGroup

Instagram:
instagram.com/RealJSterling

If you enjoyed this book, please consider writing a spoiler-free review on the site from which you purchased it. And thank you so much for helping me spread the word about my books, and for allowing me to continue telling the stories I love to tell. I appreciate you so much. :)

CPSIA information can be obtained
at www.ICGtesting.com
Printed in the USA
LVHW110622021118
595724LV00001B/54/P